Not on My Watch

Howard Gershkowitz

ISBN 13: 9781737767114

Library of Congress Control Number: 2021945697

Cover Photos: Grace Quest Graphic Design. And: https://unsplash.com/photos/P9rQn2qcEV0

Cover design © by All Things That Matter Press

Published in 2021 by All Things That Matter Press

As with my first book, I would be remiss if I failed to acknowledge the many people who contributed to its success. First and foremost, my wonderful wife of forty-two years, Lisa, who encouraged and supported my efforts as I re-worked the plot. In a close second, my son, Robert, whose advice and counsel was integral to my writing pursuits.

Editor and book shepherd, Ann Videan guided me through the various edits and updates. Her attention to detail and unbounded enthusiasm were inspirational for me.

The cover concept was created by Grace Quest (Grace Quest Graphic Design), who did a phenomenal job interpreting the story and translating into an eye-catching work of art.

My thanks and appreciation to Merry J., Eva W., and Sharon L. as my advance readers. Special thanks to Sharon who, as a fellow author, assisted me in my research. She is a retired professor and an expert on crime statistics.

As mentioned earlier, this book started as a short story, but thanks to the guidance I received from author and English professor Katy Grant, I was able to turn it into a full-length novel.

Last but definitely not least, my deep appreciation to Authors Robert Dugoni and Stephen James, who guided me through the revision process during their Novel Intensive Workshops, which they hold biannually. Their insights and coaching deepened my understanding of character and plot and allowed me to transform the original story into one which I trust you will enjoy.

~Howard Gershkowitz

Foreword

Though this is my second book to be published, it was actually written first, before 'The Operator.' It is based on a true story of Medicare fraud perpetrated by a hospital on the east coast. Written originally as a short story, I became aware of several more incidents of fraud foisted on the public through systematic schemes carried out by medical institutions. As a result, the story took on a life of its own and progressed into a novel.

Once completed, I sent out query letters to publishers and agents, but the rejection letters piled up until I became disillusioned with the project and set it aside. Meanwhile, my attention turned to the science-fiction/time travel story about a stockbroker who is whisked back to 1929, where he tries to prevent the market crash and subsequent depression. This time, I was fortunate enough to submit to Phil and Deb Harris at All Things That Matter Press and they accepted it for publication.

With the successful launch of that novel, I decided to try again with this one. As I began to review it, I discovered why it had met with failure: it wasn't very good! To my chagrin, that first manuscript was rife with errors, cliches, and suffered from generally poor technique. After a massive re-write, I sought out beta readers to get honest, independent feedback. Once again, I submitted it to All Things That Matter Press, and they accepted it.

~1~

Dateline: Boston, MA, September 8, 2021

In other noteworthy news, C & C and Associates, the local Medical powerhouse, has announced plans for another acquisition, this time in Texas. The merger, announced jointly today in the Boston Herald and Dallas Times, will be the eleventh major hospital chain to join the ever-growing empire of CEO and former corporate raider, Delbert Carter.

Dr. Harry Steinham, head of personnel for the conglomerate, spoke to reporters at a press conference at their downtown headquarters. "We are pleased to welcome Dallas General to our growing family of community-based facilities. Known for their long-standing commitment to superior treatment standards and charitable outreach programs, they represent the type of facility that C&C is excited to partner with."

Asked about growing concerns in the industry about consolidations and declining levels of service to the poor and under-insured, Steinham commented, "We are committed to helping those who can't help themselves." When pressed about disturbing reports in communities already served by C&C's affiliates, Steinham waved a stack of satisfaction surveys, claiming they contradicted the claims. "Anyone can download these from our corporate website and see for themselves. We provide only the finest care to our patients."

Steinham indicated more acquisitions were already in the works, the next one likely to be in the Southwest again. C & C stock closed at a new yearly high today in heavy trading on the New York Stock Exchange.

***

Trouble walked in wearing high heels and attitude.

Shoulder-length brown hair framed her smooth, high cheek bones. Stopping well shy of the register, she scanned the tables as if looking for someone to buy her a drink. When her eyes caught mine, they lingered a second too long. A half-smile creased her lips, disappearing so quickly I was unsure I saw it at all. Strolling casually to the periodicals rack, she picked up a *Vogue* and began browsing.

I sipped my coffee and tried refocusing on the *Journal* article in front of me, but there'd been something unsettling in her glance. Was I supposed to respond? Offer to wait in line so she wouldn't have to? If this were a bar, with its clear, unspoken rules, the choice would be easy. I was unaware of such protocols at Starbucks however, especially ones located inside a bookstore on a rainy, September afternoon.

I folded the paper and laid it down. Her dark walnut-brown eyes stayed glued to whatever page she'd turned to, her long lashes barely blinking. She wore a white silk blouse and dark-blue, knee-length skirt which showcased her slim figure and shapely legs.

Without warning, she looked up and our eyes met once more. Flashing another quick, half smile, she replaced the magazine in its rack and strode past me, the scent of Chanel mingling with the soothing aromas of cappuccinos and lattes. I watched, transfixed, as she entered the bookstore, ambling down the nutrition aisle, fingers lightly caressing the shelves.

Suddenly disinterested in the slowdown in international gold production or the market turmoil due to the aftermath of a nationwide shut down, I followed her. There was something familiar in her smile, but what? Michelle never smiled at me like that. Nor Helen. Nor any of the half-dozen others since the divorce.

I racked my brain, trying to place her. College? No, I was still too married and too naïve. My internship at Smith-Wesley Securities? That would have made sense, but by then I was too devastated by the divorce to even consider finding someone new.

She crossed into the "Relationship" section, where self-help titles like, *What to Look for in a Woman's Eyes*, *How to Interpret Her Body Language*, and *How to Get Laid Every Night of the Week, and Twice on Sundays*, were prominently displayed. These were all written by self-anointed experts, of course, who never had any of these problems. They're about as useful as a Stephen Hawking physics book. They make perfect sense, but the minute you try to practice their techniques, you trip over your own ineptitude and fall, face first, into a black hole, never to be heard from again.

Lost in thought, I nearly tripped over a stroller with a sleeping infant as it intersected my path, appearing from the aisle between *Cooking* and *Early Childhood Development*. I apologized, but only got a scowl from the young mother as she picked up her crying baby. Pivoting to see where my mysterious lady disappeared to, I found her standing several steps away, facing me with arms crossed and a broad smile on her face. She obviously witnessed my close encounter with infanticide, and I couldn't help but smile as well. Holding my hands out to the side, I shrugged to acknowledge my embarrassment and closed the distance between us.

"Hi, Steven. Long time, no see."

***

The smile fled my lips.

Nearby, a gigantic black hole started yawning at me.

"You don't remember me, do you."

No, I didn't. I would never have forgotten this woman, this symphony in silk. Yet, something about her voice ...

"I'm so sorry," I replied, "Do we know each other?"

"I'm Donna. Donna Schubell. From high school. Remember?"

I didn't. The name swirled around in my brain, but I kept drawing a blank.

"Think civics class."

Civics class? There was no one there like ... wait ... *Donna*? As in Dirigible *Donna*? The one who was always first for lunch? And first for seconds? And the only one for thirds?

I recovered as best I could. "Donna? Yes. Of course. I remember you. You've ... uh, changed. I didn't recognize you. It's, um ..."

She gently laid her hand on my shoulder. "It's okay. I didn't mean to shock you. It is kind of fun, though, running into old classmates. In fact, I was back in New York a few months ago and ran into Chad. He actually asked me out on a date."

"Chad? As in Chad Johnson?" He was a jock, as I recall, and voted most popular. He was also a qualified jerk.

"Uh-huh. I let him take me to dinner and a show."

"Why? I thought you hated his guts?"

"Still do."

"I guess I'm confused."

"He wined and dined me, like a perfect gentleman. Then, he took me back to his place and started getting amorous."

I waited for her to go on. Instead, she pulled a compact and tube of lip gloss out of her purse and touched up her makeup. Only after she'd put them away, clicking her handbag shut, did she continue the story.

"I pulled out a pamphlet from my purse on anal sex. I handed it to him and suggested he practice fucking himself. Then I left."

"What?" I said loudly. A middle-aged couple perusing books in the marriage counseling section turned to stare.

"What?" I repeated quietly.

"Oh, you would have enjoyed the look on his face. In fact, it's kind of how you look right now."

She was playing with me, but there was nothing I could do about it. Nevertheless, I took comfort in imagining Chad, mouth open, eyes wide, as the door slammed shut behind her. I'd been the foil to many of his practical jokes, so I didn't feel badly he'd been hoodwinked at his own game.

I tried to think of something clever to say, but all I could do was shift my weight nervously from side to side. I was hoping she'd say something else, but she just stood there patiently, waiting for me to speak next.

More people passed by and a teenager texting on his smart phone nearly ran me over. He broke my concentration and, as I moved out of his way, it occurred to me Donna could have done the exact same thing to me if she'd wanted to. Keeping her identity to herself, she could have let me take her out for an expensive meal, then left me holding the pamphlet, so to speak.

I regained a measure of composure. "You're right. I would have enjoyed seeing him squirm. He treated you so horribly."

"He treated *you* like shit, as I recall. Didn't he nickname you 'spaz' because you got cut from the baseball team?"

I winced. I'd totally forgotten that ineffable term of endearment until just now.

"Would you like to buy a girl a cup of coffee?" she asked, changing the subject. "We can sit and talk, and you can fill me in on what you've been up to all these years. Don't let this go to your head, but I always wondered where you ended up after graduation."

She flashed another of those dazzling smiles, and her suddenly soft-brown eyes totally disarmed me. Despite the little voice in my head whispering, *Run for your life!* I heard myself saying, "Sure. I wouldn't mind catching up."

She took my arm and we paraded back into Starbucks, past the table where I'd been sitting. Both of us ignored the round of stares that accompanied our return. After buying a Skinny Vanilla Latte for her and a cappuccino for myself, we made our way to a table in the back corner of the store where the foot traffic was lightest.

Somewhere out there, a black hole with my name on it was biding its time.

The theme song from "City of Angels" played softly from the speakers overhead.

I read once that if you hold some problem in your mind, then open any book, the answer will appear for you. I think it works with music, too. "I just want you to know who I am." That line has haunted me for years, and here it just shows up over the sound system as if I'd requested it in advance. Not that I'll ever be as angelic as Nicholas Cage, mind you.

She stirred her drink with the little wooden stick she'd picked up at the counter. What was it? Fifteen years? Twenty? Was that even possible? The awkward silence of the decades hung between us like the chill in the air before a monsoon. I lifted my cup to take a slow sip of coffee, a wisp of steam rising past my eyes.

"So, how long have you lived in Arizona, Steven?" She finally removed the stirrer and tasted her latte. She licked the foam from her lips as she set the cup back down. Reinserting the stick once more, she resumed stirring it as if it were a magic potion instead of a nonfat, caffeine-free waste of $8.95 plus tax.

"Fourteen years, give or take," I said, thankful she'd chosen a harmless subject to start the conversation. "What about you?"

"Nine. I moved here after the divorce."

"Me, too. Guess your marriage lasted longer than mine."

"Didn't you marry Shelly Crawford? You two were kinda cute together."

"Michelle. She always wanted me to call her Michelle. Yeah. The cute wore off pretty quick."

"What happened?"

"Money problems. What else?"

"Oh?"

"I earned it, she spent it, and when she found someone with more of it than me, well …"

"What a bitch."

I nodded. I had a few more expletives in mind, but I was more interested at the moment in finding out how she'd changed so radically.

"What about you?"

"You mean, what about my divorce? Or, how did I lose all that weight?"

"Yes."

She chuckled, pushed the latte aside, and leaned on the table.

"After graduating, I went to U Mass at Lowell, outside Boston. I'd had it by then with all the fat jokes and went on a strict diet. I did a lot of walking, and when it got cold out, I became a gym rat."

"Well, I have to admit you look amazing. Great outfit, by the way."

"Thanks. What about you? Where'd you end up?"

"I stayed close to home. NYU. I managed to get through college with a bachelor's in engineering, but by the time I graduated, I was disillusioned with the idea of sitting behind a desk and designing widgets. The stock market was on a bull run and I just had to be part of it, so I landed a job at Smith Wesley, became a broker, went to night school to get my MBA, and have been a stock jockey ever since."

"Managed to get through college, aye? Weren't you voted most likely to succeed? By the looks of your tailored shirt and Burberry tie, I'd say you did."

"Glad you like the tie. I wore it just for you."

"Nice try. You didn't even know it was me, remember?"

"Can't blame a guy for trying."

"So, when did you and She ... uh, Michelle get married?"

"When I was a sophomore at NYU." I took another sip of coffee, remembering. "God, I thought I had it made."

"You had big dreams, did you?"

"Doesn't everybody? What about you? You got ditched, too? Or, was it the other way around?"

"I like being single a whole lot better. Simpler, too."

"Well, I'm sorry."

"For what?"

"Sorry you didn't meet Mr. Right. And, sorry I was such a coward back when. I should have stood up for you in school. It wasn't right, the way everyone heckled you."

She reached across the table and gently stroked the back of my hand. "That's sweet of you to say, but we both know it wouldn't have made a difference. In fact, you probably would have made it worse—for *both* of us."

A flock of goosebumps flew up my arm "True, but it doesn't make me feel any better, or excuse my silence." I moved my other hand to put on top of hers, but she withdrew it before I could.

"All right, if it makes you feel better, apology accepted."

My cell phone buzzed, and when I pulled it out to see who it was, I found a text message from my partner in crime, Bill Phillips.

"Business?"

I typed a quick response before answering. "A friend. I'm supposed to meet him for a drink."

"Got some big deal in the works, I imagine."

"No, just drinks. And maybe catch the game on TV."

"I thought you stock-jockeys only talked about money?"

"No, we talk sports, too."

"We didn't get a chance to do much catching up."

"Well, maybe we can continue this over dinner? I know a quaint little Italian restaurant with great food and terrific ambiance. You free tomorrow night?"

She leaned back in her chair and pulled on a few wayward strands of hair, twirling them in her fingers like delicate cotton threads. "You're not the love 'em and leave 'em kind, are you?"

"Seems lately I'm more the love 'em and they leave me kind, but I'm always ready to make a fool of myself under the right circumstances."

It occurred to me this kind of talk was likely the key reason for my lack of success in the relationship department.

She leaned forward this time, arms crossed on the table, hair magically falling back into place all by itself. "There's always hope, Steven."

"Does that mean yes?" I asked.

"Absolutely. What time?"

"I'll pick you up at six. And please feel free not to bring any pamphlets."

She pouted coyly. "Not even the one on the sixty-nine best sex positions ever?"

"Oh, all right. If you insist, but not till after dinner, okay?"

We exchanged cell phone numbers, and I got directions to her place. I headed for my car and she disappeared once more through the winding bookshelves.

~3~

From the outside, Tiani's is just another indistinguishable storefront bistro with a faded wooden facade and tacky, checkered drapes in the windows. A manually operated "Open" sign, the kind you buy at Ace Hardware, hangs next to the tired front door. Tucked in the corner of a strip mall on Elm Street in Mesa, you could easily miss it unless you knew it was there. The obscure location suggested below-average food or service.

Nothing could be further from the truth.

Inside, it is spacious and ambient. The strategically placed mirrors and sconces on the walls gave the appearance it stretched all the way back to infinity. The soft, recessed lighting was dialed down to glow like an ocean sunset, enhanced by the undulating candlelight dancing at the center of each table. The tables themselves were spaced to permit private conversations, especially the intimate, romantic kind, and were set with spotless crystal wine glasses and sparkling silverware perfectly aligned on red-and-white linen tablecloths.

Stepping inside, we were greeted by the scrumptious aroma of fresh-baked breads and mouthwatering scents of garlic and oregano. Sonya, the maître d', stood at her usual station, gracing the podium like a dignified princess, just inside and to the left of the front door.

"Reservation for two, last name Oliver," I said, though it wasn't necessary.

"Right on time as usual, Steven," she said, glancing briefly at Donna, then discreetly nodding her approval. "Your table is ready. William will escort you and will be your server this evening." She handed two menus to the nattily dressed waiter. He bowed at the waist before leading us into the restaurant proper. From behind, Sonya softly called out, "*Bon appétit.*"

Donna wore a stunning black cocktail dress, two-inch black pumps, and a modest collection of jewelry: diamond stud earrings, a simple gold necklace, and a birthstone ring. As we made our way to our table, I noted the heads turning as we passed, men and women alike. Even the wait staff, many of whom knew me by first name, smiled as inconspicuously as they could. Donna, however, seemed to ignore it all, as if she were strolling down an empty hallway. She walked naturally beside me, holding onto my arm, her head swinging side to side, absorbing the atmosphere. I wanted to stop, hit the pause button as if we were in a Netflix video, and shout, *"Eat your hearts out."*

We arrived at last at my favorite table, located beneath the Kincaid painting, "Victorian Light." William held Donna's chair for her, the first time I recall him doing so for one of my dates. After she sat down, he reached for the linen napkin, opened it and placed it on her lap, then gently scooted her chair to the table. I watched as she met his eyes with a congenial smile, which immediately melted him. I think at that moment she could've asked him to dance naked on an adjacent table, singing "That's Amore" at the top of his lungs, and he would have obliged her.

"May I start you off with a cocktail?" he asked, taking his eyes from her long enough to acknowledge me with a sheepish grin.

"I'll have a scotch and soda. Donna?"

"A glass of red wine, please. Your house brand will do."

"Good choice." He placed the menus on the table without offering them to us individually or recanting the evening's specials. This was another break from his usual routine.

When he was out of listening range, I asked Donna, "Does it ever grow old?"

"Does what grow old?"

"The stares, the ogling, the waiters who go over-the-top to impress you?"

"I guess I don't really notice it anymore. Does it bother you?"

"No, not at all," I lied. "I just found it amusing to watch William fall all over himself." I unfolded my own napkin and laid it on my lap. "So, tell me. What have you been doing since high school, besides losing weight and attending charm school?"

I already knew the answer. The first thing I did when I finally got home was look her up in our old yearbook. *"Future Plans: Nursing,"* it said. Her LinkedIn profile indicated her current position as an operating room charge nurse at a local hospital.

"After an internship at Boston Hospital, I became a full RN, working primarily in the ER. I worked in trauma for five years, then transferred to the OR where I met Harry—Dr. Harry Steinham—and we got married two years later."

"But you got divorced after nine years?"

She pulled out her compact and looked in the mirror, adjusting a wayward lock of hair from her forehead. "A friend helped me land an OR position at SCM here in Scottsdale, so I moved to get away from it all." She clicked the compact shut, returning it to her clutch "The hours are hell, but the benefits are generous. What about you? How'd you end up here?"

"Like you, I needed to get away after Michelle dumped me. My firm was opening offices in Phoenix and they offered to pay moving costs plus a bonus if I'd relocate. That, and the prospect of not shoveling snow in the winter, sealed the deal."

William brought our drinks, but had the good sense not to stand there, waiting for us to order. The menus hadn't budged from the spot where he'd put them down. He simply nodded and said he'd be back to check on us. Good man, that William.

"Anyone special in your life right now?" I asked.

"Not really. I've been on a few dates here and there, but nothing serious. No one's in the picture, if that's what you're concerned about. And you?"

I shook my head. "I've tried, but no dice. It's like I have a 'damaged goods' sticker on my back. Maybe I'm just jaded. I funded her lifestyle for all those years before waking up. She got the lion's share of my cash and pension, and I had to start over. I kept wondering if she was screwing the judge, too."

She laughed, and when she did, her eyes reflected the light from the Kincaid painting. He was known as the "'Painter of Light" because his works seemed to glow effervescently when subjected to indirect lighting.

Tonight, it had stiff competition.

"I have a question for you," she said. "If you didn't recognize me yesterday, how come you followed me out into the bookstore? Is that how you pick up women these days?"

That faux pas had occurred to me as well, and I'd spent most of the afternoon practicing my answer.

"It's when you smiled at me the second time. It seemed to say, 'come on, walk with me.' I have to admit, I was scared to death, and no, I don't typically follow strange women into bookstores, or anywhere else for that matter. I've become extremely skeptical of relationships."

Her eyes narrowed, boring a hole through me. "And my smile persuaded you differently?"

"And your eyes" I held her gaze, mirroring her intensity. "It'll sound like a cliché, but they really blew me away."

"You're right," she said, sitting back in her chair, "it sounds like a cliché."

I picked up my glass of liquid courage and offered a toast. "To beautiful clichés."

She hesitated for a moment as my arm dangled in mid-air, then sat up straight to reach for the wine glass. It clinked gently against my scotch, barely jostling it, and we each took a sip.

Well, mine was more of a gulp.

She set her glass to the side and folded her arms on the table, not even bothering with the menu. "So, what exactly does a stock jockey do?"

I took another, longer sip of fire and ice before setting it down and cupping the glass with both hands. "Well, early on, that might have described me, but in the last eight years I've found myself working more with retirees, which meant less concern with quick profits and more attention to conservation of principal, especially after the last big pullback in '09."

"You mean you don't trade stocks anymore?"

"I do. It's just not the main focus of my practice these days."

"I don't understand. If you're a stockbroker—"

"The whole industry has changed. The big boys control most of the stock trading; the pension funds, mutual fund companies, hedge funds, and the like. With their high-speed computers and software, the little guys, including me, don't stand a chance. If you want to survive and do the right thing, then trading securities won't cut it."

"So, if someone wanted advice on, say, a corporate buyout … What? You'd say, 'no thank you, I'm not interested,' and change the subject?"

I picked up the menu and started looking through it, though I already knew what I wanted. "What kind of buyout?"

"Say, a large corporation wants to …," she reached across the table and pushed the menu down onto the table, "they want to buy a private company to get access to a state like Arizona. Is that legal?"

I sighed and let go of the menu. "So long as they pass muster with the dozen or so regulatory agencies in both states and the Feds."

"And if they, uh, 'pass muster,' as you say? It's a—what do you call it—a done deal?"

Where are you going with this?

"Any number of things could still derail it. If it's a public corporation, the shareholders have to approve it, too. Then there could be legal challenges, and so forth. Why?"

Instead of answering, she picked up *her* menu and started browsing, as if it were the Sunday morning paper. After a couple of minutes, I picked mine back up and waved William over.

"What's the special tonight?"

"Your favorite. Seafood alfredo over linguine with mushrooms and red peppers."

I handed the menu to him and looked at Donna. "Sounds great. And what about you?"

"I'll have the Mista salad. Do you have a nonfat dressing?"

"Yes, and it's gluten free. Would you like the large or small portion?"

"Small please, with the dressing on the side if you could."

"Of course. Would you like a salad as well, Steven?"

"Yes. A Caesar salad and some more of these delicious rolls and butter."

"Right away."

William bowed a second time, which is twice more than I've ever seen him do before and walked off toward the kitchen.

Donna inclined her head to one side and her lips turned up a bit. "Hearty appetite tonight?"

"Typical fare for me, I'm afraid. Are you sure you wouldn't like an appetizer? Zucchini or stuffed mushrooms? They're excellent here."

"No, the salad is fine. I just thought that filling up on pasta might, well, you know."

"Fatten me up?"

She reached over, as she had in Starbucks, and caressed the back of my hand. "Slow you down. The night is young, after all."

"Oh? *Oh.* Well, ah, I guess I could … I mean, this isn't over-the-top, really. I, uh …"

She pulled her hand back and interlocked the fingers of both hands on the table, like she was praying. "It's not a big deal. Tomorrow's another day. How did your meeting go yesterday with your friend?"

"What meeting?"

"You were meeting someone for drinks. Bill something-or-other."

"Bill Phillips. We work together. You've got a good memory."

"And."

"Like you said, we met for drinks."

"Isn't that where all the big deals are made, over drinks? Or is it on the golf course? I never really understood that."

"We talked shop, but he's in mergers and acquisitions."

"Sounds impressive. What does it mean?"

"It means he can't really talk about what he's working on because it would be a breach of confidentiality."

"I thought you worked for the same firm."

"We do, but he typically works on deals that aren't public yet. Disclosing it, even to me, invites trouble."

"Oh?"

I paused a moment as William set my salad in front of me along with a fresh plate of dinner rolls and butter in the middle of the table. To my surprise, Donna picked one up, put it on her plate, and tore off a corner of the crusty bread. She put it slowly in her mouth before starting to chew it delicately. She raised her eyebrows, encouraging me to continue.

"It's called insider trading. If Bill inadvertently told me something pertinent about one of his deals, I might be tempted to buy or sell ahead of the release. That would get both of us fired and we'd likely lose our licenses."

She continued chewing for a moment before swallowing. I don't think a sparrow would have taken as small a piece as she had. "So, even if he were working on something, say, locally, he couldn't share it with you?"

"Not without breaking any number of laws."

"But what if it was an out of state company? Or a merger he wasn't a part of?"

"If our firm was involved, it would still be taboo."

"And if not?

I stopped to shovel a forkful of salad into my mouth. I'd looked forward to this meal all day, mostly because it was with her, but at least partially because this was my favorite restaurant. Somehow, though, this had turned into an interrogation instead.

I washed it down with another swig of whiskey. "If we're not part of the deal, we'd look to see how it might affect other, similar companies. A big merger of two banks, for example, would boost the share prices of similar sized banks around the country, so there might be a legitimate play there."

She lifted her drink and took a small sip of wine. "So, you follow industry trends?"

"Of course. I didn't realize you were interested in this kind of thing?"

"I'm just making conversation. You should eat your salad before the entrées arrive."

I gathered another forkful and held it ready to shove in my mouth. "In that case, why don't you tell me what it's like working in the OR while I stuff my face?"

"Sure. We generally work in teams: there's the surgeon, of course, and often he has one or two assistants, depending on the complexity of the procedure. There's the anesthesiologist, who puts the patient under and monitors their status during the operation. Then, there are the nurses, like myself. We assist the doctor with the instruments and help maintain a sterile environment."

In between bites, I encouraged her to be more specific. "But not too graphic, please."

"Queasy stomach?"

"Let's just say the sight or sound of blood, particularly my own, has a negative effect on me."

"Okay, no gore at dinner. The surgeons have strict rules about how they like their instruments laid out on the table and even stricter protocols for how they like them handed to them. Most of them have their routines down to a science and they don't like anything out of place or out of order."

"That's a good thing, isn't it?" I managed to ask, while I buttered another roll.

"Yes. The patient's life depends on it. Anything that might disrupt the flow of the procedure or cause the doctor to go off-track, so to speak, has the potential for disastrous results."

"Hence the term 'surgical precision,' I suppose." I shoved the still-warm roll into my mouth before the butter melted all over my fingers

"Absolutely. If *you* make a mistake, someone loses money. If *we* make a mistake, someone could die."

Something in the way she said that, followed by her quietly intent stare, suggested more to this story than I was getting. Before I could probe a little deeper, however, William returned to see if we needed our drinks refreshed, and to inform us our entrees were nearly ready.

"I'll take another Jack on the rocks. Donna?"

"I'm fine, thank you."

She smiled at William and, despite the dim lighting, I thought I saw him blush.

Pushing the half-finished salad aside, I waited for William to move on. "Do you not think that what I do is important?"

She paused for an excruciating second. "That's not what I meant. Sorry."

"I admire what you do. I couldn't do it. But ask anyone about their money, and you'll often find it occupies a nearly equivalent ranking on their list of priorities."

"That's not a surprise."

"It isn't logical, or even practical, but it's reality."

"I didn't say it wasn't."

"You didn't have to."

She picked up her spoon and, for a moment, I thought she might start stirring her wine, but she simply looked at it, decided it needed polishing with her napkin, and put it down next to her other utensils. "Let's just say I've had some, uh, similar experiences to yours."

"With money?"

"With my ex."

~4~

Slapping the alarm clock to silence it, I settled into the gentle green glow of the early-morning digits. I long ago disposed of the one with the red demon eyes that stared back like some menacing drunk who hadn't been to bed yet. Today, of all days, I didn't want to wake up and return to reality. It was the morning after the night before, and I was in no rush to re-enter the world of stocks, bonds, and complex derivatives defying monosyllabic explanations.

Normally, I'd already be at the computer, checking the overseas markets, preparing a plan for the day's trades.

Not today.

I listened to Donna's gentle breathing as she lay sound asleep, resting her head in the crook of my left arm. We apparently hadn't moved since sometime after midnight, and I didn't want to wake her. Fact is, I didn't want to move at all. I considered calling in sick and spending the day right here, just like this. The subject of her work schedule hadn't come up and I was unsure what to do. Should I get her up so she wouldn't be late? Or, let her sleep in and hope she had the day off?

As if in answer to my silent question, she stirred, stretching her arms and legs. I never knew something so simple could arouse me, but it did. I reached under the covers.

"Easy, tiger," she said.

"Good morning," I responded. "I was getting ready to check for a pulse."

"Down there? Some nurse you'd make."

"My definition of 'checking your vitals' may be a little unique, but at least I don't use an ice-cold stethoscope, like they did at my last checkup."

"Seems you slept pretty soundly yourself."

"Best night's sleep I've had in a long time."

"Wore you out, did I?""

"If that's what it's like to be worn out, then feel free to wear me out as often as you like," I said, paraphrasing Bill Withers.

"What time is it?"

"Quarter after five. What time do you need to get to work?"

"My shift starts at nine. Do you have time for breakfast, or are you the 'love 'em and let 'em get their own breakfast' kind of guy?"

"I don't have any client meetings this morning, so we can grab a bite. You want me to take you home, so you can change first?"

"Sure, but not before I take a shower. I assume this dive has hot, running water."

"Complete with an obedient male servant to provide a gentle backrub while your get yourself all lathered up and steamy."

"Breakfast *and* a back rub. Now that's what I call service. Find me an extra toothbrush and you've got a deal."

Grabbing my bathrobe, I walked down the hall to the guest bathroom where I kept the extra supplies. Donna may be the best, but she isn't the first. It's amazing how little things, like not having extra clean towels or a spare toothbrush, can turn a romantic evening into the last supper. Many people keep "go-bags" in case of emergencies. I have a "please-don't-go" bag, with as many extra medicinal and personal items I imagined a woman might want.

I took a slight detour on the way back to the bedroom to turn on CNBC and check the overnight news. They reported nothing of particular import, only the typical chatter about European bankers working on another round of monetary easing. Unemployment, housing and interest-rate predictions were being revised again, and the president was facing another investigation into this or that.

Same-old, same-old.

Switching to a local channel, I caught the weather—hot; and the sports—disappointing. Just before they broke for commercial, Cindy Sue, the morning anchor, said they'd have more after the break about the pending merger of SCM Hospital in Scottsdale with an outfit out of Boston called C&C and Associates. I'd heard of C&C before. They were highfliers on the market, acquiring sleepy little community hospitals and turning them into profit engines. I might have to look into that when I got to the office.

Bag in tow, I walked back to the bedroom and knocked on the bathroom door.

"Come in."

"Here's your toothbrush, and a small collection of soaps and shampoos. Hopefully something in here suits you."

She took hold of the toothbrush as I set the bag next to the sink. "Very thoughtful of you. I rifled your medicine cabinet, of course, and there wasn't much useful in there, except the Trojans."

"I guess it's a little too late for those."

"Nobody's perfect."

"Why don't I get the shower going while you break in that toothbrush?"

Normally, I'd be over-the-top pissed off to find someone going through my stuff. It was bad enough when my mother found my well-worn, stained, *Sports Illustrated* Swimsuit Issue between my mattress and box spring as a teenager. But this felt totally different. I *wanted* Donna to rifle through me.

"Yup," she chirped, as she applied some toothpaste to the business end of the brush, "too late for the Trojans."

"Do you have any family in town?" she asked.

Traffic on the 101 North through Scottsdale was light, despite the return of the fall and the typical snowbird migration from the northern climes. She had on one of my shirts, a pair of my sweatpants, clean white socks fresh out of the dryer, and no shoes. She'd skipped the makeup, though she truly didn't need any. She looked like a character straight out of a Jerry Seinfeld episode. A small overnight bag I'd lent her for her previous night's attire lay on her lap like a pet poodle.

"No, no family in town. Both of my parents died several years ago, and I really don't stay in touch with either of my brothers."

"Oh, I'm sorry about your parents. Did their passing have anything to do with you not talking with your brothers?"

"Not really. We were a pretty typical family growing up in New York. We had our differences but got along well enough. It wasn't until the three of us got married and moved on that I began noticing problems."

"Like what?"

"We each got so involved in our own lives we didn't have time for anyone else's. We all ended up in different states: one in Maine, the other in Oregon, and I found my way here to Arizona. I tried keeping in touch but, over time, I couldn't help but notice the lack of reciprocation. I don't recall a single occasion, including holidays like Thanksgiving, when either of them ever accepted an invitation to visit. After my divorce, of course, I was expected to do all the flying, since it was cheaper for me to fly there than for them to pack up their families and fly here. That excuse wore thin, though. I finally gave them an ultimatum: make the effort, or don't count on seeing me anytime soon."

"I take it they didn't respond well."

"I was totally underwhelmed." I had a hard time paying attention to the road while carrying on our conversation. This was only my second time driving to her place, counting last night when I picked her up, and I didn't want to get lost. "They paid lip-service to the idea, but never made any plane reservations. When I realized they weren't interested enough to even try, I said a silent goodbye and haven't spoken to them since. That was six years ago. I have no idea where they are now, or what they're doing, and I don't care."

She reached over and stroked my arm gently. "That's too bad. Do you think they were jealous of you?"

"Jealous?" I glanced at her and absently wondered why I never looked that good in my own shirt.

"You're successful and free of obligations. Except to make money, of course."

"Maybe. Who knows? I never rubbed their noses in it. Besides, they're both successful in their own rights. College degrees, good-paying jobs, no real money problems as far as I could see. One of them's divorced twice now. I thought that would have brought us closer."

I turned onto the next street, noting some flashing red and blue lights ahead, indicating an accident.

"What about you? Any family here?"

"I'm close with my mom, but she still lives in New York. We get together three or four times a year. She likes to come out in the winter to get away from the cold and snow. I haven't kept up with my sisters. Like you, I have no reason to pretend to sibling sentimentality."

"Are they jealous of *you*?"

"I doubt it. I'm the only one without children, and I'm sure my divorce blew their minds. After all, I married a doctor."

"Yeah, you mentioned him. Tell me again what happened?"

She went silent. When I stopped at the light on 99th Street, I looked over to see her staring out the window. "Sore subject?"

"Oh, sorry. Harry was a lot of fun, at least in the beginning. Then, something changed. I kept trying to talk to him about starting a family, but he kept putting me off. When he got sued over a botched procedure, he became preoccupied with it. Obsessed. He started working crazy hours and stopped talking to me. We lived in the same house, but you'd never have guessed it. Finally, I couldn't take it anymore and threatened to move out, get a trial separation."

She stopped talking and, when I glanced over once more, a tear lingered on one cheek. Sometime during her soliloquy, she had turned her body ever so slightly toward the passenger door to stare straight ahead, as if her life story was flashing on the windshield in front of her.

"Then what?" I prompted, but she just kept staring as the cars and buildings flew past.

I drove on for another two or three lights before she spoke again. "Remember, when you get off the 101, it's the third street on your left, then a quick right on Jackson."

"I remember." I didn't bother pointing out we weren't on the 101. I made a mental note, however, not to test that subject again, at least not till we knew each other a lot better. "Sorry if I opened a wound,"

"It's okay. I thought I'd gotten over it. I guess maybe I haven't."

"A hot breakfast and titillating conversation with an accredited financial guru will make you forget all about it," I said to lighten the mood.

She turned toward me, a half-smile gracing her lips. "I'm counting on it."

When we pulled up in from of her apartment, I shifted the car to park, and she leaned over and kissed me.

***

While she ran inside to get changed, I tuned in to the local financial news network for the daily update. The markets were quiet today, which meant no "black swans" had shown up yet. For the second time this morning, though, I heard a report concerning the potential merger of SCM with C&C. The rest of the news was routine: the bulls calling the bears Chicken Little's and the bears calling the bulls Pollyanna's. Unemployment was down. Manufacturing was up. Blah, blah, blah.

Satisfied the world wasn't ending today, I chose an oldies station. The dashboard display flashed the station's call letters and song title in lime green LEDs. Gone were the dials and knobs I'd grown up with. For some reason, my thoughts turned to my dad, how he always listened to swing and jazz. "Why don't you listen to something more modern?" I'd ask. "I can't stand that rock and roll stuff." And, he'd reply, "Too loud."

"Sorry, Dad," I whispered aloud.

Just then, the opening strains of Blue Oyster Cult's 'Don't Fear the Reaper' filled the vehicle and I started singing along. I got lost in the lyrics, keeping beat on the steering wheel with my thumbs and tapping the gas pedal gently like I was stoking a base drum when the door opened, and Donna slid in. I reached to turn the volume down, but she got there first and turned it up, singing along, too. She drummed on the dashboard, moving her head and shoulders to the music, free as a bird.

As the last chords faded, reverberating in the car along with our slightly off-key screeching, I turned it down and looked at her. She smiled and said, "Glad you're not the elevator music kind of guy."

She was dressed in jeans and sneakers, and a T-shirt that read *OR nurses are a cut above.* This was surrounded by scalpels, forceps, and a host of other instruments with surgical significance, I assumed. Her hair, tied in a ponytail, gave her an entirely different look. She wore no makeup except some lip gloss, and no jewelry, not even earrings.

"Me too," I said. "Nice T-shirt. No uniform?"

"I'll change when I get there."

I put the car in drive and pulled away from the curb. "Busy day today?"

"Usually is. I didn't check the schedule yesterday, except to see when I was on. I'm supposed to be off at seven tonight. You able to pick me up after work?"

"No problem." I realized she could have chosen to drive her own car to work instead. "Where should we go for breakfast?"

"There's an IHOP on the way to the hospital. But, step on it—I'm starving. If you intend to keep me as a sex slave, you'd better feed me."

"I'm not sure who's keeping who, but fasten your seat belt, 'cause we're about to fly."

***

She was right, but the IHOP wasn't just "on the way." It was right across the street from the hospital. We walked in and I was glad for no waiting line to get a table.

The woman behind the counter had fiery-red hair, which contrasted loudly with her light blue uniform and gold name badge. Of medium height, and slender, she sorted and stacked menus like a croupier. I watched as her hands manipulated the slippery sheets, convinced I would have spilled all of them on the floor if I attempted it myself.

She looked up when the last stack was neatly squared off and her green eyes lit up like a roman candle when she spied Donna. "Hey, girl, where you been hiding?" She came out from behind the counter and the two of them hugged like long lost cousins.

"Crazy shifts these last few weeks," Donna said when the embrace ended. "You have a booth somewhere in the back, away from the fattening crowd?"

"Where you and your handsome new friend here can talk?" She extended her hand to me. "My name's Carol." She nodded at the window. "Nice car."

"Thanks. I'm Steven." Her handshake felt warm and firm. I saw Donna looking at me kind of strangely, so I disengaged my hand from Carol's as politely as I could. "Nice to meet you."

"Any friend of Donna's is a friend of mine, so long as you realize it'll be open season on you once you leave. I hope you don't mind being gossiped about."

"Why wait? I love hearing speculation and innuendo about myself. I assume none of it needs to be true?"

Her smile was nothing less than infectious. "Of course not. What fun would that be?"

"Then I won't tell you that Donna and I were secretly married in Vegas last night, and this is our first meal together as a married couple. Do you carry matrimonial pancakes?"

Without missing a beat, she answered, "Uh-huh. They're French blintzes, cream-filled and covered with gooey syrup. We call them Bliss in a Blanket."

"Okay, you two, that's quite enough," Donna chimed in, "If I'd known this would turn into a comedy routine, I would have gone to the greasy spoon down the street and gagged on their oatmeal instead."

Carol laughed and showed us to a booth in a back corner of the restaurant. I decided it might be a good idea to come back here again one day by myself to grill Carol.

For breakfast, Donna ordered fruit and wheat toast, dry, two Egg Beaters scrambled with mushrooms and tomatoes, and black, caffeine-free coffee. Years of discipline, I imagined, but it didn't stop me from ordering their "lumberjack special," which could have fed both of us easily.

"You didn't have to go to work this morning?" she asked.

"I will, after I drop you off." I poured coffee from the separate decanters into the cups the waitress dropped off for us.

"Must be nice, coming and going as you please. Don't you have clients or customers or something?"

"I've earned a certain amount of flexibility. Besides, with my cell phone, the computer in the apartment, and the electronic tablet I keep in my briefcase, I can work from just about anywhere. Technology, for all its glitches and aggravations, has the advantage of freeing me from having to be in the office all the time."

"Well, it's improved things in the hospital, too, but we still have to show up for the surgeries. Our patients appreciate our presence when they're cut open."

"Really? I thought I read somewhere about how surgery could be performed remotely, using robots operated by surgeons sitting in their own living rooms. That's how they operate drones in the Middle East; they fly them from nice safe caves in Nevada, right here in the good old U S of A."

"Thanks, but no thanks. They're already reducing the nursing staff to save money. Remote control operations would translate to unemployment for the rest of us."

"Hadn't thought of that. Okay, nix the robotic surgery. I wouldn't want to be responsible for mass nursing layoffs."

The waitress brought the creamer and skim milk Donna had asked for, setting them down with the silverware and napkins. My breakfast companion added a small amount of nonfat milk to hers and began stirring.

"All kidding aside, it's a serious problem," she continued. "Seems like efficiency and cost-cutting are more important than patient care. When did money become more important than people?" She kept stirring her coffee, even though she hadn't added anything else to it.

"Right after they invented money, I think." I took a sip of my java after adding some sweetener and half and half.

The expression on her face turned serious. "Isn't that what you do, Mr. Technology? Work with money all day long?" Her tone held a tinge of accusation.

Warning bells started ringing inside my brain. I had tripped over her sore spot again and rubbed it the wrong way.

"I told you; I work mainly with retirees to try to make their money last as long as they do. As far as I can see, nothing I do puts anyone's jobs at risk."

"But don't you buy and sell companies just to make a profit, sucking them dry till there's nothing left but closed factories and soup kitchens?"

"Hell no! Whatever gave you that idea?"

"Sorry. I didn't mean it that way." She stopped stirring and laid the spoon down carefully on the saucer. "It's just so frustrating to be constantly shorthanded. And now, there's a rumor going around the hospital some healthcare outfit from Boston is looking to take us over. The gristmill has it they come in and totally revamp everything—fire all the skilled nurses and doctors and bring in their own. I just don't know what to think."

I took another sip of coffee. "Don't you have contracts? I know we're a right-to-work state, but that doesn't void contracts between employers and employees."

"There's a way around it."

"How?"

"They offer you a transfer to a newly created position, with a raise and more responsibility. They don't tell you that taking the new job subjects you to a new probationary period. Then, they just let you go under some job related pretext. Or else, they eliminate the position outright, in which case they aren't even required to offer you your old job back—or any other job for that matter. You're just out."

I felt a slight queasiness in my stomach. Unfortunately, she was right. I'd seen it happen in our office. We sat quietly while the waitress returned with our meals, placing them carefully in front of us. As she did, I thought about it. No matter how many laws are passed to protect employee rights, a clever lawyer can always get around them. My saving grace? I'm in sales. That brings in revenue, which translates to job security.

"You want me to find out more about the company trying to take over your hospital?" I asked when the waitress left

"You can do that?" She paused to glance at me, then went to work on the fruit plate.

"Why not? I can leap tall buildings at a single bound, and I'm faster than a speeding bullet."

That got a smile out of her. "So now you're Superman?"

"At your service with *Truth, Justice, and the American Way.*"

"Then, yes please, look them up." She took a bite of melon. "And while you're at it, tell them to fuck off."

"For that, I'll need to call in Batman. Superman doesn't curse. Dinner tonight?"

"Since you're picking me up anyway, yes. You'll need to meet me at the south entrance, same place you'll be dropping me off, okay?"

"Deal," I said, and dug into the pancakes.

***

SCM is the last privately-run hospital in the valley. Established in 1962, it grew from a single building near downtown Scottsdale to a Valley-wide chain of medical facilities serving large sections of metropolitan Phoenix. Priding itself on its independence, it hosts outreach programs for the local community and attracts donations from local philanthropists, most of which are used to expand services. A significant endowment fund helps the poor and indigent with the substantial costs of care.

The facility Donna works at on 90th street boasts a state-of-the-art ER department and trauma center and serves as her home away from home.

I found a place to pull over near the employees' entrance and kissed her goodbye before she climbed out of the car and headed for work. She didn't cozy up to any of the others who joined her at the door, not even the cute intern in the scrubs and short, blond hair. Her gait was sure and steady, and she only slowed momentarily to wave to me before disappearing behind the door.

The morning had felt so easy, effortless, like we'd been doing this for years. I never asked her why she let me drive her to work instead of taking her own vehicle. She never questioned it or suggested she could follow me to IHOP. It was just a continuation of the night before. Things were just happening, and I saw no reason not to let them.

I thought about heading back to talk with Carol. This sudden romance popped up like a traveling summer carnival, and the voice which earlier whispered "run for your life" still nagged me, though with less intensity. As the car idled, I recalled my search on the Internet once again, and it occurred to me she could've done the same; my credentials and work history were similarly available to anyone willing to look. Was there something I was missing here?

I nixed the idea of chatting up Carol, at least for now. I didn't know the depth of their friendship, and Carol would have no reason to reveal anything negative about Donna. More likely, it would even backfire. No sense screwing it up so soon.

I headed to the office.

The 101 was running freely despite the nine o'clock hour, and I pulled into the parking garage in less than fifteen minutes. I left the radio tuned to the financial news station and, just as I pulled into my parking spot, I got lucky. I turned it up to listen to an expanded report on C&C's attempt to buy SCM. They'd gone on a buying spree of medical facilities around the country over the last several years, and this was the latest in a string of expansions westward. I'd most likely find plenty of information online.

I hurried upstairs and nodded at the receptionist at the front desk. She'd been there for two weeks now, and I hadn't learned her name yet. The turnover at our firm was quite high. So high, in fact, the office didn't even provide a nameplate until someone had been there for at least three months. Apparently, corporate policy condoned "Hey, you," as sufficient greeting for the hourly paid staff.

I found the hallways surprisingly quiet as I made my way past the cubicles and conference rooms. Then it struck me; it was Thursday. There was a free lunch-and-learn at a nearby restaurant. Each week, some eager-beaver wholesaler invited local brokers to listen to their latest investment offerings with the promise of free food at some fancy eatery. Without it, the wholesalers would be left talking to themselves, and the public would be spared hearing about yet another round of innovative financial products best left undiscovered.

I slipped inside my office and closed the door. Clearing my voice mail messages, I did a quick scan of the market to make sure I didn't need to make any significant portfolio changes. Finding nothing critical, I googled C&C Healthcare Associates, Inc. and started reading.

It didn't take long to confirm what Donna told me. In all the online news articles and commentaries, it was evident C&C's preoccupation for buying ever-larger hospital facilities culminated in the same result: mass layoffs and significant declines in services to the local communities. Additionally, quality of care issues began to show up, despite numerous "patient satisfaction surveys," which C&C's hospitals were quick to produce, showing patient satisfaction "on the rise." Within just a few months of each acquisition, C&C stock experienced unusual growth as the cost-cutting and service curtailment translated into higher profits. What stood out, however, was the growth in revenues. In corporate America, replacing highly paid employees with lower paid, less experienced ones was the norm, resulting in impressive profit growth, at least in the short term. Eventually, though, it resulted in lower revenues, reduced market share, and a general decline in the stock price. In C&C's case, however, revenue grew along with profits, which definitely was *not* the norm. Something else was going on here, but it wasn't obvious from what I could distill from the public sources.

I hit the speed dial for "Phillips."

"Hey, partner. What's the good word?" Bill always seemed to be in a cheerful mood, which put his clients and associates at ease. I often wished I could mimic his style.

"How's the new cabin coming in Snowflake?" I asked.

"Nearly done," he said, "We should have it completely furnished next week if all goes well. Maybe you can join us for a few days to celebrate? It's nice and cool up there away from the desert heat."

"What, and leave Phoenix's toasty ninety-five-degree dog days? Why would I want to do that?"

"Because it's free and because you can bring your latest fling with you. I hear she's a real knockout. What's her name?"

"How the heck did you know about Donna? I only met her a few days ago."

"Stan and his wife saw you at Tiani's. He said she was a bombshell—his words—and you didn't even finish eating dinner before leaving together. For you to leave Tiani's before they served the tiramisu means this woman is either really special or really hot. Either way, I want to meet her. Who is she?"

I wasn't about to go into the whole story with him over the phone. Frankly, my head was still reeling as it was. "We ran into each other at the mall. She went to my high school. I haven't seen her in nearly twenty years. We were just catching up."

"Like hell. You owe me more than that. I want details."

"It'll have to wait. But, if she's interested in going to Snowflake with us, I'll let you know. Meantime, the reason I'm calling has to do with the hospital she works at ... SCM. Doesn't Ellen go there for treatment?" Bill's wife, Ellen, suffers from a rare blood disorder that requires regular treatments and occasional hospital stays to keep it under control.

"Yeah, that's the one. Why the interest in SCM?"

"I heard on the radio they're being acquired by some conglomerate in Boston called C&C Healthcare and Associates. Donna mentioned it, too. She said the rumor around the Starbuck's kiosk was they typically come in and decimate the staff, with detrimental effects to local healthcare service. Have you heard anything about it?"

"I heard the story on the news, same as you, but hadn't given it much thought." His voice turned suddenly serious. "You think there's something going on I should know about?"

"Well, I did some checking, and the online accounts were pretty consistent: layoffs, followed by a general decline in services. The thing that stands out, though, is the way revenue and profits seem to be going up."

"What do you mean?"

"I mean there's none of the usual shenanigans, like heavy use of debt or pension plan terminations. The purchases are for cash, and in short order revenues grow dramatically along with profits. In the last eighteen months, C&C stock has more than doubled, and the growth numbers are extraordinary. It just doesn't feel right. Something is out of whack here, but I'm not smart enough to know what. That's why I called. Maybe you can look at their regulatory filings and figure out what's going on? You were always better at interpreting those things than me."

"Sure, I'll take a look. If SCM is in play, I need to know anyway. Ellen's doing much better now, and I don't want any surprises. I'll give you a call as soon as I have anything."

"Thanks, buddy."

"And don't think you're off the hook. I want a full report on your new fling when we get together. Understand?"

"Understood. Talk to you later."

We hung up, and I turned my attention back to the market. A long list of clients to call lay ahead of me today.

I couldn't keep my mind off tonight, however.

~6~

Five o'clock jumped up and kicked me like an overdue bill. I'd gotten lost in conversation with a pissed-off client. He blamed me for missing out on an IPO that tripled two days after going public, like I should've had a crystal ball. I promised to keep my eyes open for the next *hot stock* and rushed him off the phone. Shutting down my computer, I sent Donna a text, asking if she had any dinner preferences. Just as I pressed "send," it struck me; she was probably in surgery, or with a patient. I certainly wouldn't want my nurse answering personal texts while tending to my bandages. I'm so used to getting instant replies I forgot there are still legitimate reasons not to answer immediately. I sent another text assuring her I'd be there on time and would surprise her for dinner.

A quick stop at home for a shower and change of clothes allowed me to put together an "I don't want to go home bag." This time, I didn't want to be caught without proper protection. For dinner, I decided to take a chance on my cooking skills. That meant a trip to the grocery and the outside possibility of ptomaine poisoning, but it also meant we wouldn't have to leave her apartment.

***

"Making your famous shrimp scampi?" Randy asked from behind the fish counter at AJ's Fine Foods. The case was filled with a mouthwatering selection of fish, shrimp, lobster tails, and crab legs from the West Coast. Randy was dressed in a white butcher's coat emblazoned with the green logo, and his hair was covered in fishnet, the kind you need at the beauty salon while sitting under a hair dryer.

"Yes," I replied, watching as he picked the best prawns from the ice bed. "You have a wine recommendation?"

"How badly do you want to impress her?" He topped off the pile with a couple of extras to bring it to just over a pound.

"What makes you think I'm trying to impress a woman?"

"Come now, my culinary friend. We both know you only buy this much shrimp when you have a hot date and you're trying to get lucky. How much luck are you shooting for here? Run of the mill luck? Hope-she-calls-back-again luck? Or this-is-the-one-I'm-in-love-again luck?"

"Am I really that transparent?"

He chuckled. "You may as well have one of those banners running across your forehead like they do on the Internet."

"Okay, smart ass. Yes, I think this one might be special. What's the right wine?"

"Personally, I prefer the St. Michael's Pinot Grigio."

"You think that will impress her?"

"I have no idea. I just like pinot grigio with shrimp. You want to know what she likes, you gotta ask her," he said.

"Nice. Just give me the shrimp and I'll pick out my own wine."

I headed to the produce department for salad ingredients and some fresh asparagus. I grabbed a bag of white rice on the way to the spice aisle. Then it was time for salad dressings, fresh baked Italian bread from the bakery, and a trip to the dessert freezers for some fat-free sherbet. Finally, I scanned the rows of wine in the liquor department. Why on Earth there had to be so many selections I don't know, but I finally settled on the pinot grigio. I remembered she had ordered a glass of red wine at Tiani's, so I picked up a nice Merlot as well.

Just as I was putting the bags in my car, my cell vibrated.

"Just out of surgery. Meet u at 7. S. entrance. What kinda surprise 4 dinner??"

I texted back simply, *"On my way. u'll just have 2 wait & c."*

"Hope it's good. I'm hungry."

"Me 2. c-ya soon☺"

I kept to the surface streets on the way to the hospital to avoid the evening rush hour traffic. Even with the occasional red light, they were often faster than the four-lane interstate. Sometimes the fast lane isn't so fast.

On the radio, Madonna sang "Material Girl." I turned it off. I'd had more than my fill of that from Michelle.

I hit the south entrance precisely at 6:58 and no sooner had I come to a stop than the hospital door opened, and the latest shift spilled out, Donna among them, looking tired and ready to run.

"So, what's the surprise?" she asked as she got in. I was tempted to say something stupidly spontaneous like, "We're flying to San Francisco so we can eat at Anthony's Pier Four on the Wharf," except she might actually believe me and be disappointed with my eat-at-your-place plan. So, I opted for, "I hope you're in the mood for an old-fashioned home-cooked meal."

She clicked the seatbelt around her waist. "Oh? Whose home? And who's doing the cooking?"

I pulled away from the curb and headed for 101st Street. "Yours, and me."

"Sounds fabulous. I'm tired, and I didn't feel like going out anyway. What are you making?"

"Seafood, salad, and sherbet. Hope you're not allergic to anything."

"Just groping interns and catty floor nurses."

"Well, they were all out of groping interns at the store, and the catty floor nurses were overpriced, so I opted for shrimp scampi instead."

She laughed at that. "Just so long as I can take a shower and change before dinner."

"No problem. It will take a while to get everything ready anyway. I trust you have pots and pans and such?"

"What are those?" she replied, smirking.

"Funny, that's exactly how my ex felt. They're typically aluminum or steel, and you put them on the stove to cook food."

"Oh! *Those things*! I wondered what they were for. They're pretty basic, but they should do. You know your way around a kitchen, do you?"

"Absolutely. Just remind me—how long does it take to boil water in the microwave?"

She tilted her head and gave me a sideways glance. "What?"

"Just kidding. I stopped boiling water in the microwave after I blew up my last girlfriend's apartment."

She shook her head and sighed. A wry smile spread across her lips. "Did I mention you have a very unique, dry sense of humor?"

The lights were cooperative, and I turned onto McKenna Drive. "You just did. How was work?"

"Pretty typical. Six procedures today. We were scheduled for eight, but one coded before coming up and the other contracted strep and had to reschedule."

"So, you got to lounge through the day."

There was a short silence and I glanced over. The expression on her face said it all: chin down, eyes narrowed, and wrinkles at the bridge of her nose that threatened to swallow me alive. One more sore spot to navigate around. She takes her job *very* seriously. That's a lot different from the world I know, where gallows humor is our way of breaking the tension.

"Sorry," I said. "That didn't come out the way I intended it to."

"I hope not. We really humped today."

"You said today was typical. Is it always this stressful?"

"There's just so much we have to keep track of. Today was a good day. The remaining procedures went as planned, and it looks like all of them will recover fully."

"Well, you can tell me about them if you want, so long as you don't get too graphic."

"Ah, yes. You get squeamish about blood and such."

"Not so long as it isn't mine. I just don't want to ruin our appetites."

"Okay, I'll leave out the gory details. You're really interested in hearing about my day?"

"Sure. I spent the day working with other people's money, and it's often a thankless job. If I do something right, they're brilliant, but if a client loses money, my ancestry gets dragged through the mud. At least you get to help people recover their health."

"Yeah, but if we screw up, someone could die."

"All the more reason why your job's more interesting than mine."

With that, she relaxed and started talking nonstop till we got to her place. In fact, she was so animated, I took the long way back to her apartment just to give her the chance to totally unwrap her day. I didn't think she noticed, but when we finally pulled up to her front door, she reached over and took my hand. "Thanks for letting me talk. It's been a while since I've been able to do that. You really didn't have to go halfway around the world to get here, but I'm glad you did."

"No problem," I said. "You go ahead inside and jump in the shower. I'll grab the groceries and head for the kitchen."

***

She walked up the steps with the same, deliberate saunter as at the bookstore. It surprised me for a moment, and I toyed with the thought I was being played. Discerning the differences between women who are truly interested and those with ulterior motives was never my forte. Michelle taught me to be cynical. Trusting anyone of the feminine persuasion has been nearly impossible since her. All my interim relationships have been purposefully artificial. This time, though …

A passing car woke me from my stupor. I popped open the trunk and grabbed the grocery bags. The duffel bag stayed in the car; I could always retrieve it later. No sense jinxing myself by bringing it in. The smell of warm bread reminded me how hungry I was.

She'd left the front door open, and I found myself in a sparsely furnished efficiency apartment. A short hallway led to a living room, outfitted with a sofa, recliner, coffee table, end table with a plain lamp—the kind you find at Kohl's or JC Penney's—and a small LED television on a stand that might have been purchased at a garage sale. Another hallway led to the right, apparently where the bedroom was. Turning left, I found a cozy kitchenette and set the bags on the conspicuously empty Formica counter next to the sink. An L-shaped counter against the back wall bracketed the plain-white stove/oven, microwave, and refrigerator. I heard her call out from the empty hallway, "You can use whatever you find in the cabinets. I'm jumping in the shower now."

"Okay," I called back, wondering what she meant by "whatever you find in the cabinets." Opening the first cupboard, I found a collection of no-name cookware adequate to the task. They didn't appear to have gotten much use, so this home-cooked meal idea began looking smarter by the minute. Out of curiosity, I opened the freezer, and at once noticed the abundance of Weight Watchers dinners. Looking in the refrigerator was like stumbling onto a deserted island. Except for a quantity of fruits and vegetables in the lower crispers, some skim milk, and a container of Egg Beaters, it was empty. She either ate out a lot, or not at all. Opening a few more cabinets, I found the modest cache of seasonings, several of which hadn't even been opened, perhaps since she moved in.

I unpacked the bags, laying everything on the back counter, and got to work. I set a large frypan on the stove, depositing a generous portion of butter inside. While it melted, I searched for and found a colander that still had the original label from Bed, Bath & Beyond, and cleaned it thoroughly before using it to rinse the shrimp. Next, I turned on the oven and wrapped the Italian bread in the aluminum foil I found in one of the drawers. I popped it in to warm up while I got to work on the rest of the meal. In another, smaller pan I likewise melted some butter then added the asparagus to simmer on a low heat.

The butter sizzled in the larger pan, so I added the spices, including some Worcestershire sauce which was nearly beyond its "use by" date. I adjusted the dial to low and turned my attention to a third pot, filled with water and placed on the back burner to boil. When it roiled slowly, I added the white rice, reducing the heat so it wouldn't boil over.

The salad came next. I chopped and diced the lettuce, spinach, tomatoes, cucumbers, scallions and mushrooms in their appropriate order. There isn't an appropriate order, of course, but I impose one anyway, out of habit. Working steadily and methodically, I started to relax for the first time all day.

When the rice reached the right tenderness, I added it to the frying pan, covering it to allow the sauce to permeate the rice. The salad continued to grow in the wooden bowl I found in the lower cabinet. It, too, had required a good deal of rinsing to rid it of the layer of accumulated dust. Finally, I added the salad's fat-free Italian dressing to complete the first course and placed it in the fridge to chill.

Just as I closed the door, I heard the shower stop. It was a small apartment, so the sudden silence caught my attention. For a second, I found myself lost in the warm, sudsy memory of this morning, and nearly forgot to turn the heat down under the asparagus so it wouldn't burn. I needed everything to be succulent, not rubbery.

I had maybe ten minutes before she came out from the bedroom, so I rinsed the prawns in the colander and added them to the rice, stirring to make sure the scampi sauce was evenly distributed. I checked the bread in the oven, then pulled out a set of plates, glasses, and silverware to set the table. I wasn't surprised to discover her best china was basic white Corelle with a simple blue edging. The glass tumblers and stainless silverware were plain and simple as well, but clean. I hadn't realized I was such a snob till just now. I folded the Bounty-brand paper napkins neatly, laid the utensils on them, and placed them symmetrically next to the plates and glasses on the bamboo placemats. For the wine, the best I could do was a couple of juice glasses, which I placed next to the glass tumblers. They would have to suffice.

I placed both the wine and the salad in the center of the table and turned back to check on the stove to find my path blocked. Donna wore a halter top and tight-fitting denim shorts that covered as little of her long, shapely legs as possible.

"I'm impressed," she said, "you really do know your way around the kitchen. It smells wonderful in here."

"Not nearly as good as you do," I said.

She ignored that. "I see you pulled out my good stuff. I normally dine on paper plates and recycled plastic forks and spoons."

"I thought our first home-cooked meal should be more formal."

"And how did you know I liked Merlot?" She picked up the bottle.

"You ordered red wine at Tiani's. Just in case you're a connoisseur, however, I also brought a Pinot Grigio."

"So, your plan was to get me drunk tonight?"

"Only as a last resort. Are you more fun when you're wasted?"

She gave me an odd look, but didn't elaborate except to say, "I never remember, so I couldn't really tell you."

"Well, last night was fun, and you hardly touched your drink at Tiani's, so inebriation apparently isn't required."

"I never did have much of a taste for alcohol, but wine with dinner is a treat. I hope it wasn't too expensive."

"I didn't check the price, and I've already opened it, so I guess it's too late to worry about it." I smiled.

I still had food simmering on the stove, so I grabbed Donna and simultaneously kissed her, picked her up, spun her around and set her down by the table to give me a clear path back to the shrimp and asparagus.

"Did I distract you too much?" she asked.

"You thoroughly distract me, but I'm hungry enough to ignore it till we're done eating. I'll reengage in your distraction when we're finished."

I pulled the bread from the oven and stirred the rice and scampi again. "Help yourself to some salad," I called over my shoulder. "The dressing is a no-calorie Italian I got at the store."

"That was thoughtful," she replied. "Keep this up and I may have to hire you full time."

"No problem. I'm cheap. I'll work for sex."

She took her seat while I scooped the main course into a large glass bowl.

"You made shrimp scampi from scratch? Really?"

"Well, I thought about the Chef Boyardee canned scampi, but they haven't invented it yet, so I had to make it myself. Hope you're not disappointed."

"Nope. In fact, I think I'm in love."

"Hold on to that thought," I said, using some tongs to transfer the asparagus onto another Corelle plate. "Soup's up."

***

She sat down as I placed the last plate of goodies between us. I joined her, sitting catty-corner at the cozy, square kitchen table. When I started to ask what she wanted first, she closed her eyes, interlocked her fingers, and held them to her chin. "Thank you, God, for this food and for this day. Amen."

"Amen," I repeated

Opening her eyes, she smiled at me, a smile which sliced right though me. I was stunned speechless. All I could think to do was pour some Merlot for both of us before scooping some salad onto my plate. I watched as she dished some of the shrimp scampi onto hers.

She took a sip, wiping her lips gently with her napkin. "So, I told you all about my day, but what about yours? Did you ever make it to work, or did you end up playing hooky?"

I, too, drank some wine, though it was measurably more than her meager sip. "No, I made it to work. It was a quiet day on the markets. I didn't have any customer appointments, so I investigated that company, C&C Healthcare. Unfortunately, it appears your fears may be justified; their modus operandi is to cut staff and reduce services aggressively to ramp up revenue and profits."

She picked up her fork but didn't put it to use, just left it hovering over the plate. "In other words, they couldn't care less about people, only about money."

I stabbed a couple of pieces of lettuce and stuffed them in my mouth, chewing slowly. "Pretty much."

"How can they get away with it? What happened to serving the community? Aren't there laws and regulations? Isn't there something illegal in what they do?"

"I can't say." I stared into her piercing brown eyes. "My guess? They do everything within the letter of the law or find a legitimate loophole to jump through."

She put her fork down and folded her hands in front of her plate.

"Try some of the scampi before it gets cold," I said.

She remained still for another long moment before picking up the thin, stainless steel excuse for a fork and speared a shrimp. Rubbing it gently in the sauce, she continued. "I don't understand. How can they just fire people and cut services with impunity?"

"If you have enough money and lawyers, you can get away with almost anything." I took another bite of salad before continuing. "They can afford to make large campaign donations and spend millions on lobbyists."

"But it's not right."

"Didn't say it was. It's reality, though."

"You're not making my day," she said, finally taking a bite of my skillfully prepared concoction.

"I could lie to you and tell you what you want to hear, that your hospital will be the exception, or there's a way to deflect the takeover, but I thought you wanted the truth."

I watched as she slowly chewed her food, finally swallowing that first morsel. I hoped for a "Wow, that's delicious!" but instead she went on to say, "No, you're right. I wanted to know the truth. But it sucks. Can't anything be done about it? You asked me earlier about our contracts. What if everyone banded together and refused to play by their rules?"

"I don't know." I paused to dip a slice of bread into the sauce and took a bite. "It would only postpone the inevitable. They're run by a ruthless chairman by the name of Delbert Carter. He did the same thing in the furniture industry a number of years ago, gobbling up dozens of manufacturers and retailers. By the time he was done, several well-known, old-line companies ended up in bankruptcy. Thousands of employees lost their jobs, and their pension plans ended up in the hands of the Feds, which meant hard-earned retirement checks would be slashed. Meanwhile, Carter and his team walked away with hundreds of millions of dollars in fees and 'dividends.' How's the scampi, by the way?" I asked at last.

"I'm sorry, Steven." She reached over to touch my hand gently. "It's fabulous. I didn't mean to be rude. It's just that you're scaring me. Isn't there anything that we can do to stop this?"

I figured she'd get around to asking. The problem was, I wasn't sure. It didn't escape me, however, that she'd said *we*. Did that mean "me and my fellow employees at the hospital?" or as in "you and me?" Either way, I didn't believe there really was anything to be done.

I took another sip of wine. "First of all, it isn't a done deal yet. It needs approval from the hospital's board. Then, there are several regulatory hoops to jump through before it can move forward. I spoke with my friend, Bill, the one I mentioned to you."

"Bill Phillips, right? The one who cobbles together these things?

"Yes, that's him. I asked him to look at it. I'm still waiting to hear back. Maybe he'll have some ideas. As a worst-case scenario, however, it might be wise to get your résumé together."

She looked down at her plate, pursing her lips. Without raising her head, she said. "That doesn't sound very encouraging." She managed to gather a few leaves of lettuce on her fork before raising her chin enough to look at me with her eyebrows raised. "What about all the other nurses and employees there? What about the patients? We're all trying our best to help people. How do you work in a business like that?"

I straightened my back. "Hey, don't lump me in with Carter and his cronies. I'm just as pissed as you. He ruins perfectly good companies, screws thousands of people, and walks away a gazillionaire. That's not what I'm about, and it's not what our business is about, but we get painted with the same brush because he's so high profile. My job is to help people, too, but I don't get my name in the paper or on TV when I do my job right. I don't like this anymore than you, but I honestly don't know what can be done about it. I'm just one person."

I grabbed my juice-come-wineglass and took a long drink of wine. This wasn't going anything like I'd hoped.

She sat up straighter as well, laying the fork down to rest on the edge of the plate. "I know it's not your fault, but surely you can do better than … than …" The look in her eyes turned to fear, a child's eyes. "Isn't there anything you can do, Steven? Can't you help? Please?"

I knew I'd regret the words the minute they tumbled out of my mouth. "I'll do what I can. Maybe there's a loophole or two they haven't thought of."

The fear evaporated, replaced by a look of relief. "Thank you, Steven," she said softly. She picked up the abandoned fork full of greens and ate them. "Anyone who cooks like this can't be all bad."

I took a deep breath and let it out slowly. "Ahhh. So you approve of my kitchen skills?"

"They're almost as good as your bedroom talents," she said.

I lifted the plate of asparagus and offered it to her. "Here. Have some. It's known to be an effective aphrodisiac."

"Says who?"

"I just made it up. Now be a good girl and chow down."

The sherbet may have to wait until later. Much later.

The voicemail from Bill was skillfully vague. In this new age of indiscriminate monitoring, even the most innocuous statement could inadvertently be misconstrued, twisted into evidence of insider trading or some other breach of fiduciary responsibility. Bill was acutely aware of this. It's an odd twist of fate. We have achieved in the United States a level of "Big Brother-ism" that communist Russia never accomplished. You no longer need to be paranoid to believe someone is watching you.

Closing the door to my office, I punched his extension. "Hey, Bill," I said when he answered. "You called. What's up?"

"Where were you last night, buddy? I called the house and your cell, but there was no answer and no return call. Were you with her?"

"I didn't see any message on either phone. When did you call?"

"Around nine or nine thirty."

"I saw that someone called, but the number was blocked. Where did you call from?"

"Shit! I forgot. I got a new cell number. I was getting so much spam on the old one, I ditched it. It was easier than trying to block the bastards."

"Aren't you on the Federal do-not-call list?"

"The marketing scum don't pay attention to that. If they get caught, they pay the fine, change phone numbers, and start again. What really bugs me is they're starting to call from India and Mexico. Those countries don't enforce any lists." He gave me his new cell number, and I replaced the old one in my cell's directory. We hung up, and I called him back on his new cell so we wouldn't be on a recorded line any longer.

"So, what did you find?" I asked, hoping he'd drop the inquisition.

"Not so fast. I want to hear about last night. It's Donna, right? Is she good in bed? C'mon. You owe me."

Typically, I'd be quite anxious to share my conquests, few and infrequent though they were. Bill and Ellen got married sixteen years ago and he's been quite the faithful husband. Nevertheless, he seemed to enjoy hearing about my sexual encounters a little too much.

"There's nothing to tell. I must have fallen asleep in front of the TV before you called. I remember getting up around midnight, turning the damned thing off and heading to bed. I didn't even look at the phone till this morning."

"Sure. And I'm Mickey Mouse. This must be serious if you're willing to lie to me about it."

"She's just an old friend from high school. Really."

"And I'm your best friend, the one you share everything with. Your evasions speak volumes, Steve. Now I'm intrigued. She must really have you hooked. That's okay. I can wait. You'll come clean, sooner or later."

"You're way off base this time. There's nothing going on. Now, what did you find out about C&C?" I picked up my pen, prepared to take some notes.

There was a pause, and for a moment I thought he'd hung up. "Okay, have it your way. Like you said, they're based in Boston, and started on the acquisition trail about eight years ago. That's when Delbert Carter took over as CEO. He managed to oust the existing board and replaced top management with his own team, most of whom followed him from his last gig at the hedge fund he ran in the Nineties the one that decimated the entire furniture manufacturing industry. It was just a holding company with a few hospitals and trauma facilities in New England before he showed up. It wasn't even in the top hundred at the time. It was a small regional chain with modest revenues and reasonable profits, according to archived shareholder reports."

My secretary, Cindy, walked in with some phone message slips, but I waved her off, mouthing, "Hold my calls." She turned and left, closing the door behind her.

"What kind of reputation did they have for service? Was that documented?"

"I thought you'd ask. According to AMA and other industry watchdogs, they were pretty highly ranked, despite their size. They were recognized numerous times for their charitable outreach programs in their respective communities."

"And now?"

"A couple of the emergency clinics in poorer neighborhoods have been closed down. The remaining facilities all show dramatic increases in revenue and profit, particularly over the last four or five years. Yet service rankings have fallen precipitously with the number of patient complaints rising nearly forty percent. Looks like Carter is up to his old tricks."

"You said they're in acquisition mode?"

"Yeah. Nineteen facilities added since 2014, and two more slated this year, including SCM. Same story each time; huge revenue growth and profit expansion, with a concurrent rise in complaints and regulatory inquiries. Thus far, they haven't been indicted or fined for any wrongdoing. Their stock has soared on the big board, nearly tripling in the last twenty-four months."

I scribbled as quickly as I could, trying to come up with coherent questions. "How do they do it? Are they legitimate? Or is there something going on behind the scenes?"

"They focus on cost reductions and containment when they take over, mainly through mass layoffs and cancellation of unprofitable programs, particularly for the indigent. Then, somehow, they get revenues growing, often by double digits. The breakdown in their corporate filings isn't specific enough to say how they do it, but it smells like they're going after Medicare and insurance dollars big time, probably milking the system using high-end tests and procedures."

"Are they cooking the books?" I suggested, speculating out loud.

"No, the financials look solid enough. But the large increases beg the question. Hold on, I have to clear this other call." He put me on hold, and I went online to look at the current statistics of their firm. The numbers were impressive. Eight straight years of double-digit revenue growth. I heard the soft 'click' as he picked up the line. "Where were we?"

"You said the financials looked solid. I was looking at their revenues. They grew at nearly twenty-two percent on average since Carter went on his shopping spree. Where's all this new revenue coming from? Are people suddenly sicker in communities he invades?"

"It's not just the revenue that's gone bonkers. The bottom-line profits are just as confusing. Cost reductions only go so far; eventually you run out of people to fire. Their net increases are running significantly higher than their industry peers. I printed copies of their recent 10-K filing and 10-Q filings if you want to take a look."

"Sure. What are you doing for lunch today?"

"Meeting you at Hannah's, I imagine. Eleven thirty?"

"Absolutely. See you there." We hung up, and I began looking into medical industry trends on my desktop computer. Somewhere in the reports Bill had was the clue I needed to attack C&C, but I needed to know as much as I could about the industry as a whole before I would be able to spot it.

***

Like Tiani's, Hannah's was off the beaten path, a little bistro run by a California couple who relocated to Phoenix to get away from the crowds and smog of L.A. The Pandemic nearly cost them their business, but the food was so good that their take-out and delivery service kept them afloat during the lock-down. They specialized in homemade, not precooked, and their staff was friendly and attentive. It was a twenty-minute drive, but worth it, especially since no one else at the office knew about it. Lunchtime found it crowded with local workers from a nearby manufacturing plant. Conversation consisted primarily of sports, girls, and bitching about jobs. Our quiet discussions would be drowned out, affording us privacy that office doors and cubicle walls could not.

"Over here, Bill," I called as he walked in. He crossed the room to the corner table I bought with a twenty-dollar tip to the hostess. I've tried using charm on her, to no avail. Cold, hard cash bought her cooperation, though. She'd make a good stockbroker. I may need to introduce her to my recruiter.

We shook hands and Bill sat down, placing a large manila envelope on the table.

"What's in there?" I asked, guessing it contained the reports he mentioned on the phone.

"Everything I've pulled so far on C&C, as well some information on their top brass. Carter's a real piece of work, as is his hatchet man, some doctor named Harry Steinham."

Steinham.? Why was that name familiar?

"Are they dirty?"

"Neither one has a record with the SEC or other regulatory bodies, though there were some complaints filed against Steinham when he was a surgeon at Boston General and prior to joining forces with Carter. Nothing came of it, though. He settled out of court with no sanctions by any medical boards."

Boston General? No, it couldn't be. Could it?

"What about Carter's previous companies? As I recall, several of them ended up in bankruptcy, yet he walked away with millions in salary, bonuses, and severance packages. Was he investigated for any of that?"

"Oh, there were plenty of investigations, but he did everything legally. With the resources of the companies he plundered at his disposal, he could afford the best attorneys in Boston. The few lawsuits he couldn't beat were settled with nondisclosure agreements attached."

"That couldn't have been cheap."

"The settlements were sealed, so there's no way to know exactly how much was involved, but considering the hundred million or so he made, the five or ten million it may have cost still left him a wealthy man."

The waitress walked over, and we ordered, both of us choosing a light salad. I thought about Donna and how she barely touched her dinner last night, despite her compliments. She either lied about my cooking or is very disciplined about her eating habits. I guess I could take a lesson from that.

"And what about the SCM takeover?" I asked when she left. "How close are they on inking that deal?"

"The last three mergers took nine months, end to end, including regulatory approvals. They've got it down to a science. This one's been in the works seven months. It's pretty much a done deal."

"Any chinks in the armor? Any roadblocks with unions or local community organizations?"

"Nope. Their MO is to come in promising the moon: enhanced programs for the poor, no layoffs or significant staffing changes, and so forth."

"In other words, they say whatever they need to say to get the deal done."

"Uh-huh. After the close, though, it's a different story. They renege on their commitments, claiming conditions changed or the revenue forecasts were worse than expected. They're careful to stay within the letter of the law. By the time local management realizes they've been bamboozled, it's too late to do anything about it."

"Why can't we just go to SCM's board or the state medical examiner's office and show them these reports?"

"We could, but what good would it do?" He looked at me, his eyes tight. "Why the sudden interest in trying to stop this thing?"

"It's just not right, that's all. Someone has to stand up to these crooks."

"Someone? Meaning you? Or us? Do you have any idea who you're taking on?"

"It's a matter or principal. They can't just waltz in—"

"Hey, hold it there, buddy. First of all, who would listen to you or me? The current board of SCM is going to make a boatload of money, and money talks. Second, there are no regulatory findings against C&C, so what do you suggest we say to the state board? 'These are bad people who come in and fire nurses in the name of efficiency?' That's not their problem. Besides, C&C has a cadre of lawyers who make sure every application and submission meet state codes and standards. Unless you happen to have an 'in' with a regulator or state official, you'd just be pissing in the wind."

"There must be something we can do. I promised Donna I'd try …"
Shit.

"Ah, so that's what this is all about."

"I told you that up front," I said, hoping it would satisfy him.

"Yeah, but you've also been close-mouthed about this woman. She must really have gotten to you. How do you know she's just not using you to save her job?"

"She's not. I just want to help, that's all."

"Uh-huh. Sure. And I'm Peter Pan."

"C'mon Bill. You hate these bastards as much as I do. You said yourself their revenue and profit growth seemed extraordinary. I looked it up before leaving the office and you were right; they went from near the bottom to one of the top growth companies in the country. It can't be an accident. There's got to be some hanky panky going on. All we have to do is find it and expose it."

"'All we have to do is find it and expose it,'" he mimicked. "Suddenly you're Dick Tracy and Sherlock Holmes all rolled into one."

"That's why I came to you. If anyone can spot fraud on a financial statement, it's you. Tell me you found something. You wouldn't have agreed to come here it you hadn't."

He was quiet for a moment, and I could almost see the wheels spinning in his head.

Finally, he nodded. "Yeah, I think I see a trend. Their Medicare billings are off the chart in comparison to like-sized facilities in neighboring communities. I haven't done a statistical analysis yet, but I'm betting there's a pattern to it that might suggest fraud."

"So do the analysis. How long will it take?"

"I want to hear about this 'Donna' person first."

Just then, our salads arrived, quieting our conversation as the waitress laid the food and drinks down. When she left, I tried to answer as briefly as I could. "Like I said, she's an old high school friend, and we hit it off after all these years. What's the big deal?"

"The big deal is we've bitched about corporate greed and avarice before, but you've never been this gung-ho about doing anything about it. As far as I can see, your new fling is at the center of your newfound motivation. Before I start tilting at windmills, I need to know my sidekick, Sanchez, isn't blinded by some Dulcinea."

Blinded by some Dulcinea?

My first thought was to haul off and punch him in the mouth. I bent my head, focusing on my plate, and started shoveling the salad like I was feeding a goat. I barely chewed any of it before swallowing.

"Please don't call her Dulcinea," I said in a voice so quiet it even surprised me.

When he didn't respond, I looked up and saw his head cocked to one side with a serious quizzical expression. "Sorry. I shouldn't have done that. But you must admit, old high school friend or not, this sudden Don Quixote syndrome came out of nowhere. What is it about her that's got you so riled up you're willing to take this on? This won't be a walk in the park, and there's every possibility he could come after you big time if he thinks you're threatening his empire."

"I don't know. I admit it's out of character for me. But she's been through a lot, and I guess I'm a sucker for damsels in distress. By the way, I should probably tell you she was once married to Steinham."

***

"*What?*"

"Yeah. I thought that name sounded familiar. Back in Boston. They got divorced before she moved here."

"Let me guess … she wants to fuck the bastard over, and she's enlisting you in her witch's hunt."

"No, no, no. Nothing like that. She doesn't even know he works for C&C. I only found out just now, from you."

"Are you certain she doesn't know?"

"I haven't asked her, but she would have mentioned it to me if she knew."

"You're making a pretty big assumption there, buddy."

"You don't know her. You haven't even met her. You're the one making assumptions," I said defensively.

"Let's see … she was married to a doctor and got divorced. Now, she's dating you, which brings her taste in men into question once again and, by coincidence, she enlists you in a quest to bring down her ex-husband's company to save her job. Have I got it right so far?" Bill raised his brows.

"Except for the part about her taste in men. I'm a great catch, and you know it."

"You're a thirty-something geek who speaks Wall Street pig Latin. Some catch."

"Yeah, well back in high school she was known as 'Dirigible Donna,' and—"

"*Dirigible Donna?*" he said, loud enough for the hardhats at the next table to turn their heads and stare. "As in *blimpy?*" He started to chuckle.

Big mistake. Open mouth, insert foot.

"She isn't anymore. After graduation, she lost all the weight, became an RN, got a position at Boston General, and that's how she met Steinham."

"And how did you two reconnect?" he asked, his face still flushed from laughing.

I told him the story about running into her at Starbuck's, asking her out, taking her to Tiani's, and talking about her job. I left out the more intimate details.

"So, tell me honestly. Were you really asleep on the sofa last night when I called, or did you spend the night at her house?"

"Her house."

He ate a couple of mouthfuls of lettuce and dressing before continuing.

"I don't care about your love life, Steve. What you do at night is your business. Just don't lie to me again, not if you want my help."

"Okay. I'm sorry. I just didn't want to talk about it."

"Since when don't you want to talk about your exploits? What makes this one so special?"

"I don't know. I must admit, when I first saw her, I was totally mesmerized. If she had looked like that... well, she would have been the most popular girl in the school. When she told me who she was, I couldn't believe it. She's got an edge to her, probably from being laughed at all those years. She's got a sharp mind, though, and a great sense of humor."

"Laughing at your jokes doesn't mean she has a good sense of humor. Your jokes aren't that funny."

"Says you. Anyway, we just connected right away. I've never felt this way before, even with Michelle."

"Sure, you're just not thinking with your dick? If she's as smart as you say, maybe she was smart enough to look you up so she could seduce you. Speaking of Michelle, wasn't that the exact same problem?

Or have you forgotten she used you until you wised up, then split with your money?"

"This is different," I said, my appetite gone.

"The jury's still out on that. I want to meet her before we commit to anything."

I looked away, staring at the soda machine. Some kids were playing with the levers, spilling ice and soda all over the counter and floor. Was he right? Was I being played for a sucker? She seemed so perfect. Too perfect. Shit. It's been so long since I trusted anyone, cared about someone enough to fight for them.

"Bill, you really know how to screw up my day."

"What are friends for?" he said with a smile. "Look, I haven't even met her. Maybe she's everything you think she is. I'm just asking you to go slow here. I'll keep helping if you want me to. You're right; I'm as pissed at these corporate raiders as you are, especially now that they're moving into hospitals and medical care. I don't see anything good coming of it. I just don't want you getting hurt."

"Okay. I'll keep my eyes open. You probably should meet her. I'd appreciate your honest opinion. What are you doing this weekend? Maybe we can get together for breakfast on Saturday?" I offered.

"I'll have to check with Ellen to make sure she doesn't have anything planned for me."

I grabbed the envelope and tore it open. "Let's take a look at those reports."

~8~

I don't remember the ride back to the office. Driving on autopilot, absorbing Bill's comments, I mulled over how to convince Donna to meet him. He made it clear he wouldn't help without meeting her first, but I wasn't sure I was ready for that. This was happening too quickly, and I needed time to think.

Walking past Cindy, I absentmindedly grabbed a stack of phone messages from her and went to my desk, closing the door behind me.

I texted Donna: *"Call me when you can. re: C&C."*

I tossed the pink phone slips aside and shuffled through Bill's research. Try as I might, I couldn't focus on the graphs and official looking printouts. Dark clouds kept churning in my mind. Two hours ago, I was on a mission. Now, I wasn't sure which way was up. Bill was right – Donna could have looked up my credentials just as easily as I did hers. It's all a matter of public record. What if our chance meeting at the coffee shop wasn't really by chance?

I reached for the phone but put it back down without dialing. If she was lying to me, why would she stop just because I questioned her? If not, I could ruin any chance I had at happiness.

She's probably in surgery anyway.

I looked at the scattered phone messages staring back at me. I knew I should at least pretend to care about work. Instead, I swept them into my top drawer and closed it. I returned my attention to Bill's research. *Someone* should do something to stop C&C from polluting the local medical community.

***

It was four in the afternoon when my cell phone started dancing on the desktop, startling me back to reality.

"Got your message. On a break. Can u talk? Call me."

I hit re-dial and she picked right up. "Hi. How long is your break?"

"What happened to, 'Hello, darling. How are you?'"

"Hello, darling. How are you?" I said, feeling thoroughly domesticated.

"Just fine, dear. And you?"

"Lonely and lost without you." I smiled.

"Now, that's better," she said. "So, what did you find out?"

"Looks like C&C is well on its way to acquiring SCM, probably within the next couple of months."

"And the rumors about layoffs and program closures?"

"All true."

The line went quiet.

"Donna?"

"That's not good news, is it?"

"'Fraid not."

"Is there anything we can do about it?"

She said "we" again. Just like that. We.

"When's the last time you updated your resume?" I asked.

Shit. I forgot. It wasn't funny the first time, either.

"Really?"

I bit my lip.

"This is a powerful, well-funded corporation run by a ruthless, greedy bastard. I just spent the last two hours reading up on it. If you're expecting a fairy tale ending where the poorly armed villagers fend off the hordes of invading barbarians, I'm afraid you're in for a disappointment. No one has successfully opposed their buyouts in the last four years, and with each takeover, they get bigger, richer, and stronger. Bill thinks it would be suicide to wrestle with them."

"Bill?" she asked.

"The friend from work I told you about," I said. "He's great at researching this kind of thing and I respect his opinion."

"And he doesn't think there's any chance to prevent this?"

"He's got some ideas. Problem is, he doesn't believe any of them will work."

"Can I talk to him?" she asked.

"Uh, what do you mean?"

"I mean, can I talk to him? You know, like on the phone? Unless you'd like to introduce me in person."

I paused for a moment, tapping my pen on the desk.

"Well, I'm supposed to meet him for breakfast on Saturday. If he doesn't mind, maybe you can join us?" I didn't mention it was Bill's request, his requirement for helping.

"Can you ask him and let me know tonight? I assume you're coming over for dinner?"

"Seven o'clock?" I asked.

"Perfect. What are you cooking this time?" she asked.

"You'll just have to wait and see."

***

I stopped at My Ching, my favorite Chinese takeout restaurant. The food isn't particularly incredible—in fact, it was predictably typical—but I really liked the name. It was a twist on the *I Ching*, a book outlining a venerable Eastern philosophy. I've always been intrigued by its simple, direct approach to everyday life. It teaches patience, detachment, compassion, and harmony as cornerstones of living. I searched the hexagrams painted on the wall for some insight, but I didn't see any that recommended "walk away while you still can."

When I got to Donna's, I rang the bell.

"Come in, it's open."

I put the box of takeout on the counter next to the sink in the kitchen.

"You expecting an army?" she asked. "What's with all the food?"

"I didn't know what you liked, so I got one of everything. Well, almost everything. I hate seaweed soup, so I took a chance it wasn't your favorite."

"You got moo goo gai pan?" she asked, eyebrows raised in anticipation.

"Of course. I love its name. What other food group lets you speak gibberish, yet sound so mysterious?"

"There's that unique sense of humor again. You should have been a stand-up comic. "Come here." She wrapped her arms around my neck and kissed me.

As my mind bent, I swore I heard Bill Withers singing in the background.

Finally, she let go. "Let's eat. I don't want the *moo-oo goo-oo gai-i-i pan* to get cold."

She scrounged up some plates and utensils, and we sat at the table to chow down. If we were going to end up together, I would need to do something about the lack of basic cutlery and earthenware.

"So, what else did your friend, Bill, find out" Donna spooned out the rice and apportioned the various shrimp and chicken delicacies into the Corelle plates.

"Tell me about your ex, Dr. Steinham," I said, sampling the shrimp with lobster sauce, my personal favorite.

"Harry? Why do you want to know about Harry?" she asked, her eyes narrowing. "I thought we were going to talk about the takeover, not ancient history?"

"We *are* talking about the takeover. Harry works for C&C. He's their head of staffing."

"Oh? I didn't know that. I knew he left Boston General, but I didn't know where he ended up. After the divorce, I lost touch."

I couldn't tell by her blasé reaction if she had known all along or truly didn't care. So much for my amateur attempt at an ambush.

She opened a hot-mustard packet and mixed it with some sweet and sour sauce to dip her egg roll in. Watching her lick her fingers afterwards momentarily cost me my concentration, but I recovered enough to say, "Well, he apparently is the one who comes in after a merger and performs the staff evaluation. It's on his recommendation that people are hired and fired … mostly fired."

Around another bite of eggroll, she mumbled, "Harry? You're kidding. What does he know about staffing?"

"I was hoping you could tell me. You were his wife. What's he like? Does he have any background in this sort of thing? How did he treat his staff in Boston? Were there any complaints? Is that why you left him?"

"No. I told you. We split over our differences of opinion on having children, especially after … uh, well, anyway, he was a surgeon. I know he ran into some trouble when a couple of surgeries went south. He was angry about the restrictions the hospital imposed, but I never saw him as vindictive."

"People change, Donna. You of all people should know that. Maybe after you left, he decided to get back at his employer by joining forces with Carter so he could seek his revenge."

"But that still doesn't explain how he could suddenly become a staffing expert. Why would they hire Harry to do that? He has no training or background in personnel or business."

I thought about it for a moment, savoring the lobster sauce and rice. It was better than I remembered. Or maybe it was the company. Anyway, I swallowed, took a sip of saké, and continued. "That might be the precise reason. Having a surgeon as head of that department might give it an air of legitimacy. The regulators might be impressed if a medical professional was part of the team responsible for facilities staffing. From Carter's point of view, Harry might be the perfect foil. Since he has no background in staffing, he could easily be manipulated, especially if it meant he got to be the hatchet man when the merger was complete."

"But what does Harry get out of it?"

"Personal satisfaction? Power? I'm sure he makes a lot more money, and if he gets stock options, well, he'd be wealthy by now. I've never known a surgeon who didn't believe they deserved to be rich."

She nodded her head. "As cynical as it sounds, I have to agree with you. I see it all the time at the hospital … surgeries and procedures ordered for problems that could as easily be addressed by less expensive treatments. I often wondered whether Harry really enjoyed what he was doing, or if he was only in it for the money. Still, I can't picture him as Ebenezer Scrooge."

"Well, there's one way to find out," I said.

***

I hesitated, wondering if this was the right time. "How would you feel about calling him up and asking him out to dinner?"

The forkful of white rice and chicken stopped halfway to her mouth, hovering in midair like a traffic helicopter surveying an accident scene.

"What? You mean like on a date? To ask him to back off? *Are you crazy?*"

"No, I'm serious," I replied.

She put the fork back down.

"What good would it do? I haven't spoken to him in years. Why would he want to see me again? And even if he did, surely you don't think he'd listen to my advice, do you?" Her speed talking seemed totally out of character.

"Slow down." I held up a palm toward her. "I'm just asking. I'm sure he wouldn't listen, even if you asked him 'pretty please.' He might not even agree to talk to you, though I'm guessing he would. He thought enough of you to marry you, and with the typical ego of a doctor, he probably thinks you still love him. Just like our old friend Chad from school, he'll do it just for the prospect of having sex. Just another conquest to prove he can still have you if he wants."

"You're not suggesting—"

"That you seduce him? No. I'd have to kill him if he touched you. But, if he thought there was the possibility, well, maybe he'd open up a bit, and you could find out what's really going on. You could milk him for information, then give him one of your 'pamphlets' before you walked out the door."

"You're serious."

"Why not? If he's their pawn, maybe we can use him to gain some inside information."

"I meant you'd kill him if he touched me?"

"That, too."

She sat back and visibly relaxed just a little. She looked at her food for a minute, stirring it aimlessly. "I wouldn't want to be alone with him. He's stronger, and I might not be able to fight him off if he got violent."

"I'm thinking dinner, in a public restaurant, maybe with some company."

"Who? You? That would be very awkward."

"No, Bill. He would know what questions to ask. You could introduce him as an acquaintance, someone interested in investing in C&C. We could come up with some excuse. You wouldn't be alone, and we might get something useful to help stop the merger."

"Does Bill know about your hair-brained scheme?" There was a faint hint of enthusiasm behind the questions.

"We'll break it to him on Saturday," I said.

Picking up another of the little white cardboard containers, I offered it to her. "Want to try the Kung Pao chicken? It's extra hot tonight."

***

Her refrigerator stilled looked empty despite the seven white boxes of mostly unopened entrees and rice we placed in it. After cleaning up, we retired to the living room to continue our discussion. She sat on the love seat opposite me on the sofa. I didn't want to sit that far away, but it was probably a good idea. If we were going to talk, the physical distance would keep us from premature extracurricular activity.

She took a sip of the merlot. "So, what makes you think this'll work? I mean, if Harry is their hatchet man as you say, I don't see how my meeting with him could do any good."

I cupped my own, fully refilled wine glass in both hands. "I'm not sure it will, but we need to find a weak spot, and the weakest link in any corporation is always a human being. If we try to take C&C head on, either with some legal action or by confronting Carter, we'd get nowhere. Remember, they have a cadre of lawyers and a boatload of money at their disposal. This takeover will make them millions, and they're not likely to let a couple of locals derail their plans. But if we attack from the inside somehow, create some dissention in the ranks, we might be able to create some leverage. As a worst case, maybe we can get Harry to reveal some of their tactics, share some useful inside information we can take to the Feds for further investigation."

"Now you're starting to sound like a lawyer."

"No need to insult me," I chided. "Fact is, I work in a regulated business, and I spend more time taking CE classes on new compliance requirements than I do with clients. As a medical corporation, C&C is subject to an even more stringent set of regulations and laws. No matter how good their lawyers, or how creatively devious their upper management, there must be some rule, some regulation they've somehow overlooked. Even the great Al Capone was taken down for tax evasion."

"You think Harry forgot to pay his taxes?"

"No, but you get my point. If they're doing something illegal, then we need to find a way to prove it, and quick. We don't have time or the resources to do it ourselves and, if it were blatant, the government would already have opened their own investigation. Our best chance is to get a peek inside the machine, and the only open door I can see is through Harry."

"And you think your friend Bill would be willing to help us?"

"I can't speak for him, but I know he's as tired as I am of this bullshit. Besides, his wife Ellen gets treatment at your facility for a rare blood disease. If they get taken over ..."

She reached for the glass of wine, but just swished it around, her eyes studying the eddies in the burgundy liquid. Finally, she put it back down and bent forward, elbows on knees, hands clasped in front of her. "Do you know what she has?"

"Not offhand. Maybe you can ask him when we meet on Saturday."

She shook her head and sat back in the chair. "Fair enough. I'll consider calling Harry. But I don't have his phone number. I don't even know where he lives."

"I'm sure we can find it. As a corporate executive, it's public record."

"He isn't stupid you know. Once he finds out I work there, he'll figure out what I'm up to."

"Maybe, maybe not," I said. "Here's a thought. We disarm him. You tell him that right up front. Use it as the reason for the call. Someone saw his name and recognized him as your ex. You thought it might be nice to get together and rehash old times. Feed his ego. He'll respond, I'm sure of it."

"And Bill? How do I introduce him?"

"He's the friend who put two and two together. C&C is a public corporation and Bill is an investment pro who's interested in investing in C&C. It sounds logical enough."

"Sounds too complicated to me," she said.

"I'm guessing it will get more complicated before it's done."

I took a gulp of wine, then re-read the little strip of paper from my uneaten fortune cookie: *"An adventure awaits you."*

~9~

Dateline November 10, 2015, Trenton, New Jersey

A team of federal agents swooped into Good Spirit Memorial Hospital today, removing cartloads of computer equipment and file boxes. The Chief Administrator, Dr. James Horwitz, and the Chief of Surgery, Dr. Samuel B. Higgins, were seen exiting the building in handcuffs, surrounded by FBI agents. They ignored questions from the press, which quickly gathered when wind of the sting operation reached the media earlier in the day.

When this reporter contacted the Lead Investigator, Arnie Stromble of the Medicare Fraud Unit, he revealed that GSMH had been indicted in federal court of Medicare Fraud for fraudulent billings for non-existing surgeries to the tune of $100 million. He was unable to share further details, but stated, "These types of crimes cannot go unpunished. To anyone scheming to defraud the government to line their own pockets at the expense of the taxpayer, know that we are every vigilant and you will pay dearly for your crimes."

***

Dr. Harry Steinham came from a long line of family physicians, dating back three generations. A sturdy man of five-eight with a full head of hair and a neatly trimmed mustache, he considered himself stern and competent, though by most standards he wasn't very imposing at all. Like his father, he chose orthopedic surgery as his specialty. Unlike his father, he was motivated by the income and status and not by any genuine desire to help people. He plodded through medical school, his pedigree helping him limp along. His skills as a surgeon proved to be adequate to navigate his residency and obtain the necessary licenses and certifications.

For the most part, his career was unremarkable, at least up to the end when he was nearly forced out of medicine altogether. A moderate drinker, he didn't embrace the workaholic attitude endemic to his profession. You'd as likely find him at a bar at three in the afternoon as in an operating room. His lack of ambition and a general malaise toward attending conferences to learn the latest techniques and procedures only dulled his skills further.

He'd met Donna at Boston Memorial where she worked as a nurse. He found her both beautiful and sassy. He still had some ambition in those days, and Donna seemed like the kind of woman who could motivate him to work hard and make lots of money. At first, things went well, and his practice steadily grew. Donna wasn't much of a cook, but she was explosive in bed—a thermonuclear reactor at full tilt—and he thought he had everything he ever wanted out of life.

Then, she started talking about having children. Her persistence grew annoying, and he found himself avoiding her, staying out later and later at his favorite pub to avoid the inevitable conversations at home. Perhaps that contributed to the mistakes he started making in the operating room. They were minor at first, but then, almost simultaneously, three patients filed lawsuits against him for malpractice. His insurance premiums skyrocketed, the state medical board opened an inquiry, and the hospital restricted his privileges. He was required to have an attending surgeon supervise all his procedures until the state's investigation was complete.

Finally, in an attempt to re-energize his marriage—and perhaps convince Donna there was more to life than nursing rug rats—he took her to Paris on an ill-fated vacation. He never got around to telling her the depths to which his career had sunk, and she didn't press for a large financial settlement after the divorce, so they went their separate ways in disrespectful ignorance.

Things went from bad to worse. The hospital put him under stricter scrutiny, prohibiting him from the lucrative procedures that served as the backbone of an orthopedic surgeon's practice.

The state board recommended disciplinary action, which might include forfeiting his license, and a fourth lawsuit was opened by a family whose son had died several months earlier, following complications from a botched bone graft.

As the roof caved in, he grew increasingly bitter. His anger at both administrators and regulators ate at him day and night, and he started drinking more heavily. He was spiraling into depression when he received a mysterious, if fortuitous, phone call.

"Is this Harry Steinham?" the booming, authoritative voice on the other end of his cell phone barked.

"Yes, this is Dr. Steinham. Who's this?" he said, downing the last of the Jack Daniels from the eight-ounce tumbler. Holding the phone to one ear, he got up from the table to retrieve another bottle from the kitchen pantry.

"You don't know me, doctor, but my name is Delbert Carter. I run C&C Healthcare Associates here in Boston. I'm sure you've heard of us."

"Yup. I've seen your ads. You just took over that facility in Bingham, New York, right?"

"That's correct. We think healthcare in this country needs some serious changes. Our objective is to make hospitals more efficient. We streamline their operations in order to focus more on patient care by eliminating unnecessary administrative fat and removing obstacles for physicians such as yourself—obstacles that take away your freedom to do your job as you see fit."

Pushing cans and boxes out of the way, Harry located another bottle of whiskey. He pulled it out and sat down again. To Delbert, he said, "And to what do I owe the privilege of your phone call?"

"We're looking for someone with experience, someone who's been through the ups and downs an overly regulated and uncaring bureaucracy can impose. In the search for a director of staffing evaluations, my people looked through hundreds of files, and your name rose to the top. You come from a family of physicians, you graduated from a prestigious university, and you ran a successful practice until the system turned against you."

"That's right. *I was* doing just fine till the state board gave credence to those nonsense lawsuits." Harry adroitly opened the new bottle and poured another drink.

"Well, I think I can help you with that. Would you be free for dinner tomorrow night at the Meritage? I have a proposal for you to consider."

Harry's arm, glass in hand, stopped midway between the table and his lips. Slowly, he placed it back down.

"What time?" he inquired, experiencing a sudden clarity despite his inebriation.

"Seven o'clock, and don't be late. The offer expires at seven-ten."

With an audible click, the line went dead.

***

The Meritage is a landmark on Boston Harbor, sitting directly across from Logan Airport. Considered one of Boston's finest eateries, it is often crowded, but the award-winning food is always worth the wait. Harry had been there on several occasions and fully expected to park at the bar for an hour or more before a table could open up. That didn't bother him since it meant running up a serious drink tab on Carter's credit card. When he arrived and introduced himself to the hostess, however, he was immediately escorted by the attractive woman to Carter's table. Harry followed her, his moustache twitching noticeably. She led him to a corner booth positioned a discreet distance from any other diners. Sitting alone at the table was an impeccably dressed businessman in his sixties, sporting a Rolex Mariner on his left wrist. Clean shaven with closely cropped salt and pepper hair, he was just finishing a phone call when he noticed Steinham's approach. Standing up, he towered several inches over Harry. He reached out and they shook hands.

"Nice digs," Harry said, referring to the semi-private table Carter had sequestered.

"Rank has its privileges," Carter shot back. He pointed, and Harry took a seat. Carter sat as well and folded his hands on the table, the diamond studded onyx ring on his right hand sparkling brightly despite the subdued lighting.

Harry noted the lack of a smile on Carter's face, and the hair on the back of his neck stood up, accompanied by unwelcome chills down his spine.

"I've already ordered for you. The menu is extensive, and I felt certain you didn't want to waste time sorting through it. I hope you like clams and sea scallops," Delbert stated.

"They're my favorite," Harry said, resisting his inclination to reply sarcastically. He would've preferred the prime rib, but what the hell. It was a free dinner, complete with an offer of employment. He could suck it up for a couple of hours if he had to.

A waiter stopped by and delivered drinks. "I also took the liberty of ordering drinks. I understand you're partial to Jack Daniels. So am I. I like a man who drinks his whiskey straight up. Only sissies dilute it with soda water."

"What shall we drink to?" Harry asked, hoping to get Carter to say something useful.

"To my new director of staffing. I assume you read the proposal I faxed to your office."

"Of course," Harry said, lying with a straight face. Carter tilted his glass at Harry, who did likewise, and they each took a substantial sip before setting the tumblers down. "When do I start?"

"Immediately, if the pay package is acceptable to you. I assure you, with the plans we have for C&C, your stock options should be worth millions before the year is out."

Stock options? Harry hadn't read the proposal, giving it instead a perfunctory glance. He'd expected to have a conversation about it and get the pertinent details verbally from Carter. He knew what they were but was clueless how they worked. Over the years, he had dabbled in the market, mostly in penny stocks that did nothing but lose him money.

"Yes. Absolutely. I can see the value in being a team player."

"Good. Then it's settled. I'll expect you to be at your desk Monday morning at seven sharp. We have several facilities we're studying as takeover candidates and need someone to review the personnel records for opportunities to consolidate and reduce needless overhead."

"I have a schedule conflict on Monday. Perhaps I could begin on Tuesday? I need to take care of a pressing matter of some urgency—"

"Ah yes, that little matter of the investigation into your inadvertent miscues in the operating room. I've had our attorneys contact the state board and the matter is being handled out of court. The hearing has been cancelled, so you're free to show up on Monday. Our legal department will let you know if they require anything further from you, but I doubt they'll need to bother you."

The first course arrived, a mouthwatering seafood salad with freshly baked crab cakes and an assortment of butter spreads.

"Where's Mr. Carter's salad?" Harry asked, wondering why the waiter only brought one serving.

"I won't be dining with you Harry. I have other matters to attend to. Enjoy your meal and have another drink if you'd like. The bill's been taken care of already, so no need to leave a tip. See you on Monday." With that, Carter abruptly stood up and left.

"Busy man," he mumbled to himself before draining the glass and ordering another.

Bill's enthusiasm for the fight, though welcome and reassuring, seemed a little suspicious to me. Despite his adventurous spirit, I wondered what was really going on in his head. I thought about his wife and two kids. Jeopardizing his job on my say-so, merely to help me win a battle not of his making, should justifiably have scared him off. Our shared view about corporate shenanigans hadn't been sufficient in the past. Ellen, of course, had a serious medical condition requiring ongoing treatment and occasional hospitalizations, though he'd been closed mouthed about it in recent months. Could it be clouding his good judgement?

Now, ironically, Bill and Donna each wanted to meet the other as a condition of continuing the fight. A knot weighted my stomach as I laid out the bagels and cream cheese spreads from Einstein's Bagels on the kitchen countertop. I brewed fresh coffee—including a carafe of caffeine-free for Donna—and set the table. Unlike Donna, I preferred stainless steel flatware and dinnerware. For a moment, I considered pulling out some cheap, plastic plates I kept for outdoor barbecues so Donna wouldn't think I was showing off but thought better of it. If this thing between us was real, she should see the real me.

Bill got there first, carrying another, overstuffed manila envelope.

"Been doing some homework, I gather?" I said, as he stepped inside.

Like me, he was dressed down in jeans and a T-shirt. His read *I'm not saying I'm Batman. I'm just saying nobody has ever seen me and Batman in a room together.* I've got one that reads, *I'm not schizophrenic. And neither am I,* but I chose to wear a plain, dark pullover instead, on the off chance I might truly be schizophrenic.

"Yeah, lots of it," he said. "Hey, it smells great in here. Where's Donna?"

I grabbed the envelope and opened it. "She'll be here in a few minutes. So, what are all these?" I leafed through the graphs as Bill poured himself of cup of java. He offered to top mine off, and we sat down at the kitchen table.

He pointed at the top copies. "Those are the more pertinent printouts on C&C. I've started to get a picture of their operation, and I'll explain it to Donna, best I can. I think you'll find these interesting in particular, I analyzed their Medicare billings, and my initial gut reaction was right. They're nearly triple what other similar-sized hospitals claim, particularly in heart stent procedures. I hope Donna might shed some light for me."

"Why her?"

"She works in the OR. She should have a feel for the mix of procedures there."

"You're thinking they're targeting her hospital because they have a higher percentage of Medicare-approved heart operations?"

"No. Just the opposite." He reached over and pulled out the comparison graph, handing it back to me. "Their ratio of stent procedures is actually *lower* than the average."

"You lost me. If they have a lower ratio—"

"That's where the opportunity lies. They'll refocus the hospital's attention on these higher-profit procedures."

I looked at the two columns he'd highlighted, and the disparity was obvious. "I see. Instead of searching for companies with overfunded pension plans they can loot, they're looking for facilities with below average Medicare billings, with an eye to rebalancing the mix toward the higher-reimbursable operations?"

"Why not? It's free money, at least until they get caught." He pulled another page from the packet, this one a tabulated list of medical codes with dollar prices next to them. "That's a chart of Medicare's reimbursement rates for heart procedures. It wouldn't take a rocket scientist to figure it out; drop the less profitable ones, then deliberately institute a policy to recommend the more lucrative ones."

I reviewed the list, and it was clear as day. The government had inadvertently provided a roadmap for systematic misdiagnosis in the guise of procedural classification. "But they'd have to reduce or stop other tests and procedures as well."

"Exactly. They couldn't eliminate all of them, but they don't have to. It's all about finding the right mix: enough low-end billings to satisfy the regulators, while substantially increasing the high-profit operations.

By finding hospitals where the mix is upside down, like SCM, they can come in and do the double shuffle—reduce the low-end procedures while simultaneously increasing the high end. That would explain the huge swings in revenue and profits."

"But why all the firings?" I asked, looking to see if there were any reports on staffing levels.

"You won't find anything in there on staffing," Bill said, reading my mind. "I haven't gotten to it yet. Nevertheless, I can think of two reasons. Replacing higher-paid staff with greener, less experienced personnel immediately boosts the bottom line. Also, by bringing in their own administrators and staff, they save time since the newer folks are already trained follow orders."

I laid the reports aside, shaking my head. "Damn. But so far, nothing you've said seems illegal. Choosing to only offer high-profit-margin tests and operations isn't a crime."

"I agree. But if they're deliberately ordering unnecessary tests and operations just to get higher payouts, that's fraud. Plus, if they're billing for phantom procedures—just conjecture, I have no proof—*that's* criminal. Either way, it's the only avenue worth pursuing if we're to have any chance to derail them."

Just then, the doorbell rang. I called out, "Come on in, it's open."

Donna walked in, dressed in skinny jeans and a plain, white halter top. I saw the look on Bill's face change instantly. He went from stone serious, business formal to an oh-my-God-are-you-kidding-this-is-Donna stare. I'd thought about showing him a picture from my smartphone but opted instead to see his reaction when they met in person. Now, I wasn't so sure this was a good idea at all.

He stood up and approached her, hand extended, palm up. "So, you're Donna."

She high-fived him. "So, you're Bill." She poked him in the chest. "Or are you really Batman?"

He shook his head. "No. At least, I can't tell you I'm Batman. Otherwise, I'd have to swear you to secrecy."

She chuckled before coming over to kiss me lightly on the lips. "Smells good in here. Is there coffee?"

"Dark roast and decaf" I replied, "Grab a cup and we'll sit down to breakfast. No sense working on an empty stomach."

Pouring herself a cup of decaf she turned back to Bill. "Steven has told me a lot about you. When it comes to financial matters, he thinks you're Houdini."

"Steve has bouts of delusional thinking, as evidenced by his unusual sense of humor, so don't believe everything he says."

"He said you had an idea about stopping the takeover of the hospital by my ex-husband's company." She poured a small amount of nondairy creamer into her cup and stirred it. Peering at him over her coffee mug, the steam somehow curling its way past her cheeks, she ran her teeth over her bottom lip.

"There's always a way," Bill said, still unable to peel his eyes off her. "The question is, is there enough time to act before the clock runs out and they break out the champagne and pink slips?"

"Steven thinks it might be useful for me to talk to my ex. Do you think that's a good idea, too?"

He finally broke eye contact long enough to look at me. I nodded to let him know I had broached the idea with her already.

"Well, I guess that's up to you. Our only chance might be to sabotage the merger from the inside. If you're willing to try, maybe we can get him to reveal something useful."

There was that word "we" again, this time out of Bill's mouth, as if the three of us were childhood friends, playing cowboys and Indians with cash registers and cell phones instead of saddles and six shooters. Seeing the effect she was having on him, I began wondering.

"This is starting to sound like a spy novel," Donna said, taking the words out of my mouth.

"It's more like corporate espionage," Bill said.

Donna stopped stirring, removed the spoon, and set it down. "Isn't that illegal?"

Bill and I exchanged glances.

"You'll need to be careful about the questions you ask," I answered. "You sure you want to do this?"

She nodded and took a sip of coffee. "Just tell me what I need to do. I'll do my best."

I grabbed a plate and a bagel, slathered it with cream cheese, and added a slice of tomato and a helping of lox. They did likewise, and we sat. I took my usual spot at the head of the table, and they sat on either side, facing each other.

We sat in silence for a couple of minutes as we each attacked our breakfast.

Bill took a long drink of coffee, then turned to me. "I think your idea for me to go with Donna to meet with Harry makes sense."

"I think I'd feel better if you were there," Donna interjected.

"Okay, it's settled. Except, I don't think I should go as me."

I nearly spilled my coffee on the table. "*What!*"

"You gonna wear your cape and cowl, Batman?" Donna asked, apparently unperturbed by the idea.

"No, though it's an interesting suggestion."

"Who the hell do you plan on going as?" I asked, confused.

"Jim Adams."

"Come again?"

"Jim Adams. Let me explain. During my research, I found an article in a Dallas newspaper. During their last major acquisition, Dallas General, our good Dr. Steinham ran some kind of con game on the side."

Donna furrowed her brows. "What sort of con game?".

"Well, a couple months before C&C closed the deal, Steinham contacted a local investment broker and convinced him to hawk 'Participation Notes' with promises of quick profits. During the final week leading up to the merger, Steinham swindled the broker and at least six of his clients out of $15 million by selling them private, secured, convertible bonds to help fund the purchase. Problem was, they were bogus, and both the broker and his clients lost all their money."

Donna shrugged, confused. "So, why didn't they go after Harry?"

"They did, but the broker had never met him in person, and they couldn't prove he was running the con. The contracts and money changed hands by overnight delivery to a privately-owned postal storefront outside Boston. At the last second, the investors were instructed to wire funds to an account in the Caymans, and the trail quickly went stone cold. The money was gone with no provable ties to Dr. Steinham or C&C."

This didn't make any sense to me either, and I held up my hand. "What makes you think Steinham did it? Anyone could have pretended to be him. He might be legitimately innocent."

"Because I spoke to one of the investors who was scammed, and he sent me a copy of the bogus contract. I compared it to the offering statement C&C had to file with the SEC. The contract contained much of the same language as the official one."

"So? The perp copied the wording from the official doc. That doesn't prove anything."

"Except the contracts were drawn up and signed *before* the SEC filings were made public. Only someone on the inside could have known what was in them. My money's on Steinham."

"That still doesn't explain this Jim Adams character," Donna said.

"I'm betting Steinham's gonna run the same con here in Arizona. What if we set up our own con? Except this time, we use a *real* fictitious name," Bill said, so matter-of-factly it nearly made sense.

Donna got it before I did. "You mean, present yourself as an investment broker. Set yourself up as his next mark."

"Exactly. That could be the excuse you use to call him. You have this friend, Jim Adams, who noticed C&C's interest in SCM, and he wanted to get in on the action. If your ex hasn't already found someone to scam, this could be our opportunity to catch him red-handed."

"That's fine for screwing Harry," I said, "but how would that help stop the takeover? C&C would just distance themselves from him and move in anyway."

"Maybe. But I'm guessing he'd sell his soul to keep from going to jail. I think he'd turn state's evidence first and rat out his corporate buddies. That's how we stop C&C," Bill said.

"I always thought you had an overactive imagination, my friend, but now I think you've worn that T-shirt a little too long."

"You got a better idea, buddy?"

I didn't know what to say. It was crazy, the kind of thing that only happens in movies and pulp fiction. Of course, even pulp fiction has some basis in reality. Still, I couldn't see how it would be possible for us to pull this off.

"We're real brokers, not criminologists or con men," I finally said to Bill. "What makes you think we stand a snowball's chance in Phoenix of succeeding with this hair-brained scheme of yours?"

Donna nodded her head, slowly at first, then vigorously. "I think it could work. What have we got to lose, Steven?"

"You mean aside from our jobs? How about fines and jail time? And as for this scheme of Bill pretending to be 'Jim Adams, investment broker?' Bill, have you lost your mind? If Steinham catches on, we're up shit's creek."

Bill waived me off. "Who care if he catches on? He's the one running the scam. He can't very well go to the police claiming we were trying to out con him, can he? That'd be suicide."

"It's still nuts," I said.

"If it's our only chance, I think we ought to at least try," Donna said insistently.

"Yeah, Steve, where's your sense of adventure? Aren't you the one who's always reading me the riot act about 'corporate irresponsibility' and 'standing up to these thugs?' Well, here's your chance to do something. Come on. Let's stop these motherfuckers. They're arrogant and over-confident. They won't even see us coming."

"Now who's Don Quixote?" I said to no one in particular. I took another bite of my bagel, chewing it slowly, though it'd lost its flavor somehow. I could feel Donna's stare, but I kept my eyes on Bill. Washing down the now tasteless food, I figured, what the hell. "All right, we'll try it your way. But we better have a backup plan, just in case." I reached over and grabbed Donna's hand. "You're *sure* you want to do this?"

She squeezed gently. "Yes, Steven, I'm sure."

No doubt lingered in her voice or in her eyes. I wasn't entirely sure if we were the modern version of the *Three Musketeers* or the *Three Blind Mice*, but it didn't matter now. She was sure.

"Okay. Game on."

***

"Hello, Harry. It's Donna. How have you been?"

We watched from the sofa, listening in on the cordless extensions from the other bedrooms. We had them on mute to prevent any inadvertent sound from tipping him off. Donna faced away from us, her hastily scribbled conversational notes in front of her.

"Donna? Donna! Is it really you? It's been nearly five years!"

"Six, but who's counting?"

"How amazing you called. How'd you find my number? It's a good thing I was in the office today." Bill and I looked at each other, shaking our heads. Harry sounded just like a used-car salesman, the phony sincerity dripping like synthetic molasses. "Saturdays are my day to catch up on paperwork."

"Actually, it was a friend of mine who found you, not me. He's a local investment broker. Said he spotted your name in the business section of the paper."

I wanted her to slow down, not sound like she was reading from a script, but there was no way to catch her attention.

"He recognized the name and put two and two together," She glanced back at us, and I motioned for her to ease up. She paused, then continued in a more natural voice. "Are you really looking to take over the hospital in Scottsdale?"

"If you're talking about SCM, that's true. I'd forgotten you'd moved to Arizona."

She threw a furtive glance at us. I just shrugged. She knew him better than us; the fact he lied so easily shouldn't come as a big surprise. "Are you still in Boston?"

"Beantown's been good to me."

"So, you won't be coming to Arizona yourself, then?"

"Coincidentally, I will. But only to help with staff evaluations. I'm flying out a week from Monday. Maybe we could get together for a drink?" It sounded like he was reading from the same script.

"Actually, I was thinking dinner." She turned her chair toward us, and Bill gave her a thumbs up while I smirked. I knew what the plan was, but suddenly the thought of her meeting him for dinner soured my mood. She nodded at Bill and continued, "There's a fabulous Italian restaurant here named Tiani's. We could relax and … you know … catch up?"

Good thing the phone was on mute. I nearly gagged.

"Even better. The only night I have free is Wednesday. If you wouldn't mind making reservations, I could meet you around seven thirty. I'll have my secretary print up directions. Tiani's you said? Now who's this friend of yours? What did you say he does?"

"His name's Jim. Jim Adams. He buys and sells businesses, helps clients find investments, that kind of thing. It's way over my head."

"You said he found us in the paper. Do you think he might be interested in an opportunity related to SCM?"

"I don't know."

She looked up and down the page of notes in front of her. We figured she'd have to sell him on Jim Adams, but he threw her for a loop. She spread her hands in a question, mouthing the words, "What do I say now?"

I mouthed, "Fake it," at her.

Without taking her eyes off me, she responded, "I suppose I could ask him."

"Please do. We're always looking for local talent to help with funding,"

"I kind of thought it would just be you and me, Harry," she said in a sultry voice.

"Don't worry. After dinner, we'll go out for a nightcap. Just you and me, like old times."

Over my dead body.

"Well, I'll ask him, but if he can't make it, don't be disappointed. He's a busy man."

"Just tell him we have an extraordinary opportunity for his clients, and he doesn't want to pass it up. Once I have him hooked, we'll ditch him. Hey, he's not your boyfriend, is he?"

"No, no. Just a friend. I'm not really seeing anyone right now." She avoided my stare. "Besides, you ruined me for other men."

"Then it's settled. I'll see you and your friend Jim on Wednesday. God, it's good to hear your voice. I can't wait to see you."

They exchanged cell numbers along with a few insincere compliments and said goodbye.

***

We were back at the table, fresh coffee in hand, letting it all sink in. "Well, what do you guys think?"

"Well, I guess Batman here was right. It worked." Donna skootched a little closer to me, resting her hand on my knee.

Bill picked up the sheaf of papers we'd been working on and reassembled them into a neat stack before re-inserting them in their envelope. "We don't have a lot of time to prepare. We should get together again to lay this out. What about tonight?"

"Why don't we just keep working now?" Donna asked. "We're here already."

Bill shook his head. "I can't. I promised Ellen and the kids I'd take them to a matinee."

"All right. We'll find something to do to keep busy," Donna said. "What time?"

"How about six?" I suggested. "I'll order pizza, and we can work as late as we need. Maybe you can pick it up on the way back here?"

"Will do." He reached his hand out to Donna who gave him a firm handshake. "It was nice meeting you. I can see why Steve tried to keep you a secret."

"Nice to meet you too, Bill. Or should I start calling you Jim instead?"

He laughed—a little too easily, in my opinion. "You'll have to practice."

"Seriously, though, I really can't tell you how much I appreciate your help. I know we only just met, but if anyone can pull this off, you can."

"Don't pass judgment yet. I've never done anything like this before, and there's no guarantee it will work. In fact, I'll be surprised if it *does* work."

"We'll make it work," she said, letting go of his hand. Her sudden, unflinching conviction disconcerted me. She'd only just met him. Hell, we'd barely met ourselves. There were forces at work here beyond my comprehension.

I stood up and forcibly shook Bill's hand, pulling him out of his chair as I did. "See you later, buddy. Say hi to Ellen for me."

I escorted him to the door and closed it behind him. I stood there for a moment, trying to gather my thoughts.

I heard Donna's footsteps behind me. Putting her hand on my shoulder, she leaned in close and whispered, "It's such a beautiful day out. Why don't we go for a walk?"

~11~

Kiwanis Park has always been my private refuge. Sheltered from the noise and commotion of the city in a quiet residential neighborhood, it forms a sequestered oasis in the middle of a bustling college town.

We walked by the lake, hand-in-hand under an anonymous sky. The smell of burgers and franks sizzling on nearby grills reminded me of simpler times. The summer monsoons with their torrential downpours and mile-high thunderheads were a distant memory.

Our own, private thunderstorm may be headed our way, in the looming confrontation with Carter and Steinham, but right now the park's majestic palms and towering shade trees smiled down on us, sheltering us from the pending turmoil.

"It's been a long time since I've done this. Good choice, Steven."

She tossed a handful of birdseed to the waiting ducks who hungrily snapped them up. A flock of pigeons swarmed around us, fighting with their feathered adversaries for every morsel.

"Thanks. This is one of my favorite spots. I come here nearly every morning."

"Oh?" she said, "So this is why you disappear at oh-dark-thirty?"

"Yeah. See the ramada up there on the hill?" I pointed. "That's my fortress of solitude. Each morning, I bring my journal and my coffee, and watch the day take hold. It's been a habit of mine for more than ten years now."

"Just you?"

"Well, there are usually some joggers down here by the lake, even before sunrise, and there are always dog walkers. Most of the regulars live nearby. Everyone minds their own business, though. It's some unwritten rule of the park. If you want your peace and quiet, don't disturb anyone else's."

"What do you do while you're here?" she asked with apparent genuine interest.

"Depends on my mood. Sometimes I meditate. Sometimes I read something spiritual. Mostly I write. I keep a journal and it's like a staunch friend. It never interrupts me or lets me down. I can say anything I want to it, and it never belittles me, or curses, or talks back. Truth is, I'm probably my own worst critic, so being able to write things down keeps me from exploding."

"Anything in there about me?" she asked.

"What do you think?"

"I think one day I'd like to see it."

"Maybe one day you will."

"Okay. When you're ready, I guess."

She hooked my arm and we continued around the lake, past other ramadas filled with families celebrating birthdays and enjoying the ambient temperature. A handful of them stared at us—or, more likely at Donna—but I didn't care. Lost in the moment, I was unfazed by how easily Donna and I had become a couple; just two happy-go-lucky lovers in a dime-store romance novel.

"I didn't picture you as religious."

"Not religious, really. I used to be, but the endless drudgery of rituals turned me off. Lots of people derive solace from attending regular services, but so much of it is just a Broadway production. I used to go, but I gave it all up. I prefer to come here. I can read and study whatever I wish, and if I want to take time to say a silent prayer, there's no stopwatch on a pulpit to tell me time is up."

"Is that why you're so upset with companies like C&C? It's a moral thing for you?"

"I suppose. I hadn't thought of it that way. Look," I said, nodding in the direction of a man carefully tending a grill, "I don't know anything about him or his family, but it's obvious they're here to enjoy the day, just like us. He's preparing sustenance. His wife over there is watching her kids wear themselves out playing." I inclined my head toward a young woman sitting in a folding chair a short distance from her children. "I can't picture them plotting the overthrow of the government or raping a local business so they can line their pockets. Yet, people like Delbert Carter take advantage of others without regard to any moral or ethical moorings."

"So, why did you decide to become a stockbroker? You couldn't beat 'em, so you joined 'em?"

"Gotta make a living, right?" I answered flippantly, not wanting to revisit my reasons for my career choice.

She had other ideas, however. "But if you're interested in spirituality, shouldn't you pursue a career that lets you express it? Seems to me you're at cross purposes, no pun intended."

I steered Donna toward an inviting bench tucked beneath a shade tree and we sat facing the lake. "I've thought about it. But I've always liked business and had a flare for sales. My 'spiritual awakening' didn't happen till later. It's not so easy to make a change in mid-stream. In any event, I wouldn't want to become just another clergyman stuck in the same, dull routine."

A few pigeons landed nearby, and Donna reached for the bag of seeds and threw the few remaining crumbs their way. "Do you think your divorce had anything to do with it?"

"Maybe. Who knows? It was difficult, especially when I realized how big a fool I was. But I don't think it caused me to seek repentance from God, if that's what you're implying."

"It was just a thought." She crumpled the empty bag and deposited it in the nearby trash can. She sat back down. "I haven't been very devout, either so I'm not one to call the kettle black. I was just wondering ... is this why you're helping me? You're bucking for sainthood?"

"Hardly. I've had more than enough opportunities to stand up for principles, but never did anything about them. I'm doing it for you."

Her eyes lasered in on me with gale-force intensity. "Why?"

"Because I think you're worth fighting for. And because I'm falling in love with you."

She fell quiet, and I regretted saying it out loud. She got up and I followed her past the pier jutting into the lake, where two fathers were teaching their children to fish for rainbow trout and cod. There was something touching about it, and I felt myself choke up, wondering if I'd ever have children of my own to teach.

"I'm flattered," she said at last. "I think you're sweet to say it but, really, how can you be in love with me? You don't even know me."

"I intend to change that," I said, still thinking about the budding fishermen and their fathers on the pier. "You've affected me more in two weeks than any other woman I've met in the last ten years. Bill thinks I'm just infatuated with you, just like he is. But my gut tells me there's something more here, and I've got to follow it."

"You sure you're following your gut and not your penis?"

"Pretty sure. If I'm wrong, then I'm wrong. I'm sure you'll tell me if I am. I know how I feel, and that's got to be enough for now."

"Okay," she said, "but I hope you understand. We've had some fun, but I'm not ready for any long-term commitments."

"I understand," I said, not meaning it.

We kept walking, the silence hanging in the air like the empty pedal boats that bobbed gently on the water, waiting for customers to get in and power them with their legs. Finally, she asked, "What did you mean, 'Just like Bill is?'"

"C'mon. You saw how he looked at you. Surely you noticed."

"You're exaggerating."

"No, I'm not."

She just stared at me, and for a second, I thought I might end up in the lake with the paddle boats.

"You think I was flirting with him?" she asked at last.

"Were you?"

"No," she shot back, angrily. "I can't believe you're jealous of your best friend."

"I'm not jealous. Bill's married. He'd never step out on Ellen. It's just a fact of life."

"Just a fact of life," she repeated.

"Sorry," I said, "I didn't mean to upset you. Forgive me."

"I'll think about it."

"Let's stop at the cantina and get some ice cream." Changing the subject seemed like a good idea.

"Do they have Italian ices?" she asked, but her eyes said, *I'll let it slide this time, but don't do it again.*

"Yes, I believe they do."

***

Bill showed up promptly at six, pizzas in hand. "So how are the lovebirds this evening?" He spread the boxes on the kitchen counter, dumping the packets of cheese and seasonings next to them.

"Refreshed," Donna said, giving Bill a peck on the cheek. "Steven took me to a park in Tempe today, and we spent the day relaxing."

"Did he introduce you to his duck friends?"

"You mean Manny, Moe, and Jack? Yes. It's bad enough he has names for them, but I just couldn't believe it when they waddled up to us from the lake's edge. He said they had great memories, for ducks," Donna said.

"I don't know what his fascination is with them. It's not like he doesn't eat *duck a l'orange* occasionally for dinner. Maybe he likes playing with his dinner before eating it, like cats do with mice."

"Okay, you two," I interrupted. "Enough duck bashing. I note you didn't bring any wings with the pizza, so let's enjoy dinner and get to work without getting all fowl mouthed."

"Ouch!" Bill said.

"Double ouch," Donna said. "That was two thirds of a pun: P U! You need to get some better material. Which one of these is vegetarian?"

"This one." Bill opened a box. He deftly scooped up a slice and put it on her plate. Their eyes met for a moment, and he turned away, biting his lip.

He grabbed an *everything* slice, dusting it with some oregano and pepper flakes. "Did you two get a chance to talk about the reports I left here?"

I grabbed a couple slices of plain cheese pizza. "Yes. Donna confirmed your suspicions."

Donna took a nibble of pizza and swallowed. "Yeah, it's amazing how much more animated the surgeons are when they know they're actually getting paid decently for their work."

"That doesn't make it illegal," I added.

"Not if it's done for legitimate reasons," Bill replied.

"But you're convinced they're promoting unwarranted surgeries?" Donna asked.

"That's my working theory. The question is, can we prove it?"

"Can we?" We both responded in unison.

"Not from the outside, we can't. Not in time, anyway. That's why we've got to get Harry talking."

"Well, he was always tightlipped about his practice, so unless he's changed, I doubt he'll give too much away. Assuming he knows of course."

"That's why we've got to make this believable. Assuming you're right, he won't intentionally incriminate himself, but if he's as greedy as I think he is, it shouldn't take much to get him to take the bait."

I took a couple small bites of pizza, careful not to burn the roof of my mouth. I downed them with a large gulp of water. "I agree. Harry's never going to come right out and admit to anything illegal. He won't jeopardize his private game."

Bill nodded. "Nevertheless, it's our best bet." He watched as Donna, who had taken up a knife and fork, cut up her slice into smaller pieces. "You'll need to ask a couple of leading questions and see what he does with them. Steve's been in sales longer than me. He'll think up some simple, open-ended ones for you."

"You mean like, 'How long have you been out of the insane asylum?'" I replied.

"Cute. I mean like, 'These are really terrific numbers. How do you guys do it?'"

"Okay, you two," Donna said, putting the utensils down and picking up a small square of pizza. "Cut the comedy act. What exactly do you want me to say? Or do I just bat my eyes and fondle him under the table while you try and milk him?"

Both of our mouths dropped open as we stumbled over our epileptic tongues.

"Uh, no, of course not," I managed.

"That's not what I meant," Bill choked out.

I gained some semblance of control. "You're the reason he's coming; you're the most important one there."

"So then, tell me. What do I say? How do I introduce 'Jim?' Are you really ready to act the part? Do you need me to distract him with something really low cut?" Donna asked matter-of-factly.

"Couldn't hurt," Bill said, his eyes straying. "Maybe even a little flirting. The more relaxed and in control he feels, the more likely he'll fall for our charade."

"When did you become an expert in psycho-cyber-bullshit?" I asked, following his gaze and starting to boil inside.

"I read a lot of books, okay?" He said, re-directing his eyes toward me.

"How are you going to convince him you're for real?" Donna interjected, leaning in closer.

Bill looked back at her, keeping his eyes up this time. "I have a separate mailing address, a mail drop at the local UPS store. I added the name Jim Adams to it for purposes of our little escapade. Along with my virtual phone and fax line, it'll look like a legitimate business, at least from Boston. I'll have some cards printed up, and a good friend of mine can rig a bogus social media account, complete with testimonials from satisfied customers."

"A separate *what*? Why do you have a different mailing address?" I asked, dumbfounded.

"I've had it for a couple of years for convenience."

"Is there something you'd like to share with us, Batman?" I asked, suddenly forgetting about his wandering eyes.

"With Ellen's illness, I needed a place where her prescriptions could be delivered without disturbing her when she was resting. We get ninety-day supplies through a mail-order pharmacy. I couldn't have them sent to the office. They won't sign for medications, and I didn't want some clueless receptionist refusing it, sending it back to the pharmacy. The local storefront's open six days a week. They'll sign for any delivery regardless of the carrier, then text me when it arrives. It works better than trying to be home when the medicine's delivered."

"Okay, that makes sense," I said slowly, unconvinced he was totally forthcoming on this clandestine mailbox.

"But didn't you tell us Harry uses a similar kind of address for his con? Won't he recognize it immediately when he sees your card?" Donna asked.

"Nope. Just like his, the address is a simple street address, and the box number looks like a suite number. Unless he physically shows up there, or Googles it, he won't be able to tell the difference. Remember, in past scams, he didn't show up in person. He ran the whole thing remotely, just as we will. The fact he's letting me meet him in person means he's getting sloppy."

"And what about this virtual phone and fax?" I asked, unwilling to let go of these new revelations.

"I got rid of the fax machine at home a long time ago. It's cheaper and more convenient to have one set up on the computer. I can send and receive faxes wherever I have access to the Internet, including my tablet or smart phone. It saves paper and doesn't tie up my home phone. The virtual phone is also cheaper. I can make long distance calls for free. I'm surprised you don't already use one, Steve. You're the techno-geek."

"I don't do much faxing from home, and my cell has unlimited long distance," I answered. "I didn't realize Ellen needed to have medicine delivered by mail. How long has that been going on?"

"About two years now. The insurance company won't pay for her med's unless I use their mail-order prescription service. It's all about saving them money."

"I'm sorry to hear about your wife, Bill," Donna said. "Do you mind if I ask what she has?"

"It's a blood disorder. Polycythemia Vera."

Her facial expression softened as she thought about what he said. "I've heard of it. It's serious. I can understand why she needs constant maintenance drugs. I attended an in-service a couple of months ago, and there's some sort of clinical trial scheduled at the hospital later this year. One of the drug manufacturers is testing a new treatment protocol. Were you aware of it?"

"Matter of fact, Ellen's doctor got her into the initial trial group," he said, his eyes growing distant. "We're hoping it will reduce the amount of time she has to go through infusion therapy."

"I hate to be the bearer of bad news, Bill, but if C&C takes over ..."

His chin dropped to his chest. "Yeah. Yeah, that occurred to me, too."

Donna reached over and put her hand on his. "We can talk about this later. Why don't we get to work? How would you like me to introduce you to Harry?"

***

I started the third pot of coffee, using an espresso roast to get a little more kick. Graphs and reports covered the coffee table and half the living room floor. Bill sat on the sofa, working on the last of the now-cold pizza, while Donna and I knelt amidst the sorted piles searching for scraps of evidence about Harry's extracurricular activities.

In addition to the Texas scam, we found two more instances of brokers and investors claiming Steinham ripped them off by offering "notes of participation" for local hospital takeovers. Each time, the pattern was the same: someone identifying themselves as Steinham offered a local investment professional a get-rich-quick scheme. The ruse was based on legitimate-looking offerings with above-average, riskless returns. Tied to C&C's recent successes, it was easy enough to pull a fast one over these so-called experts, proving there's a sucker born every minute, regardless of their pedigree.

As for C&C itself, there was an abundance of evidence, circumstantial but compelling, which pointed to corporate malfeasance. Bill somehow secured billing schedules and usage charts, all cross-referenced to industry averages on elaborate spread sheets. He was quite thorough, which wasn't surprising, though I wondered how he managed to get all this information on such short notice.

As if reading my thoughts, Donna questioned him on it. "Where did you get all this?"

"They're part of C&C's public filings." He washed the last of the pepperoni pizza with a glass of wine before handing her another spreadsheet.

She took it and rubbed her eyes. "These are way over my head. What do they mean?"

Bill got off the sofa and knelt next to her. With one hand on her shoulder, he pointed to the various lines on the paper. "Basically, it's a plot of C&C's percentages versus their industry peers, using a logarithmic scale, adjusted for state specific anomalies."

Donna leaned into him, resting her cheek on his shoulder. "And you think they're fake. What is it you called it? Cooking the books?'"

I coughed and they separated.

Slightly.

Bill folded the paper and put it on the coffee table, then picked up another and handed it to her. "That's a possibility, though it would be hard to prove without direct access to their computers. What's more certain is their pattern of cost cutting." He pointed again at the squiggly lines. "They fire staff across the board at every acquisition, which I'm afraid is a legitimate concern for you and the rest of the folks at SCM." He traced one of the red lines. "Every dollar in salary they save translates to more than two dollars in increased profits." He put that one aside and picked up a third graph, this one a bar chart labelled *Procedures.* "More troubling is the increase in nonemergency surgical billings. Take a look at this. The last hospital they took over had a three-fold increase in heart stent procedures in just the first nine months alone. This is a real money maker, both for the physician and the hospital."

I reached across to grab the page he was holding, wrapping my free arm around Donna's waist. "The question is, why did the local population suddenly experience more heart problems than in the previous ten years?"

She leaned into me this time. "So, either the local doctors were under-diagnosing serious heart problems, or C&C deliberately encouraged more of these operations."

I gave her a little squeeze but directed my next question to Bill. "That constitutes fraud, right?"

Bill pivoted, grabbed the coffee table to pull himself up, and sat back down on the sofa. "If the operations were unnecessary, performed with the express intent of bilking Medicare, yes."

"What about the patients? Why would they go along with this?" Donna interjected.

"Come on, Donna, you of all people should know," Bill said. "Most people follow the advice of their doctors. Despite all the information available online, if your doctor says you need a heart stent or bypass procedure to save your life, you're not gonna question him or her."

"True enough," Donna agreed, "I just don't get why any doctor would knowingly perform unnecessary procedures."

"Really?" I shook my head. "Seems we had this conversation. Surgeons are as human as you or me, and just as motivated by greed. An hour in the OR is worth ten times more than sitting in an office seeing patients."

"What about your ex," Bill asked. "He was a surgeon. Did he ever complain about the money he made seeing patients in his office versus the operating room?"

"No, but it was pretty obvious. Right up to the end, he spent very little time in the office, preferring to do surgery. 'It's what I'm trained to do,' he'd say."

"Well, it's the same way in our business," Bill added. "Ideally, we help legitimate companies raise money to grow and expand which, in turn, helps the economy. The financial pressure to do more business often overrides even the most altruistic of motives. I've seen too many questionable deals where the only reason to proceed was the fat payday when the deal closed.

Donna gave me an accusatory sideways stare while she asked Bill, "And you think Harry's at the heart of it?"

"Maybe. Maybe not," he replied, "but he's the key. Catch him red-handed and dangle him in front of the FBI."

~12~

Dateline, Phoenix, Arizona, September 28, 2021

Continuing stress in the medical industry, still reeling from the effects of Covid-19, have resulted in several closures of small to medium-sized clinics valley wide. Cost cutting measures have forced the valley's larger facilities to lay off nurses and support staff as standard medical procedures slowly ramp back to pre-pandemic levels.

In related news, a proposed merger of Scottsdale's SCM system with C&C Associates from Boston appears to be moving rapidly ahead. Sources indicated there could be a much-needed infusion of capital, protecting patients and staff from further cuts to services. A spokesperson for C&C lauded the combination as being in the best interests of the local community.

At time of release, SCM had not yet responded to repeated requests for comment.

***

By Wednesday we were ready—or, at least as ready as we were ever going to be. Bill showed up at my place with an assortment of cleverly designed microphones, recording devices, and video transmitters purchased from the local "I, Spy" store.

For Donna, he provided a new, stylishly sequined clutch containing a camera whose lens blended in perfectly with its sparkling fake gems. Next, he pulled out a Mont Blanc pen, which served as a wireless transmitter. He installed a thumbnail receiver on my laptop, so I could watch and listen from home, recording the whole thing. Finally, he produced two small earpieces he and Donna could wear so I could communicate with them as well. I questioned the wisdom of wearing anything visible, which Harry might take note of. After a short discussion, we decided against them. Instead, if I spotted something fishy, I'd send a text to Bill's cell to alert him of trouble.

He pulled out a couple of high-quality, professional-looking business cards, bought at OfficeMax, complete with his fake business address and virtual phone and fax. If Harry bothered checking his story to locate his "investment company," the jig would be up. We were counting on him being so cocky, and Bill being so convincing, no background check would occur until it was too late.

Donna wore the same black evening dress from our first date. She'd tried on several other blouse and skirt combinations for me that were more revealing, but I convinced her too much cleavage might tempt Harry to be overly aggressive. We wanted her to distract him, but not to the point he didn't engage with Bill.

Before they left, she put those lovely arms around my neck and whispered in my ear, "Don't worry. Harry's no competition for you."

I nearly told Bill to go by himself so I could keep Donna with me. Instead, I simply wished them good luck and walked them to the door.

By design, Donna called Harry just as they were leaving to tell him they were running a little late and would he please go ahead and secure a nice table. Bill was also a regular at Tiani's and we didn't want his cover blown in front of Harry should Sonya say something like, "Hello, Bill. Where's Steve? Isn't this his latest flame?" We should have chosen a different restaurant, but it was too late now. Who knows how many other details we screwed up in our hurried preparations?

I watched as they drove away, my heart in my throat.

***

"We're here."

I stared at the text. They were fifteen minutes late, as planned. Bill turned on the microphone in his fake pen, and sure enough, I heard Sonya's voice as she greeted him warmly. "Regular table? You didn't make a reservation, so you'll have to wait till its free tonight, maybe another twenty minutes."

"No, we're meeting someone," Bill responded.

I pictured Donna scanning the tables to spot Harry.

"Would it be okay if we just walked back?" Donna asked. "I know we're late, and he's probably here already."

"Stocky, balding guy? Twitchy mustache?" Sonya asked.

"That's him."

"Yeah. He's near the back, to the right. He's a little creepy. I think he tried to pick me up. Is he a friend of yours?"

"A business associate, that's all," Bill said.

"Well, if I were you," Sonya said to Bill, "I'd sit between him and your date. Wait. Aren't you Donna? You were here with Steven the other night."

"Yes. Yes, I am. You've got a good memory. Harry's my ex. He's a bigwig from Boston and Bill wanted to meet him, so I agreed to introduce them."

"If he's your ex, then you have my sympathy. I can see why you dumped him."

"That's a story for another time," Donna replied. "He has an unsavory reputation, so I suggest you steer clear of the table. He's been known to shamelessly hit on maître d's."

Good thinking, Donna, I thought.

"Thanks. I will," she said, "*Boun appetito.*"

It got quiet, except for the clinking of glasses and silverware. After a couple of minutes, I heard Donna say, "There he is. The table there in the corner. Do you think he could have picked a darker spot?"

"For a corporate bigwig, he doesn't look the part. His suit doesn't quite fit him, or am I seeing things?" Bill whispered back.

"He was never a fashionista," Donna whispered back, "but he likes expensive restaurants and Jack Daniels, hence the girth."

"Well, it's showtime. You ready?"

"Roger that, Batman."

"You can be my Robin anytime. Now, just Relax. You look gorgeous. He won't even notice me prying into his affairs."

"Thanks, Bill. Uh, I mean Jim. Sorry."

"No problem. Here we go."

After another short break in the conversation, I heard Donna again. "Hello, Harry."

"Donna! I'm so glad you could make it. You look fabulous. The years haven't changed you one bit. I must have been a fool to let you go."

God, he sounds like a used-car salesman. I wonder how long he rehearsed that?

"You look terrific yourself, Harry. This new job must really agree with you." Donna's lines were, in fact, rehearsed. "This is Jim. Jim Adams, the friend I told you about on the phone."

I pictured them shaking hands. Bill wore a tailored suit, one that fit like it had been embroidered on. He was meticulous about his health and worked out five days a week. Too late, I realized he should have looked more like a country bumpkin than a polished securities analyst.

"Nice to meet you, Jim. Donna told me you're in investments." Harry said, wasting no time getting to the point.

"Brokerage, actually. Here's my card. I handle clients of some means who are always on the lookout for opportunities outside the norm. One of them pointed out an article about C&C's acquisition of SCM and I thought it worth looking into. I saw your name and remembered Donna was once married to a Dr. Steinham. Turns out it was true and, well, here we are. I'm flattered you agreed to meet me."

"Just out of curiosity, who was this client of yours?" Harry asked.

"Sorry. Confidentiality prohibits my using his name. You understand. If it turns out there's a way for him—us—to participate in the deal, of course I'll introduce you."

That's right, Bill. Stick to the script.

"Fair enough," Harry said, "though I'm not quite sure what you mean about participating. Why don't they just buy C&C stock? It's listed, you know."

"Yeah, but that's not where the real action is, is it? I mean, don't you have any private equity financing? That's what my investors are looking for … an edge. Isn't there something you could do?"

"Well, now that you mention it, Jimmy— Can I call you Jimmy? Why don't we sit down and discuss it over some drinks and lasagna? I've been sitting here for twenty minutes and the smell from the kitchen is driving me half-crazy with hunger."

I heard the shuffling of chairs, followed by the waiter's voice taking their drink orders. Harry ordered a Jack Daniels on the rocks—a double. Bill ordered a glass of Chianti for himself and a red wine for Donna. *How did he know?*

At that point, the computer screen started streaming the scene. Donna had deftly placed her clutch on an empty spot at the table, positioning the wide-angle lens so I could see everything. Harry was exactly as Bill had describe him. His suit coat hung on him, and his belly kept him several inches from the table. He already had a nearly full glass of hooch in front of him and I wondered why he ordered another. Bill pulled the Mont Blanc from his shirt pocket and laid it on the table along with a small note pad.

"Hope you don't mind me taking some notes as we talk," he said, propping the pen against the pad so the neatly disguised microphone in the clip pointed up.

"No, no, not at all, Jimmy" Harry said, but his eyes stayed focused on Donna. Sure enough, his mustache was twitching, and I saw Donna squirm slightly in her seat.

The hair rose at the back of my neck.

A mouth-watering basket of freshly baked breads arrived. I could nearly taste the garlic and homemade dipping sauce. I was tempted to go into the kitchen and get something to eat, but I didn't want to miss anything, so I sat there salivating.

Bill's Chianti arrived, along with Donna's Merlot. They toasted the success of the takeover, and Donna launched into her list of carefully practiced questions. She leaned in, a little too much as far as I was concerned and smiled warmly.

"So, isn't it exciting? How long will you be here in Phoenix, Harry?"

"Just a few days. I've got to be back in Boston this weekend."

"You said you were looking over the staffing at SCM. Does that mean you'll be working with Dr. Johnson? He's our HR director."

"Already been in touch with him. We'll be working closely together for a few months. Our technicians will be introducing some new systems to help your staff become more efficient, while increasing the care levels for the patients. Maybe while I'm here you could show me around?" Harry's mustache was dancing uncontrollably.

"Sure. We can catch up on old times, and you could teach me some of *those new systems* you've developed." Her voice dropped to nearly a whisper when she said, "those new systems." Harry broke out in a wide grin. I knew it was part of the act and, in 20/20 hindsight, it was a good thing Bill went with her instead of me. I might have knocked his teeth out then and there.

"Speaking of systems," Bill said, right on cue, "your results were impressive in the last two facilities you took over. Your stock price nearly doubled in just eighteen months. Revenue increased forty percent and profits jumped nearly seventy-five percent. That's huge. How did you do it? Do you think you can do the same thing here?"

"No reason we can't," Harry said, without shifting his stare. "Once you find a winning formula, you just need to apply it over and over. No real secret there." He took a bite out of one of the rolls and, without swallowing, continued talking with his mouth full. "Don't you agree?"

Bill took a sip of wine before answering. "Agreed. These increases are just spectacular. You've gone well beyond anyone else in the industry. Are you willing to discuss any of this with my investors?"

"That depends." Harry finally swallowed, followed by a long swig from his tumbler. "Just what kind of capital are you and your investors capable of raising?"

"Ten million dollars, maybe twenty, depending on the terms. But I have to go back to them with more information."

Harry's mustache stopped twitching and his eyes narrowed as he studied Bill closely, "What kind of information?"

"Well, for instance, what are the pro forma projections for SCM? Just because you were able to increase profits at the other facilities, there's no guarantee you can do it indefinitely. I think they'd like to see what changes you have planned to achieve your aggressive cost savings and revenue gains, especially in light of the current environment."

"What do you mean, 'the current environment?'" Harry asked.

"Come on. The pandemic decimated the local economy, including the hospitals and clinics here. On top of that, the insurance companies have been squeezing them even harder. It would follow that profits would be shrinking, not expanding. It's just counterintuitive you could buck the industry trends, and my investors want to be sure it isn't just an accounting trick."

"It's no accounting trick, I assure you, but I'll need to run this by my executive committee, and they'll want to know if your clients are accredited. Can they put their money where your mouth is?"

"No problem," Bill said. "I'll show you my list if you'll show me yours."

Harry sat back and smiled, mustache active again. Bill was a decent poker player, and I hoped he caught the man's "tell" signal. I wanted to text him, but I dared not interrupt the flow of the conversation.

"You have a deal," Harry said. "I'll be back in my office on Saturday. Perhaps we could exchange our 'lists' by secure email."

"I'll have to clear it with my customers first, but I'm pretty sure they'll agree. They'll want to know what terms are available. Any chance I can get that from you as well?"

"I'll include it with the reports I send you Saturday. Is this a secure email address on your card?"

"Yes," Bill said. "Just give me a call first and we'll coordinate the exchange. If your numbers ring true, I'm sure we'll be able to do business."

I dialed his number and the cell in his pocket started buzzing. Bill excused himself as he answered it.

"Hello dear," he said into the phone. "What? When? How high was his fever? No! Okay, I'll meet you at the clinic. Fifteen minutes, twenty tops … Yes … Yes, it's okay, I'm sure they'll understand. Okay, bye."

Bill hung up the phone and stood. "I'm so sorry. That was my wife. Our youngest wasn't feeling well after school, and she said he has a fever of a hundred and three. She's heading for the nearest urgent care center. I'm sure you understand. I'm so terribly sorry about this."

Harry and Donna both stood as well. "Is it Josh?" Donna asked, her face mirroring Bill's pretend concern.

"Yes. Probably caught something at school." He held a hand out to Harry, who took it firmly in his own.

"You go take care of your family, Jimmy. I'll call you on Saturday. What should we do with your dinner?"

"Maybe one of you can take it home in a doggy bag. Here," Bill said, reaching into his pants pocket and producing a money clip. He peeled off two hundred-dollar bills and laid them on the table. "This should take care of the tab. Again, I'm so sorry, but I really must go."

"I look forward to working with you," Harry said, and sat back down.

Bill replaced the money clip in his pocket. "It was good to meet you, Doctor. Good night, Donna."

"Good night, B ... Jim," Donna said, catching herself just in time. "Call me tomorrow and let me know if Josh is all right."

"Will do. And I'll speak with you on Saturday, Doctor."

Harry said goodnight once more, and Bill strode away.

Harry reached for the two bills and slipped them in his pocket.

***

I barely noticed him when he walked in thirty minutes later. He slung his jacket across a chair and sat down. My eyes remained glued to the screen. Donna kept switching back and forth between flirting and plying Harry for information. It was obvious from his damn facial hairs what he found more interesting, though.

"At Boston General we had our fair share of indigents come through the ER. Is that still the case?" Her chin rested in her hands with elbows on the table, eyes locked on his.

"I wouldn't know," Harry said. "For all I care, they can have all the indigents in the whole damn city." Harry leaned over and slowly trailed his fingers up and down her exposed arms. "Why don't we talk about you? It must be lonely here in Arizona. I can't imagine you finding anyone to keep you warm at night in this godforsaken place."

Bill reached over and muted the conversation. "We can watch the video while we talk," he said, nodding at the image on the laptop. "Donna seems perfectly capable of handling Harry."

"Oh? And when did you become an expert all of a sudden?" I tried to turn the sound back on.

Bill pushed the laptop out of reach with one hand and shoved the stack of unopened reports in front of me with the other.

"I'm not in the mood to look at any more of your freaking charts and graphs. You know what you can do with—"

"Donna told me she hated Harry."

"Wait. What? When?"

"In the car. You have nothing to worry about. Let's get some work done."

"Did she say anything about me?"

"Yeah. She said you were a geekazoid. Now, can we please get to work? She'll dump him in an hour or so and, when she gets back, you'll expect me to leave."

My shoulders loosened a little.

"All right. So long as you understand."

"I'm married. I'm not dead. Now. Can we get to work?"

"Yeah. Sorry."

Bill pulled out another incomprehensible spreadsheet labeled "Private pay insurance reimbursements vs. Government sponsored programs; Medicare and Medicaid." He pointed to a column marked "Cross referenced by facilities category."

I squinted at the closely spaced percentages, trying to make sense out of them. "How'd you get this? Some of these hospitals are privately held, and the information isn't publicly available."

"I got it from the Social Security database."

I glanced at the screen. Donna had moved her chair closer to Harry, and they were holding hands.

"What the hell is she doing?"

"She's doing what we told her do."

"Well, I don't like it. I'd rather just kill him and take my chances with Delbert Carter."

"*Look at me!*" Bill raised his voice.

Startled, I jerked my head hard in his direction.

"She's a big girl. She can handle herself. Now, what do you think of these numbers?"

I forced myself to focus on the chart, though the numbers were just a blur. "Where'd you say you got these stats?"

"The Social Security database."

"Really? When I looked online yesterday, all the data was at least two years old: consolidated, not broken down, facility by facility. How the hell did you get this?"

"I have friends in low places," he said, smiling ear to ear like he'd just won the Nobel Peace Prize for clandestine research.

"Oh? Like who, for example?"

"Like a computer hacker named Jeremy. He has a way, shall we say, of coaxing sensitive data from uncooperative computer systems."

"Legally?"

"I never ask, but his intel is always current and deathly accurate."

"How can you be sure?"

"I've matched his findings with available quarterly filings by public hospitals. They're within pennies of each other."

"Including C&C?"

"Especially C&C."

I took a closer look at the data on the page. "Wait a minute." I ran my finger down the column, then across to the dates. "The current quarter isn't over yet. Where'd you get these figures?"

"Jeremy got them for me."

"And where'd he get them?"

"Someplace reliable, I'm sure."

"You mean to say he's broken into their mainframe?" My mouth dropped open in disbelief.

"I didn't ask, and he didn't tell me."

This wasn't the Bill I thought I knew. How'd I miss this? He always seemed to be one step ahead of his peers when it came to investment research. Now I think I know why.

"So, if the numbers match, doesn't that mean they're *not* committing fraud? I don't understand. How are we going to catch them committing a crime if they aren't committing any crimes?"

"Just because Medicare pays the claims doesn't make them legitimate. By law, they're required to pay all claims within fifteen days, without first verifying their accuracy. This is why there's so much fraud—the crooks know how the system works and they milk it. They submit fraudulent claims with current procedure codes, and they get paid, no questions asked. By the time the enforcement division catches on, the scammers have closed up and moved on. So long as it's pay-first-investigate-later, this type of fraud will continue unabated."

"And you think C&C is submitting false claims?" I grabbed the spreadsheet, my interest peaked.

"No, they're not that stupid. I believe their scheme is more sophisticated. Like I told you before, they take over existing facilities then deliberately implement policies targeting the most lucrative Medicare procedures, while reducing the number of routine low-profit programs and operations."

"But—"

"Here. Read this article from the *New Jersey Herald*. It chronicles how St. Anastasia's did just what C&C is doing, just on a smaller scale. Since it takes so long for Medicare to react, C&C might be able to do this for years, skimming billions from the Medicare program before they get shut down."

"No wonder they're in such a rush to get these mergers done."

"They're minting money at the expense of the U.S. taxpayer."

I shook my head in disgust and, when I did, I noticed the computer screen was blank. Instead of the camera feed from Donna's purse, there was nothing but static.

"What the hell!" I stood up and reached for the laptop. I fiddled with the video controls, but the screen stubbornly refused to focus in.

"Here, let me." Bill shoved me aside, swiveling the computer towards him. He found the 'rewind' control and we both watched until the picture reappeared. He let it go back another few seconds, then stopped it and hit Play. The action resumed, this time at normal speed. There sat Harry, holding his drink in one hand, and Donna's hand in the other. I reached over and hit the mute key, turning the sound back on.

"It shure is nice to sheeeee you again," Harry said, slurring his words. Donna reached for her glass of wine, knocking it over. Like a red tidal wave, it swam straight at the camera, washing over it. The image warbled on the screen for a second then turned to static.

Bill pointed at the signal strength indicator. "No incoming signal. It must have shorted out."

"Dammit," I said, drums pounding in my ears. "He's drunk. I've got to get to Tiani's."

Bill grabbed my arm. "Hold on, buddy. Let me make a call first."

"Call? Call who? Who you gonna call?" I tried to wrestle my arm away.

"Calm down, partner," Bill shouted.

I stopped. Bill never shouts.

"Let me call Sonya and have her check on them. Then we can decide what to do." He pulled out his cell and dialed Tiani's.

"Sonya please. Hi, Sonya; it's Bill Phillips. I think I forgot my pen on the table when I left this evening. Would you mind checking to see if it's there? No, I had to leave early. My son had a fever and my wife called. Yeah, he's okay. The doc' said he just had a touch of bronchitis, gave us a Z-pak. Okay, I'll hold."

"She's checking," Bill said as I headed to the hall closet. "What are you doing?" he asked.

"Getting my jacket. I'm heading down there."

"I said wait," Bill exclaimed, stepping around the side of the table to follow me.

Holding up my hand, I said, "You wait here, while I drive. If you hear from her, call me and I'll turn around."

"Don't be a fool. If you show up and make a scene, it will blow the whole operation."

"The operation," I shouted. "The *operation?* I don't care about the fucking operation. If he touches her, I'll kill him. Screw the operation."

I snatched my coat out of the hall closet, and turned to find Bill blocking the door, still holding the phone to his ear.

"Get out of my way," I growled, trying to squeeze past him.

He shoved me hard in the chest. "I said wait."

I fell back, stumbled over the leg of the hall table, and fell on my backside.

As I was about to stand up to punch him, he started talking into the phone. "They left? When? Five or ten minutes ago? Did everything seem okay? No. No, I mean were they. You saw it? A taxi? What about Donna? Yeah, yeah, she had a car. What pen? Oh yes, thank you. One of them probably took it. I'll check with them in the morning. Thanks Sonya."

He lowered the phone.

"They've left Tiani's already, in separate cars. She'll be here in twenty minutes. You better get your act together, Steve." He pocketed his phone and headed back to the kitchen. "And pick up your damn jacket."

***

At quarter to ten, Donna stepped in, shoes in one hand, wine-stained purse hanging limply in the other. She dropped them just inside the door, then threw her arms around me, pressing her cheek into the hollow of my shoulder.

After a few minutes she pulled back and I could see the exhaustion in her eyes. Did she see the relief in mine? Before I could tell her how glad I was that she was back, she kissed me, long and tenderly. When she was done, she whispered, "Miss me?"

For a second, I totally forgot Bill was there and tried to draw her closer, but she put her hands on my chest, thwarting me.

Then I heard him clear his throat. "Okay you two love birds. Can we do a quick critique? Then I'll leave you to, uh, well …"

Donna stroked the stubbled on my chin. "Sounds good, Bill. What do you say, Romeo?"

"I guess I can show a little restraint," I took her hand and led her to the kitchen table. Donna nearly slipped on a pile of papers on the floor.

"You boys have some sort of disagreement?" She bent down and picked some of the charts up, adding them to the ones disarrayed next to the laptop.

"We had some problems with the video feed," Bill said, joining us at the table. "Did you have any difficulties with Harry after I left?"

"None at all. Why?"

"We thought Harry was getting a little too assertive," I said.

"You mean *you* thought he was a little too amorous," she said. "You're jealous."

"Who? Me? Of course not."

Bill harrumphed. "He was getting ready to mount his steed and ride off into the night to rescue you."

"Says you."

Donna reached over and took my face in her hands. "That's sweet, Steven, but unnecessary. I can handle Harry."

"But he was reaching out, running his fingers up and down … Then I saw him holding your hand, and he was drunk. What if—"

"Harry is an alcoholic. Normally it would take a few more drinks for him to get truly inebriated—"

"I heard him right before you spilled your wine and the picture shorted out. He was slurring his words."

She reached into her dress, above her left breast. When she withdrew her hand, she had a small plastic baggie with a couple of small, white pills in them.

She laid it down between Bill and me.

Bill picked it up and examined it. "What are these?"

She took the packet from him, shaking it so the pills danced inside. "I brought my own secret weapon, agent Adams. I slipped a Mickey into his drink while you and he were exchanging goodbyes." She got up and deposited them in the trash. When she sat back down, she pointed at the computer. "I'm surprised you didn't see it on the screen, Sherlock. Some spy you'd make."

"But the wine? I could swear you spilled it on purpose."

"I meant to spill it on *him*, so he'd need to go clean up and I could slip out. I missed, but it worked anyway. He thought I spilled it on myself, so I used it as an excuse to go home. I tucked him in a cab outside before heading here. I wouldn't be surprised if he passed out in the taxi."

"Why didn't you call and tell us?" Bill asked.

She walked back to the door and retrieved her purse. Opening it, she pulled out her cell phone. A drop of wine escaped from it and hit the tile floor. "Can you stop by Verizon tomorrow for me and pick up a new phone?"

"Of course," I said. "I owe you that much."

"For now, I'll take a cup of hot tea."

"You need me to doctor it up a little?"

"No thanks. I've had enough liquor for one night. Just put in a little lemon and a half packet of Sweet'n Low." She sat down at the table next to Bill, pushing some of the papers aside. "Did you get anything useful out of tonight?"

"Not directly," Bill answered, "but if he's willing to use Jim Adams as his next sting victim, we have our in."

She frowned. "You think he's going to show his hand based on one dinner meeting?"

Bill shook his head. "Of course not. But I think he's running out of time to run his little con. Once he's given us the dummy documents, we can go after his company, and especially his boss, Delbert Carter."

"I still don't know why you think he'd turn on them. He works for them, for God's sake," she replied.

"You're too used to working with people who actually cooperate in their jobs. In the world of big corporate business, it's every man for himself. If Harry thinks he's facing real jail time and the loss of all his ill-gotten gains, he'll turn like a sour cabbage."

"Well then, I want to be there when it happens. Steven, is the tea ready yet?"

~13~

Thursday turned into a headache without an aspirin. Verizon didn't have an exact replacement for the wine-drenched cell, and Donna had given me specific directions not to buy anything unless it was teal. By the time I tracked one down, I was late for my first client meeting of the day. Harvey Barstow couldn't care less about my excuses. The market was down, and he wanted to know why I hadn't moved "the damn money into cash."

The day went downhill from there as the continuing market volatility prompted hostility from concerned investors—real ones, not the fictitious, Jim Adams, kind. Common swings of hundreds—sometimes thousands—of points in a single day caused lots of people to question the validity of equity investing at all. I kept hearing, "Why should I invest? Isn't the game rigged to favor the banks and the wealthy?" It is, of course. High-frequency trading was the new threat to market stability.

"No, Mrs. Jones, the market is regulated by the SEC, so your investments have as good a chance as anyone's to grow," I heard myself answer more than once, like I was on autopilot.

I shuffled the papers on my desk, reviewing the year-to-date analysis of the Hubert's portfolio. *Yes, Mrs. Hubert,* I practiced in my mind, *your portfolio is down six percent this month, but last year you were up eleven percent.* I stood and walked to the window. Donna was pulling a double shift. She snuck in only five hours of sleep last night and had to rush home to change to make it in by eight. She kept forgetting to bring a change of clothing to leave at my place for just such occasions, despite repeated invitations to do so. Maybe she thought I was a cross dresser and didn't want me trying on her things. Or maybe I'm just too dense. Leaving clothes at my place meant commitment.

"Hope you're having a great day," I texted to her, knowing she wouldn't see it till quitting time.

Returning to my desk, I phoned to confirm dinner with Bill after work. I wondered how much Bill's wife, Ellen, knew about what we were doing. She was a terrific lady, but I could always see her eyes glaze over when Bill and I got together and started talking shop. I hoped he wasn't keeping her in the dark this time. If things went south, I didn't want to be responsible for trouble in the Phillips family.

***

"So why are we meeting at IHOP?" Bill asked as we walked up to the front door.

I held the door open for him. "You'll see."

At the counter, we waited while the hostess led a large family of four to their seats. The mother and father were outright obese, and the two teenage children well on their way to achieving supersized proportions. Was it really possible Donna looked like that once? The mother turned and caught me gawking, so I picked up a menu and pretended to read it.

I had my nose buried when a familiar voice said, "Hi, may I help you?"

I put the menu down and smiled. "Hi, Carol."

"Well hello there." She grinned broadly. "It's Steven, isn't it? You're Donna's new friend."

"I'm flattered. You remembered me."

"Donna talks about you all the time."

I leaned on the glass counter. "Really?"

"Sure. She started coming in here a few years ago, and we've been tight ever since. She says you knew each other in high school."

I nodded. "Uh-huh. Back in New York."

"What took you so long to get together?"

"After graduation, she ended up in Boston and I ended up out here. It was pure coincidence we ran into each other."

She held her hand to her chest. "Surely you noticed her?"

"You know how it is. We went to a big school, ran in different circles."

"Yeah, she told me. Apparently, you didn't even recognize her. Has she really changed so much? I can't imagine anyone could forget her. I'm so jealous, she's so gorgeous."

Donna must have conveniently neglected to mention her weight challenges.

"Yes, she is. I guess I was just too shy to approach her."

"Well, that makes sense. She must have been the most popular girl in school, with guys three-deep waiting in line. Too bad she ended up marrying that jerk."

"I thought he was a doctor."

"Ha. Some doctor. He was a real … anyway, I'm glad the two of you found each other. I liked the way you treated her when you were here."

"Thanks. I think she's really special."

"Table for two?" she asked, looking over my shoulder. A line had formed while she chit-chatted with me.

"Yes. By the way, this is my friend, Bill. Is there somewhere we can spread out and do some work while we eat?"

She reached out and he shook her hand. "Nice to meet you, Bill." Picking up two menus, she started walking. "Right this way. I've got just the table for you."

After we sat, Bill pulled out another set of spreadsheets and reports.

"More research?" I asked.

"Always, though I'm a little confused about your choice of venue. Was that short conversation with Carol worth eating dinner at a breakfast joint?"

"They serve burgers and stuff here. That's dinner, kind of."

"Why don't you just come here at an off hour and ask her whatever it is you want to ask her?"

"Because the first thing she'd do is call Donna and tell her all about it."

"So, I'm your interrogation excuse?"

"Something like that."

"And you think my Adams' act is over the top. Sheesh."

The waitress came by, and we ordered, though by the look on his face, I was in debt for at least one meal at Ruth's Chris steakhouse. When she left, Bill grabbed one of the graphs. "The deeper I look, the more I find. Every facility they've taken over—"

"Hold that thought."

"But—"

"Looks like Carol's going on break. Give me ten minutes. I'll be back."

***

"Well, it's about time. I hope you don't mind; I was hungry." Bill's plate was half empty, but there was no trace of my food. "The waitress took yours back. I don't know if it's still under the heat lamp, but you may want to ask her to make it fresh, unless you like nuked eggs."

As if in reply to his command, our waitress came over and asked if I was ready to eat.

"Yes. And could you make it fresh? I'll pay for the original if you need me to."

"That won't be necessary. I've seen you in here with Donna. If you're good enough for her, that's good enough for me. I'll have your dinner here in a jiffy."

Bill took a drink of soda—I felt bad because otherwise we'd have gone someplace with alcohol—and commented, "Looks like everyone here knows you. You're a real IHOP celebrity."

"Cute. Let's get some work done."

"Not so fast, my friend. What did Carol say? You can leave out the niceties, just the skinny on Donna." He gathered up his cheeseburger and took a huge bite while I choked back a retort about Donna being skinny.

"Not much, really, except—"

"Not much?" he mumbled with his mouth full. "You were out there for almost twenty minutes!"

"Not much except that Harry is an even bigger asshole than we thought. She told me the divorce had something to do with Harry's, uh, proclivities towards deviant sexual behavior."

Bill swallowed hard and took another drink. "Wait, what?"

"I don't think Donna told her all the gory details, but what little she shared painted an ugly picture. She used the term 'Mickey' too, which may be why Donna was familiar with its use."

"Sounds like there's more than meets the eye, here. You'd better be careful. You sure she hasn't used one on you?"

"One what?"

"A Mickey Finn. You fell in love pretty quick, even for you."

"Ha-ha. No, I'm sure she didn't use any drugs on me. She didn't have to. Anyway, maybe there's something here we can use."

"Like what?"

"I don't know. But if he has a weakness for sexual fetishes, there might be a way to exploit it."

He hesitated a moment, chewing on his lip. "Okay. Okay, you're right. That's useful information. I'll keep it on the back burner in case the investment scam goes south. I guess I owe you an apology."

"Well, that's a first. Why?"

"I thought you were only interested in yourself and pumping Carol for ways to worm your way into Donna's heart. Instead, you came away with ammunition for the cause. Good job, Steve. Good thinking."

He was wrong, of course. I *was* only interested in getting Carol to reveal something—anything—that I could use to win Donna over. But I wasn't about to disillusion him. "Thanks. Now, let's have a look at what's in that envelope."

***

The waitress appeared with my dinner, and while I started to chow down, he pulled out a series of reports. Choosing one and laying it in front of me, he pointed to one of the long columns of numbers. "Look at these from Illinois." He moved his finger rapidly from column to column. "And these from Florida. And Ohio. It can't simply be luck or superior management."

"But that's just your opinion. We need confirmation from an official source."

"I've got a call in to the head of the Medicare fraud unit in DC, but I haven't heard back yet. If it's this obvious to me, maybe there's already an investigation underway and we can call in the cavalry."

"I assume you aren't holding your breath."

He sighed. "No, I'm too much a realist for that."

"Good." I wasn't as hungry as I thought, so I wiped my mouth with my napkin and pushed the plate aside. "Now, before you bore me to tears with more facts and figures, I've got to ask you a question."

"No, I'm sorry, you can't talk to my computer guy, Jeremy the geek."

"That's not it, though I want to revisit that issue—we may need his help later on. No, I wanted to ask you about Ellen. Why didn't you tell me how bad it was? I mean, jeeze, Bill. Clinical trials? Experimental treatments? What's going on? I thought we were friends?"

He lowered his head until his chin nearly touched his chest and lowered his voice. "Sorry, Steve. I didn't mean to leave you out." He paused, and I thought for a moment he was going to cry. Raising his head, he continued. "It's hard enough trying to explain it to the kids. Until I knew more about it, I guess I just didn't want to talk about it to anyone. Don't take it wrong. Please"

"I won't. But I want you to know I'm here for you. Is she gonna be all right?"

He shrugged. "According to her doctors, it's controllable with medication and regular blood treatments. She's got Polycythemia Vera, PV for short. Her body overproduces red blood cells which causes a variety of side effects, including fainting spells. Her primary care physician works at SCM, too. That's how she got into the trials in the first place. If C&C comes in and forces him out, we'd have to find a new facility, maybe a new doctor, and this is a pretty rare disease. I'd rather not make a change right now, especially since they've finally found a workable treatment regimen for her."

"And the trial for the new, experimental procedure would be cancelled too, right?"

"I can only assume so. Trials aren't big money makers, especially if they don't produce results. C&C is interested in quick profits today, not iffy payoffs years from now."

"Don't look now, but you could say that about us. We've had more layoffs and staff reductions in my office this year than the previous ten. I'm sure it's all about the bottom line."

He nodded. "Same story with my department. I don't know how they expect us to get anything done with insufficient resources. We've lost two of our best analysts to the competition this month alone."

"You're not going anywhere, are you?"

"Nah. I thought about it, but I need the medical benefits. No one else offers coverage that comes close to what we have. I've just got to make it work here."

I took a deep breath, exhaling slowly. "All the more reason for you *not* to do this. If this thing blows up in our faces, medical insurance will be the least of your problems."

He raised his eyebrows at me. "What about you? You're sticking your neck out, too. You ready for the unemployment line?"

I shrugged it off. "I'm single, no obligations, except to myself. I've got enough stashed to last me quite a while if I get canned. I'd feel really guilty if anything happened to you, and especially to Ellen if this goes south."

"Put your guilt away. I'm aware of the consequences. I'll find my way if I get fired. Right now, I'm just mad enough at the world to want to push back. They're threatening your girlfriend, my wife, and the entire community, not to mention what they're doing nationally. Someone has to stand up to them, and it may as well be me."

"Okay, maestro. It's us against them." I pushed the report back across the table, no longer interested in discussing it. "Just one more question. Have you told Ellen about our little scheme?"

"I'm working on it. Once I know how far we have to go with this thing, I'll tell her."

"Don't wait too long, buddy. She deserves to know what's going on."

"I'll tell her on the way up to the cabin this weekend. You two still coming?"

I smiled at the thought of a quick getaway out of town. "Sure. Can't wait to check it out," I waved the waitress over and reached for my wallet, but Bill grabbed the check and handed her a credit card.

"This one's on me."

I nodded and got up to leave as he stuffed all the charts back into the envelope. "Thanks. I think I'll accidently get lost and stroll by the front desk. Maybe Carol wasn't done telling me how much Donna adores me. See you tomorrow."

~14~

The soothing hum of the pavement did little to calm the queasiness in my stomach. Snowflake was three hours away, assuming no accidents or traffic jams. The steep grades and occasional switchbacks hugging Salt River Canyon demanded my continuous attention, despite the welcome change of scenery. The break from routine would do the four of us some good. The trap for Harry was firming up, but I still had my doubts. Soon it would be too late to turn back.

"Do you know if they caught it early?" Donna asked, checking her makeup in the vanity mirror. "The quicker they treat it, the better the result."

"I'm not sure. Bill's been tight-lipped about it." I kept a reasonable distance behind their SUV, which seemed to float effortlessly along despite weighing twice as much as my BMW. "She was misdiagnosed several times before her doctor nailed it. Maybe you can ask her this weekend? You'd understand it better than I."

Snapping the compact closed, she put it back in her purse. "Only if she brings it up. People don't like to talk about their condition, especially with strangers."

"You're a nurse. Why would she mind? Besides, it's the reason he's doing this. One of them anyway"

She went quiet and started fidgeting in the seat. Had I hit another hidden chord? I've learned to wait her silences out, but patience is not my forte.

She reached over and took my hand. "He's doing this for Ellen?"

"Pretty much."

"And you're doing this for me?"

"I thought you knew that."

"I don't have a rare blood disorder." With her free hand, she smoothed the slight creases in her jeans for the umpteenth time since we left Phoenix. "Ellen's a lucky woman. A lot of men, when their wives get sick, walk away."

I snuck a sideways glance at her, careful not to take my eyes off the road for too long. "I don't believe that."

"Well, it's true."

"Really? Based on what?"

"Experience."

"Meaning Harry?"

"No, not Harry, although … I've seen it way too often."

"At the hospital, then?"

"When a man is sick, his wife always shows up first thing in the morning, staying till after dark. She's pays attention to every detail of his care. If she's the one who's sick, her mother or sister or BFF shows up. Stays."

"So? What's your point?"

"Dear hubby visits less and less frequently. 'Gotta make a living,' he'll say, followed by, 'A man needs some physical attention, ya know,' as he screws around with his secretary or visits Tiffany's." She stopped, and all I could hear was her breathing. "The divorce is just a formality."

We drove for a few miles in silence, past hundred-foot, rock-faced cliffs.

"You don't really believe it do you? That men are such—"

"Assholes?" She was staring out the passenger window. "Wendy was my best friend. She taught me the ropes, showed me how to handle the stress. One day, she told me she'd been diagnosed with cervical cancer. The Doctors …," her voice cracked, "the doctors gave her twelve months to live, maybe eighteen if she did the chemo and radiation. She lost her hair, constantly sick and vomiting. Before long, her husband of seventeen years had a honey on the side. By the time she was bedridden … well, he just left a note on the kitchen table saying how sorry he was and walked out."

"Yeah, but—"

"I hated him. I still hate him. I watched Wendy die, and all I wanted to do was cut off his testicles and nail them to their front door so everyone could see what kind of heartless bastard he was."

I resisted the urge to reposition my hand to protect myself from the imaginary pair of shears. My mind raced for something to say, some platitude to offer. It didn't make sense. Why would he have done that?

When my father died, my mom stayed by his side day and night, right up to the end, just like Donna said. If their fates had been reversed, I don't think it would have even occurred to him not to stay.

I eased our car a little closer to the Bill and Ellen's, close enough to see their heads bobbing in conversation. "Bill's not like that." I twisted sideways to look at her. "Why are you so cynical?"

It was only for a half-second, but a piercing *honk* startled me.

"Keep your eyes on the road, Romeo. I want to get to Snowflake in one piece."

"Sorry." I reached over and took Donna's hand. "Bill would never do that to Ellen." I squeezed progressively harder until I felt her squeeze back in response. "And neither would I."

I glanced over again, not sure wat to expect.

A single tear rolled down her cheek.

"Promise?"

"Promise."

~15~

Dateline, Boston, MA October 1, 2021

The markets suffered yet another setback as the widely anticipated vaccine for Covid-19 appeared to have unexpected side-effects, particularly in young adults and specifically women of child-bearing age. Several other trials are still ongoing for competing compounds, but they are at least three-six months off before they could be considered viable for distribution. Amongst the losing sectors in this afternoon's rout are the cruise lines, airlines, and other travel-related segments of the world-wide economy, which were counting on a return to normalcy following the promising ascent of the wonder drug, CoronaFlex.

In related news, several area hospitals have added capacity for the anticipated increase in Covid cases. C&C Associates, when contacted by this reporter about their response to the potential surge, sent out a press release indicating their facilities in the Northeast were 'well prepared for any contingency,' but did not directly address their readiness for any unexpected assault on their Emergency room from Covid victims.

***

Another muggy Saturday in Boston. A stubborn nor'easter dumped almost two inches of rain overnight, then cleared enough for the sun to heat the air to a sticky ninety degrees. Nevertheless, Harry felt refreshed and ready to get back to work. He kept wondering why he didn't end up in bed with Donna, considering her constant flirting, and he suspected there was more going on with Jim Adams than she admitted. Just as well. He couldn't stand the thought of being nice to her again. Soon, she'd get the pink slip from C&C, and he'd arrange to be there to watch as they escorted her from the premises.

In any event, he'd made other plans, just in case. Before flying back to Logan on Friday, he stopped in Las Vegas. Staying at his favorite hotel, he started with room service, a T-bone steak with all the trimmings from the Wolfgang Puck restaurant downstairs along with a bottle of Johnny Walker Black. Next, he pulled out a burner phone and dialed the unlisted number.

"Twisted Kilts. How may I help you?"

"Daphne? Harry Steinham here. Are the Swedes available tonight?"

"Hold on a moment, Doctor, I'll check for you."

Daphne wasn't her real name, of course, but if she didn't recognize you, you didn't get past her. Their security was tighter than the hotel's. Any hint of a violent reputation or the slightest whiff of an undercover alias got you blacklisted, electronically barred from the constantly changing, secure phone number.

Harry objected initially to the background check, convinced his credentials with C&C should have been sufficient, but he ultimately relented. The inquisition was worth it, as his position—and bank account balance—qualified him for their "trusted" list.

"Yes, Doctor, they are. Are you staying at the Venetian, as usual?"

"Room 9801. Have them come around nine o'clock and clear their dance calendar for the rest of the evening."

"Yes sir. Marie and Ralph will be there at nine. Enjoy your evening."

***

He slept like a baby on the red-eye back home. The champagne had flowed, and he watched as they performed on the sofa. Aroused, he'd invited them to join him in the king-sized bed, spending several blissfully depraved hours enjoying their skillful attention.

Now, however, he had to get back to reality and decide what to do about Jim Adams. He looked like the perfect stooge, but he'd never dealt with one of his marks in person before. He fingered the business card, turning it over and over like it was a Magic 8-ball, but no prophetic advice materialized.

Putting it aside, he got on his computer and downloaded the acquisition file for SCM from the mainframe. He transferred the pertinent details of the merger to the doctored "Participation Notes," fictionizing the sensitive names and dates just in case someone actually read the damn thing and tried to verify their validity.

Confident they looked legit, he massaged the "offering statement" further to increase the interest rate to nine percent, the equity sharing to eighteen percent. These were slightly higher than the last one, but Scottsdale was a more affluent community, and he felt the need to show higher returns to attract enough investors to make it worth their while.

He printed a copy and admired his handiwork. "Perfect. Even Mother Theresa would want a piece of the action." He saved the document on an encrypted flash drive which he locked in his desk draw before deleting the original.

He reached to turn the computer off but hesitated. Picking up the business card, he googled 'Jim Adams, Investment Advisor." Hundreds of 'Jim Adams' popped up, so he narrowed the search to Scottsdale, Arizona. There were still several results on his screen, but one matched the address and phone number on the card. He dialed the number but only got a recording. He hung up and googled the 'Better Business Bureau' and searched their database.

Nothing under Jim Adams.

Next, he tried the Arizona Corporation Commission, which regulates businesses in the state.

Three Jim Adams came up, but none of them listed 'investments' as their main source of income.

He picked up the phone again and called the number on the screen.

"You have reached the Arizona Corporation Commission offices in Phoenix Arizona. If you've reached this recording, we are either closed or are experiencing high call volumes. Please try again later. Our business hours are—"

He banged the phone down. "God-damn it."

The cursor on the computer blinked at him defiantly, counting down the seconds. The merger was less than two weeks away, three at the outside. He'd never find a willing patsy before the ink dried on the deal.

He'd have to chance it.

~16~

He wasn't kidding. Bill's new cabin was nothing short of spectacular. Situated off the highway just outside of Snowflake, it took twenty minutes of tire-squealing, hairpin turns up a winding driveway lined with creosote bushes and junipers. I don't know what I expected — a Lincoln Logs look-a-like maybe—but we rounded a sharp corner and the cabin rose up in front of us like a mountain man's dream. The subtle angles and lines of the roof and irregular contours of the walls melted seamlessly into the surrounding pines. The forest floor rolled gently up to the sides, and it was difficult to distinguish where the brown ground cover ended, and the cabin's walls began. The windows, recessed with dark shades, gave the illusion of secret entrances to animal lairs. A simple flagstone walkway led to the front door from the detached garage, where we parked our vehicles.

I piled both duffle bags with our clothing on top of a wheeled cooler and struggled along the rough ground as Donna walked on ahead. The wheels kept jamming on the flagstones, and I ultimately had to carry everything in one at a time. By the time I laid the last bag on the floor of our room, Donna was already in the shower.

I grabbed the cooler, which glided smoothly on the parquet floor, and wound my way through the interior of the cabin in search of the kitchen. The bedrooms were located on the western end of the structure to take advantage of the views, so I had to walk through the vaulted, great room to reach it on the far side. An eight-foot-wide fireplace graced the southern wall, complete with a thick, slate mantel sporting framed pictures of Bill's family. I stopped for a moment to look at them. They'd been sequenced to show how his children, now twelve and fourteen, had grown over the years.

The rest of the room was filled with sofas and armchairs arranged so several groups of adults could engage in coy conversations without disturbing the others. Oak beams soared twenty-feet high at the room's apex giving it the feel of a hunting resort, rather than a vacation home. I passed a full-sized pool table, complemented with a well-stocked wet bar on the wall behind it, and a floor-to-ceiling entertainment center which housed a fifty-two-inch, 5G TV.

I knew Bill was successful, and guessed he made nearly double what I did, but this was more elaborate and luxurious than I anticipated. My mind drifted back to that post office box and virtual phone line.

Finally, passing through a set of French doors, I found the kitchen. With a host of commercial-grade appliances—including the stove, refrigerator, and dishwasher—Bill could have hosted a party for our entire office with ample cooking and storage capacity to prepare a restaurant-quality meal.

A wooden island in the center sported a five-foot diameter "lazy Susan," and stools to accommodate eight adults comfortably.

"Finding your way around okay?"

I turned and smiled at Ellen who stood there holding two grocery bags.

"Let me help you with those," I said, walking towards her. "Where's Bill?"

"Outside, checking around the property." She handed me the two, heavy sacks. "He's a stickler for detail and wasn't satisfied with the weatherproofing to the southern wall. He told the contractor to strip it and reapply the waterproof stain. For their sake—and ours—I hope they got it right this time."

She was dressed in jeans and a light-blue sweatshirt, though it wasn't particularly cold inside. I could see why Bill fell in love with her. She had liquid blue eyes, which matched the color of her sweatshirt, and drew you in as they flickered like a well-lit campfire. Her light-brown hair was cropped short and tight, in a Demi Moore sort of way, and she wore very little make-up. Though near my age, she'd recently started using concealer to hide the hints of wrinkles around her eyes. She'd also lost some weight over the last couple of years, no doubt another side-effect of her struggle with the PV.

I put the sacks on the center island and we both started unloading, storing the perishables in the fridge and the canned goods in the cabinets above the countertop. Ellen hungrily eyed the packages of steaks she removed from my cooler, gently placing them in a separate meat drawer. "So, tell me about Donna."

"Not much to tell. We knew each other in high school but went our separate ways after graduation. I met her a few weeks ago at the mall, and we hit it off. I'm sure Bill filled you in on the juicier details."

"You mean the part about how she's got you wrapped around her pinkie, and you've fallen head over heels for her?" Ellen smiled.

"Is that how he put it?"

"Something like that."

She transferred the produce to the crisper. "You know, I've always found it interesting how both of you always answer a question with another question. Is it some sort of secret technique men learn so you never have to give a straight answer?"

"Does it seem like that to you?"

She laughed. "Now I know why you two are such good friends. You never have to talk; you just keep swapping questions."

"All right, allright. Tell me what you want to know." I slid one of the stools out and took a seat.

She closed the refrigerator door and did likewise. "Tell me what attracted you to her. Is she smart? Sensitive? A good kisser? What?"

"To be honest, she's all three of those things, at least to me. What really gets me is her strength. She's been through a lot, including a divorce nearly as devastating as mine."

"Bill mentioned something about her ex … Harry something or other. He was a doctor, right?"

"Still is, but he works as a personnel executive now for a large conglomerate in Boston."

"Bill said he met him. Says he's a real piece of work."

"I haven't had the pleasure, but from all accounts, I'd have to agree."

"He also told me this company is trying to take over the hospital where she works. Is that true?"

"Not just trying. They're likely to succeed."

"And that's why Bill's been so hush-hush, isn't it? That's the hospital I use for my treatments."

I just nodded. She leaned in a little farther, and those hypnotic eyes of hers turned dead serious, threatening to burn a hole through me. "What aren't you two telling me?"

I took a deep breath, climbed off the stool and turned back toward the refrigerator to get a bottle of water. "You want something to drink?"

"No thanks."

I sat back down and took a long, slow drink. "This company, C&C, has a nasty habit of reducing services in the name of expense control."

"Meaning?"

"Lots of people, including Donna, are going to lose their jobs."

"Hmph. I see. And what else?"

I fiddled with the bottle and the thin plastic crackled, so I put it down. "And, uh, some patient services might be affected."

"I see." She lowered her eyes.

The air in the room grew uncomfortably still, and the ticking of the stove's clock sounded like cannon fire.

"We're trying to stop it," I said, breaking the silence.

"Are you now."

"Uh-huh. We have a plan. Sort of."

She raised her eyebrows. "Really. And you two think there's something you can do about it?"

I chewed on my lip for a moment. "There's no way to know unless we try."

"Uh-huh. You know, I've known you two characters for a long time. This isn't some lame-brained adventure to settle a bet, is it? Like when you raced to LA to see who would get the corner office?

I shook my head. "No. This is serious."

"Well, then. I'm guessing it's way above your pay grade. If I must find another hospital, I'll find another hospital. It's not worth your careers."

"Is that what Bill told you?"

"Not in so many words, but he's nearly as transparent as you."

"We'll be careful. You're right. It's not worth our careers."

"Damned straight. If I catch either of you—"

"I got it. 'nough said. Now, can I ask you a favor?"

"Depends," she replied.

"You asked me about Donna. One of the reasons I wanted to come up here this weekend was for you two to meet. I'd like your honest opinion."

Ellen leaned back in the stool. "You having second thoughts?"

"No, but I trust your judgment. I'd like your impression."

She thought about that before nodding and leaning forward again. "Fair enough. But only if you promise to pull the plug on this kooky scheme of yours if things start falling apart."

If this falls apart, there might not be time to pull the plug before we're all sucked down the drain. "Agreed."

"Agreed to what?" I heard Bill say.

We looked up to see him and Donna coming into the kitchen. He was dressed in Bermuda shorts and his Batman T-shirt, while Donna wore capris and a form-fitting T-shirt that read, *"Nurses know how to operate, too."*

Ellen stared at her for a moment before turning her attention to Bill. "We agreed it's too nice a day to spend inside. All the groceries are put away, and there's nothing much to do but enjoy the sunshine." She stood up, gave Bill a quick peck on the cheek, and turned to Donna. "Feel like a taking a walk? Something tells me our men are about to start talking shop, and I get enough of it at home already."

"Sounds good to me." Donna raised her eyebrows at me. "Unless you had other ideas?"

"No, I think it's a great idea. You two can get acquainted while Bill and I have a beer and sit on the porch, working."

"Then it's settled." Ellen headed for the kitchen door and opened it. "Come on. We don't want to waste a second of this glorious day."

The door closed gently behind them, and I suddenly wished I had kept my mouth shut.

***

A brisk breeze swirled around them. Ellen pointed the way along the gray and brown flagstones toward the pine forest surrounding the property. She pointed out the local flora and fauna as they followed the man-made foot path until they found themselves on a well-worn dirt trail next to a crystal-clear stream. Pine needles crunched beneath their feet amidst a flurry of grackles and quail dutifully collecting them for their nests somewhere in the branches above. Despite the sunlight filtering through the maze of junipers, both women found it necessary to walk with their arms crossed to ward off the chill.

Rounding a copse of blue-green firs, a mountain lake came into view and Donna's breath caught in her throat. "Wow. No wonder you decided to build here.

"Bill won't admit it, but he was raised in a small town back east. He spent his childhood exploring the backwoods and fell in love with this place as soon as he saw it. He couldn't wait to build the cabin and spend time reliving his youth."

They stopped by the lake's edge, enjoying the pristine view.

"Did you enjoy the drive up?"

"Yes. It was, uh, eye-opening." Donna slowly scanned the Norman Rockwell scene before here. "This reminds me of where I came from as well."

"Steve tells me you two went to school together."

Bending down to pick up a pinecone, Donna turned it over and over in her hand before gently tossing it into the water, watching as it floated away. "That seems like such a long time ago now."

"How'd you two get back together? Were you a couple back then?"

"No. Not a couple. Just friends. Acquaintances? He was the class geek, and I was overweight and, well, let's just say we traveled in different circles."

Ellen gave her the once over, trying not to be too obvious. "That's hard to believe. I'm sure you're exaggerating."

"Uh-uh." She smoothed out her T-shirt, tucking it where it had pulled loose from her jeans. "My sisters inherited the thin genes. They got the stares and the dates. I got to stay home and watch TV."

"Sorry."

"No need. Ancient history. I envied them, even wanted to be just like them, but it was hopeless, so I figured I could eat my way to oblivion."

"But look at you now. I see the way Steve looks at you. Hell, I saw the way Bill looked at you. I'm gonna have to do hand stands in bed this weekend just to keep his mind off you. How did you do it?"

Donna stuck her hands in her pockets to warm them up. "One day, after seeing my therapist, I'd had it. He told me, 'Unless you accept yourself the way you are, you'll never be happy because of your low self-esteem.' That pissed me off so much, I never went back to him. I vowed to lose the weight—all of it—and keep it off."

Ellen eyed Donna again. "Well, it obviously worked."

"I went on a strict diet, walked five miles every day, bought a gym membership with the money I saved on food. I got sick to death of vegetables and salads, but it worked. After graduating, I met Harry— that's my ex—and I thought I had it made. Funny how things work out, huh?"

A curious squirrel bounced his way out of the woods and stood on its hind legs. Holding its front paws still, it wrinkled its nose as if trying to figure out what they were saying. Donna bent down to get a better look, but that was enough to scare it off, and it scurried back where it came.

"There are lots of interesting critters out here," Ellen said, pointing towards the sky where a hawk was circling the lake in search of a meal. "C'mon. let's keep walking; it's too chilly to stand in one spot too long."

Ellen led her east along the path.

"Speaking of doctors, Bill told me about what's going on at the hospital. He said they're being taken over by some outfit in Boston, and your ex-husband's involved somehow?"

Searching the perimeter of the trees, Donna watched for signs of movement. "Yes. The good Dr. Harry Steinham."

"You two married long?"

"Long enough. Too long."

"And now?"

"Now he's in charge of staffing at this new outfit."

"Oh?"

"Yeah. He's their hatchet man."

Donna gave her the short version of how they'd met in Boston but split after a rift over starting a family.

"So you divorced him? Because he didn't want to have children?"

"Partly. We were in Paris for our anniversary—"

"Paris is so beautiful. Bill took me to there for our tenth anniversary, and it was one of the best times of our lives."

"Well, I suspect he didn't do what Harry did." When Ellen didn't respond, she continued. "We got to the hotel, and the first night, he had them send up chocolates and champagne. I'm pretty sure he slipped something into my drink because I don't remember anything at all about the rest of the evening. All I know is I was sore in places I had never been sore before. On the last night, he tried it again, except this time, when he wasn't looking, I emptied the glass in a planter and refilled it myself from the bottle. I pretended to be woozy, and he started pulling out all sorts of crazy things: handcuffs, a dildo, and an assortment of toys I didn't recognize and wanted no part of. Suddenly, I knew what he had done. I told him to go to hell, grabbed my coat, and left. I filed for divorce as soon as we got back to the states."

Ellen stopped in her tracks. Donna kept going for a couple of steps before stopping and twisting around to face her. "Oh my God, Donna. I'm so sorry. I had no idea. It must have been *horrible*."

"Like I said, ancient history. C'mon. Let's keep walking."

Ellen caught up, and they continued around the lake. "And you haven't seen Harry since?"

"Other than in divorce court, no. As soon as I could, I found another job as far away from Boston as possible. That's how I ended up here."

She fell silent and they continued their journey, matching footstep for footstep until they reached the far side of the lake. There was an old, wooden bridge over a tributary stream and the weather-worn planks creaked beneath their feet. Stopping midway, they stood together, looking down at the mountain runoff as it merged into the deeper waters.

Ellen leaned against the railing. "And now you've met Steve. How'd that happen?"

"I was wandering through the bookstore at the mall when I noticed him reading the paper," Donna replied. "When he glanced up, I could see he didn't recognize me. I decided to leave, but he followed me. I thought he'd figured it out, but when he caught up and I told him who I was, well, it took a few minutes for his head to catch up with his mouth."

Ellen chuckled. "Yeah. That sounds like him. It's nice you two hit it off so well. Steve is a great catch."

Donna picked up a small stone and tossed it into the water below, watching it bounce off the rocks jutting from the surface before disappearing out of sight. "He's okay. But he only sees what he wants to see."

"Wait a minute. I thought you two were a couple?"

"He certainly thinks so." Donna watched the vanishing circles from the stone's submersion.

"Say what? I don't understand." Ellen said, scratching her head.

Donna just shook her head. "He's desperate for a happily-ever-after ending, and I'm not so certain—"

"Hold on a minute there. Has this got something to do with your ex?"

"No. I told you. I divorced the bastard. This has nothing to do—"

"You just told me he's in charge of the takeover. Does Steve know that?"

"Of course. He's helping to stop the takeover from happening. That's why—"

"So you're just using him? Is that it?"

Donna held up one hand. "Slow your freight train down, there. No, I'm not using him. He's sweet and funny, and he's still the smartest man I've ever known. I'm just not as convinced as he is about the future. I don't mind having a good time, and God knows I could use his help with this situation, but—"

"Stop right there," Ellen said, both hands on her hips. "He's a good man, not just someone who's sweet and funny. And he's not some toy for you to play with."

"I never said— "

"And to make matters worse, my husband's involved in this now, too. You apparently have him fooled as well. What are you exactly? A nurse? Or an actress bucking for an Emmy?"

Donna backed up a step. "Slow down, Ellen. I'm not out to fool anyone, and I'm not using anyone. Steven volunteered to help, and he asked Bill, who's doing this as much for you as he is for me. Your treatment for PV at the hospital could be in jeopardy. This is as much about you as it is about me."

"How do you know about my PV," Ellen shouted, caught off guard. "Bill didn't say a word to me about telling you—"

Donna raised her hand again, pointing her finger this time. "He's just protecting you. Just like Steven thinks he's protecting me."

Ellen swatted Donna's hand to the side and moved in so close their noses almost touched. "You're just taking advantage of Steve, and now you've dragged my Bill into this. I won't let you do it. I'm going back to talk to Steve. He needs to know what kind of witch you are."

Ellen spun on her heel and started stalking back up the trail.

"Wait! Ellen, you don't understand," Donna shouted, trying to catch up.

"Wait for what?" Ellen swiveled back. "I think I understand perfectly well."

Donna strode up to her, stopping nose to nose once again. "How? How can you possibly understand? You and your charmed life and your cozy little cabin. What do you know about anything?"

Ellen tried to walk away but Donna grabbed her shoulder and spun her back around. "Steven told me about your PV. He said Bill's hung in there, fought for you. You have someone, and I have no one. I saw the way you looked at me when we met in the kitchen. I've seen it before; that look. What do you know about me? Nothing. Just like him. All he saw when we met was smooth skin and silk stockings. Why should I respect that? I'm just like you. I want what *you* have. All I've got, though, is an ex who wants to screw me, and a starry-eyed dreamer who thinks he's found nirvana."

Ellen shoved Donna back with one hand. "He's an honest, decent man. Yes, he's a dreamer. And he's brilliant. And … he's in love with you, you dumb bitch. Head over heels. You say you want what I have? You wouldn't know a good thing if it hit you over the head with a rock. You're the one living in fantasyland—a dark, ugly one. You'd better wake up, Ms. Prima Donna, 'cause I'm not going to let you hurt him."

"He only thinks he's in love with me."

"No. No, I saw the way he treated at you back there, the same as Bill treats me. With respect. Doesn't that mean anything to you?"

"You call it respect. I call it lust."

"Steve was married before, too. Did he tell you?"

"Of course. He told me she was a cheating gold-digger."

"Well, except for the cheating part, grab a mirror and take a good, hard look."

"I'm not like that," Donna shouted.

"You're *exactly* like that," Ellen yelled right back.

Donna shouted right back. *"No, I'm not."* Then, bowing her head, she repeated, in earnest, "No, I'm not. You're right, Steven has been good to me, and I don't deserve it. But I need his help." She looked up and her eyes softened. "I don't know where else to turn."

"Then you better be straight with him, starting with telling him the truth. Either you come clean or I'm going to crash your little party and you can go straight to hell."

~17~

Dateline, Florida – October 1, 2021

The Florida Sun reported today that St. Andrews Hospital in Miami was raided today by the FBI in a sting operation orchestrated by the Medicare Fraud division. Agents were seen carrying boxes and computers from the premises. No arrests have been made, according to sources in the agency, but sealed indictments have been presented to the Federal Court in Broward County in connection with an ongoing investigation.

When reached for comment, Arnold Stromble, lead investigator, refused to give details, but re-iterated the agency's stance on Medicare abuse and fraudulent schemes, 'We will pursue, indict, convict and close down every criminal enterprise attempting to take advantage of the US Taxpayer at the expense of the vulnerable, medical public which relies on these programs for timely and appropriate life-saving procedures."

***

The sweet smell of pine tar and fresh-laid mulch calmed me as much as the beers we drank. The wrap-around redwood porch was the perfect place to unwind, complete with an unobstructed view of the dense forest cloistering the cabin from civilization. A chilly sixty-eight degrees forced me into long sleeves, but the strategic orientation of the cabin's southern flank sufficiently deflected the breeze from the mounds of paper spread out on the picnic table in front of us. For good measure, Bill grabbed some stones from the carefully groomed rock garden and deposited one on each pile.

I sat facing the trailhead yawning between hundred-year-old Ponderosas. "Think the girls will be okay?"

"Yup. Ellen's been wanting to meet Donna. She's glad you finally found someone," Bill said, nursing his second beer.

"How's she doing, by the way? Does she know about the takeover?"

"Essentially." He took another swig of ale. "I told her as much as I dared. She's got enough to contend with."

"Well, don't keep her in the dark too long. Something tells me you'll need her support and help through this. I just hope we can pull it off."

"Me too. Let me show you what I found yesterday."

Bill put the bottle down and grabbed a folder from one of the piles. He'd been busy. He managed to contact Steinham's last victim, a broker by the name of Sam Penderton in Dallas. The copies of correspondence were on C&C stationary, as were the contracts and wiring instructions. It all looked legitimate.

Except it wasn't. Bill pointed out the discrepancies. "The address and phone numbers don't match up, and the logo is altered, see? After the scam was perpetrated, the phone numbers were disconnected, and the phony mailbox address cancelled."

I took the bogus forms and held them side by side with their legitimate origin. The shade and weight of the paper were different as well, as was the font used for the header. Everything was intentionally imperfect, like a paper phishing scam.

I placed back them under one of the stones. "If Penderton had bothered doing any due diligence, he would have discovered the discrepancies."

"Well, his greed trumped his good judgment. The inflated returns Steinham dangled in front of him were just too good to pass up."

"Not to mention the hefty commission he likely charged his clients,"

Bill drained the bottle and reached for a third. "Classic con. Now Penderton's reputation is mud, and he's on the hook for the money his clients lost."

"If we're not careful—"

"Yeah. I know. By the way, do you know where the term 'con man,' comes from?" When I shook my head no, he pulled his watch off and held it out to me. "It's short for confidence man. It dates back to 1849, when William Thompson, a grifter, started approaching people on the streets of New York and, after engaging them in casual conversation, asked if they had enough confidence in him to allow him to hold onto their watch for a day. People—more trusting back then—just complied. Thus, the 'con' was invented. They never questioned his motives or his actions until they found themselves lined up at the jewelry store to buy themselves new watches."

Turning it over in my hands, I admired how thin his Jaegar-LaCoultra was. "That's interesting, but this isn't 1849, and we're talking about more than timepieces. A lot more." I handed it back to him, wondering how he got it. A gift from Ellen? An award for some deal he put together? "You said the money Harry stole just disappeared. Is it really that easy to wire money offshore and have it vanish? I thought that kind of thing couldn't happen anymore."

He slipped the watch back on. "Compared to drug money or terrorist bankrolls, which are tracked more rigorously, this is peanuts. Besides, his company is a recognized market leader, with billions in revenue and profits. Why would a bank question the legitimacy of a wire transfer under that banner?"

"But it still doesn't make sense," I said, finally finishing off my first beer. "Surely someone at C&C or at the FBI is wise to him by now."

"I've left several messages at the local FBI office, but no one's called me back."

I popped open a fresh brew. "What about C&C itself?"

"Who knows? Maybe Carter's in on it. Or maybe it's Carter's scam and Harry's just doing the dirty work."

"I hadn't thought of that. Nevertheless, I still want a back-up plan. I want to talk to that computer friend of yours."

"Who? Jeremy?" Bill shook his head. "I don't think that's a good idea."

"Why not? Maybe he can—"

"I said it's not a good idea."

I plunked the beer down and leaned on the table. "Really? Like *Jim Adams* is a great idea? If that backfires, we have nothing. *Nothing*. We can't afford to put it all on your acting ability. If you were working a deal, you wouldn't rely on one source for your research, would you? You'd challenge it from all angles, looking behind every curtain for skeletons."

"What do you think all this is?" he said, pointing at the piles of reports on the table.

I held up my hands. "Hey, I'm not questioning your work, but you're an analyst. You deal with paper; reports, graphs, projections... This is the real world, Batman. We're dealing with real crooks. Get your nose out of your paper mâché world and start treating this like it's life or death. We need door number two."

"And your idea of a backup plan is breaking the law, hacking into their mainframe again? Even if he could, anything Jeremy uncovers would be thrown right out of court as illegally obtained."

"We're not going to court, remember? Unless there's something you're leaving out, our plan is to frame Harry and get him to do a Benedict Arnold. I'm just looking for some extra leverage. If Jeremy's as good as you say he is, we have nothing to worry about."

He picked up my beer and handed it to me. "Last famous words, General Custer?"

"Just get me his number. I'll make sure he understands the need for prudence and discretion."

***

The sun crossed the apex of the cabin at some point, casting long shadows on the backyard before we stopped to grab some pre-made deli sandwiches from the kitchen. I wasn't sure if it was the quiet calm of our surroundings or the third beer I polished off, but I relaxed and let Bill ramble on through his extensive research. I was an egghead in high school, and I could just picture him hunkering down in the library to read up on some arcane aspect of history instead of joining a pick-up game of basketball in the gym. By the time he'd gotten through all four piles of carefully labelled folders, the breeze had become a steady wind, chilling the air uncomfortably. I felt cold and worn down to the point I couldn't stifle a yawn.

"I think I'd like to take a quick nap before dinner. What do you say we pick this up again tomorrow?"

He smiled and started putting the folders into his briefcase. "Sounds good to me. We covered most of what I wanted to show you already. What do you think?"

"About what?"

He stopped midway through transferring the files, holding the next to last one in his hand. The smile disappeared. "About what I just shared with you."

Oops.

"You've always been better at analysis than me. I couldn't have put it all together like that. I'm more a shoot-from-the-hip type."

He finished putting the last one away but didn't say anything.

"That's why I became a stockbroker; I don't have the patience to do what you do: reading reams of reports, searching for that one detail, that one overlooked provision in some boring prospectus that makes or breaks a deal. I need to be where the action is."

A half-smile returned to his lips. "You do have the attention span of a fruit fly."

"It's my one, endearing feature."

That got a laugh out of him. "Go. Get your beauty rest. But don't forget, you're cooking dinner tonight."

"I'll be sure to set the alarm."

I got up to go inside while he reached for another beer, stretching his legs out in front of him and leaning back in his chair. I was closing the porch door when, without looking my way, he called out. "Hey."

"What?"

"Thanks for listening."

***

Neither Bill nor I heard the women return, so when I entered our room, I was surprised to see Donna lay napping on the bed, obviously tired out from her walk. I considered joining her, but she was lying catty-corner, and I didn't want to wake her, so I went in search of one of the living room's several sofas.

Entering the great room again, I marveled at the eclectic combination of rustic and modern. On the one hand, it felt like a Revolutionary-era retreat, the windows placed just so along the north and south walls to allow ample light to enter. On the other hand, the fireplace was gas fired and operated by remote control. I checked out the switches and knobs on the control panel built into the arm of the all-leather sofa. It alternately turned the lights on and off, as well as the stereo system and TV. I tuned the stereo to a soft-rock station, dimmed the lights, and adjusted the flames in the fireplace to give off a warm glow. I was just getting comfortable when Ellen walked in and sat down opposite me on one of the recliners.

By the look on her face, I realized my nap would have to wait.

I yawned and sat up. "How was your walk?"

"It was good," she said without elaborating.

"Donna's out cold. I guess she's not used to this high-country air."

"You're probably right."

"What did you two talk about?" I prompted.

"You mean, did we talk about you?"

I raised my eyebrows.

"Uh-huh."

I was full awake now, the fatigue replaced by a sudden rush of adrenaline.

"She's very nice."

"You think she's very nice," I echoed.

"Yes."

I started chewing my nails. "You really don't like her, do you?"

"I didn't say that." She reached over and pulled my hand from my face. "That's very unbecoming. What are you, twelve?"

"Sorry." I folded my hands in my lap. "Ellen, I known you too well. When you say, 'very nice,' you mean 'totally unimpressed.' What gives?"

Ellen folded her hands as well, looking down at them as if to check to make sure they were still attached to her wrists "She's a very attractive woman."

Uh-oh.

"Come on, talk to me."

She raised her eyebrows without lifting her head, her blue eyes unreadable. "There's not much to talk about. We just don't see eye-to-eye, that's all."

"First Bill, now you." I paused for a second. "I'm making porterhouse steaks for dinner tonight. Am I going to have to beat you over the head with a T-bone to get you talking?"

"What do you mean, 'first Bill?'"

"Bill didn't like her either. Not initially. He thought she was just using me. But after he met her, he changed his mind. That's one of the reasons he's helping us fight C&C."

"Bill's entitled to his opinion."

I took a deep breath. "Jeez, Ellen, if you have something to say, just say it."

She tilted her head and her voice softened. "You really want my opinion?"

"No, but I guess I need to hear it."

She laid her right hand on mine. "Steve, I can see you're smitten with her. You're a big boy. You don't need my approval. She's certainly very beautiful, and I understand you two have some history together. I'm just don't think she feels the same way about you that you obviously feel about her."

"In other words, you think she's using me, too?" I unfolded my hands, encircling hers in mine.

She bit her lip. "I didn't say that. I just think … I mean, you hardly know her. Maybe you should take it slow. It takes a woman longer to, ah, realize what she's got than a man does. You're all such pushovers."

The pounding in my ears eased a bit.

"Okay," I said, nodding. "Thanks. I appreciate it. And I promise, I'll take it slow."

"I don't want to see you hurt again like you were with Michelle."

"Donna isn't Michelle."

"I'm sure she isn't."

She wasn't smiling. Extricating her hand from mine she got up. "I'm not your fairy godmother but, if I were, I'd make sure you weren't confusing the fairy princess with Grimilda."

***

I waited till she disappeared through the door separating the two sections of the cabin, then reached over and shut off the stupid stereo. Stretching out, I closed my eyes and tried to nap, but I couldn't.

I don't want to see you hurt again, like you were with Michelle.

I sat up and rubbed my eyes. The pictures on the mantel caught my attention and I walked over to take a closer look. Most of them were of the kids, but there were a couple of group shots, as well as a cameo of Bill and Ellen against a backdrop of an exotic, seaside resort. I couldn't tell how old the photo was, but the sparkle in their eyes was unmistakable. They were in love.

I thought I was in love, too. Michelle, for all her flaws, had me hooked. I should have known better. Was I too blind? People fall in love, right? They meet, there's chemistry, they have sex, and get married. They live the happily-ever-after fantasy.

But my fairy tale turned into a Halloween nightmare. I swore I'd never let it happen again. I picked up the framed photograph, studying their happy faces.

"I want what you guys have. What's your secret?"

***

As chef *du jour*, I was responsible for preparing the evening's fare. Tonight's dinner included thick-sliced porterhouse steaks—except the one for Donna, of course, which looked like it was hand-shaved with a razor blade. These would be paired with ten-ounce Maine lobster tails, accompanied by freshly prepared rice pilaf, steamed broccoli and cauliflower topped with my home-made scampi sauce.

The kitchen contained a full complement of utensils for every imaginable contingency, a stark contrast to Donna's scanty collection. I'd brought a small arsenal of spices and cooking liquids, but the provisions arrayed in the more-than-adequate cabinets dwarfed my purchased selections. It was simply awesome, considering I've never seen Bill ever barbeque a hamburger or sauté a single vegetable since we met. Ellen was a good cook, but this was over the top.

I pushed the thought aside as I began pulling out everything I needed, spreading the meal's ingredients on the island countertop. Wishing the rest of my life was this easy, I distributed the appropriate pots, pans, and dishes to their intended destinations on the stove. I've cooked in small spaces, and it's always a pleasure to have everything out at once, in plain sight. To some people, cooking is work—a drudgery to be done with as quickly as possible. To me, it embodies the essence of creativity and challenge. Mixing the right kinds of spices and sauces, applying them adequately to meats and pastas to create flavors that tantalize and satisfy the palate, then observing their effect on the taste buds of my dinner guests. In some Asian societies, an audible burp is expected to signify satisfaction, I merely look for smiles and unabashed kudos. Always tell a chef you love his cooking if you ever want him or her to cook for you again.

The rice, vegetables, and scampi sauce simmered on the back of the six-burner stove as the kitchen filled with the mouthwatering smell of French bread warming in the oven. Evidently, the scents wafted sufficiently throughout the house, finally reaching the sleeping quarters at the other end. One by one, Donna, Bill, and Ellen drifted into the kitchen, noses first, to ask, "So when do we eat?"

"Patience, please," I answered, "can't you see there's an artiste at work?"

"It smells amazing in here." Donna ruffled my hair with one hand and stroked my stirring arm with the other.

"Yeah, it does," Bill added, grabbing a beer from the refrigerator, "and I'm famished. So, what's on the menu, Chef Steve?"

"A feast fit for financial wizards and their enchanted ladies," I remarked. "But all of it will go to waste if someone doesn't start setting the table."

To the clink of glasses and silverware, I grabbed the steaks and lobster tails and headed for the back door and the waiting, propane-fired barbeque grill. Also of commercial pedigree, it would pre-heat quickly, so I adjusted the control knobs and waited. When the thermostat reached the *"Broil"* marking, I began placing the fare on the grill's shiny-new surface and basted the lobster liberally with the scampi sauce. I heard the door open again and looked back as Donna stepped out. She glanced at me with a look I hadn't seen before—inquiring, yet with an air of detachment.

"Something on your mind?" I asked with Ellen's words still reverberating in my head.

"When did you learn to cook?" she asked, ignoring my question.

"After Michelle left. It was either learn to cook or spend a lot of money on restaurants. I make a good living, but it seemed wasteful, and embarrassingly lonely, constantly eating out by myself. Why?"

"It's just unusual to find a guy who cooks like you."

"Don't tell that to Wolfgang Puck or Rocco DiSpirito."

That brought a smile to her lips. "Pardon me. I didn't realize I was in the presence of culinary genius."

"In my next lifetime, I was thinking of coming back as a gourmet chef."

"As long as you promise to keep the portion sizes small and fat free, look me up."

I liked this banter. I wanted nothing more than to keep it light and playful, but I needed more.

"Maybe after dinner you and I can take a walk down to the lake. I can tell you about my cooking exploits, both successes and failures."

Her expression changed back to detachment. "Sure."

I grabbed one of the long, stainless steel forks hanging on the side of the grill and flipped the steaks over. I basted the lobster tails again, wishing for better mind-reading skills.

Just then, Ellen stepped outside as well. "You two okay out here alone?"

"If you're asking if we need a chaperone, the answer is no," I said, trusting she knew what I meant.

"In that case, is there is anything you need me to do in the kitchen? I think the bread is just about done."

"Why don't you take it out and start slicing it? The surf and turf is nearly done, so you can ladle the rice and vegetables into the serving dishes if you wouldn't mind. We'll be right in with the main course."

"Will do," she said, and stepped back inside.

Cutting into a couple of the steaks to see if they were ready, I said to Donna, "So, did you two have a nice walk this morning?"

"It was invigorating," Donna replied.

"Maybe you can tell me about it later."

"Maybe I will."

We stood there, listening to the steaks pop and sizzle, watching the butter sauce bubble on the surface of the tender, white meat of the lobster tails.

"I think they're ready," I said finally. "Let's eat."

***

Donna held the door as I carried in the platter. I could see the steam rising from the bread and vegetables on the center of the table. The crystal water glasses were filled and two bottles of wine sat on either end of the table. *So that was what was clinking in Donna's bag.*

Bill and Ellen shuffled the plates around so I could set the main course down. "The steaks are all medium, except for mine, which, if you listen carefully, can still say 'moo.' Donna, this one's yours." I pointed to the petite steak on one side. "The lobster tails are all about the same size, so help yourselves." I moved back to the stove and poured the remaining scampi sauce into two serving boats. "I made extra sauce, so you could add it to your own liking."

"It all looks scrumptious, Steve," Ellen said. "If I wasn't already married to Bill, I'd grab you up in a heartbeat and lock you away in my kitchen."

"Hey, I can cook, too, you know," Bill said, with a faux hurt look on his face.

"Sorry, boiling water for tea and burning bread in the toaster doesn't qualify you as a cook," she replied.

"I have other, more noble attributes.'

"I know." She threw a sideways glance at Donna. "That's why I keep you."

The conversation fell victim to our hunger, and the food magically disappeared in-between snippets of casual conversation and the occasional, "Mmm, that's good."

As Bill grabbed the last of the bread and dipped it in what remained of the scampi sauce, Donna lifted her wine glass and tilted it at me, so I grabbed mine as well and clinked in a private toast. "Did you two accomplish anything while we were out?"

Bill answered before I could. "Yeah. We worked through the billing divergences and found a couple of likely pattern distortions that might add up to fraud on C&C's part. I think we're ready to go to the authorities with our pre-lims before the board approvals are finalized and the 10-Ks are filed."

"Can you say that again, only in English this time?" Ellen asked.

"Sorry. I—"

"He meant there's evidence they're deliberately ordering unnecessary procedures to boost the bottom line. We're hoping we can get the feds to listen before the merger is final," I said.

Donna pointed to the plate of vegetables, and I reached over and handed it to her. "Does that mean we don't have to catch Harry in his little scam?"

Bill shook his head. "No. Just the opposite."

"But didn't you just say you had enough evidence?" Donna responded, lading a small helping onto her plate.

"Having evidence and going to court are two different things. We need to flip Harry, and to do so, we need back up."

"Why" Donna asked.

"For one, the feds have surveillance equipment. We got away with our little charade at Tiani's, but we may need to tap his phone or infiltrate his computer." His eyes darted in my direction for a second before continuing. "There's no way we can handle that."

"But there's more, isn't there?" Donna prompted.

He paused long enough to drain what was left of his beer. "If Harry calls our bluff and wants us to pony up to the trough, we'll need their resources. Neither Steve nor I have enough scratch to convince him we're high rollers, even if we combined our liquid savings. Harry would bolt and we'd be left high and dry. We can't chance it. We need the Feds in on this."

Ellen remained quiet through this exchange, but finally chimed in, "You didn't tell me anything about putting our money at risk, Bill. And what's this 'con' thing all about, anyway?"

"I told you, Ellen. Harry's running a con game, and we're setting him up in a con of our own. Once we catch him red-handed, we can blackmail him to give up C&C."

"Well, I'm suddenly not comfortable with the whole thing." She grabbed my arm, threatening to cut off circulation. "Steve, how can you let him get involved in something like this?"

I pried her hand off my arm and held it in mine, "He's a big boy. You told me so yourself."

"Don't be cute, Steve." She let go and withdrew her hand. "You're single, with no responsibilities. If something goes wrong, no one's relying on you for a paycheck. We've got children at home, and Bill can't afford to screw up his career. What on God's Earth are you two thinking?"

"Calm down, Ellen." Bill held his hand up. "There's more to it than you think."

"Like what? Tell me. What's more important than our family?"

"Nothing's more important than our family. You just have to understand— "

"What? What do I have to understand? That you're taken in by this … by Donna's sob story?"

I could see Donna's face turning red.

"She didn't convince him to do this," I chimed in, "I did. Blame me if you have to, not Donna." Motioning towards Bill, I said, "Buddy, if you want out, I'll understand. I'll figure something else out."

"Stop," Bill said, raising his voice for the second time in a week. "Let me speak, please."

We all looked at him, Ellen with daggers, Donna with disappointment, and me with despair.

"Ellen, honey, the one thing I didn't tell you was the merger will likely screw up your treatment. Your doctors, and most of the staff in your department are gonna lose their jobs. And you know that new study you got accepted into by the drug company? It almost certainly will be canned. That new protocol has the possibility of giving you back your freedom, not to mention extending your life. Have you forgotten what your doctor said? Do I need to remind you? I want to spend the rest of my life with you, but that means you have to be here long enough for that to happen. I can't let them get away with it. This really *is* about family. It's about *you*. Can you understand that?" He panted out the last few sentences, nearly on the verge of tears.

Ellen softened visibly. She reached out to take his hand. "Why didn't you tell me?"

"You have enough to worry about. I just wanted to keep them from setting you back. I love you."

A hush took hold of the kitchen, the kind of quiet you find in deep chambers of your own mind when no one's around, or when you see the night sky for the first time without the whitewash of big city lights. Only the hum of the refrigerator and the methodical clicking of the wall clock over the stove made a sound. The angry blush on Donna's face dissipated, replaced by an expression of stoic compassion. Did she understand what just happened?

I tapped Donna lightly on the shoulder. "How about you and I go for that walk? I think I'd like to check out the lake."

"She pushed her half-eaten dinner plate aside and stood up. "Sure."

"You two want to join us?" I asked, knowing the answer before I asked.

"You two go ahead," Ellen answered. "We'll stay here and clean up. You may want to take a sweater, Donna. It's probably going to be chilly."

Donna hooked my arm as we retraced the path she and Ellen must have traveled earlier. Her soft flannel hoodie fit loosely over her blouse, and it smelled of roses and pine needles—though the scents more likely came from the actual pine needles and roses we passed rather than her sweater. The only sounds were the slight crackling of the twigs and groundcover beneath our feet, married to a soft breeze strumming the branches above.

"Bill and Ellen were lucky," I said softly. "They found each other in college. Except for a short breakup as sophomores, they were inseparable. In the years I've known them, I don't think I've ever seen them fight, at least not in public, and certainly not in front of me."

"Oh?"

"Yeah. Bill is really dedicated to her and the kids."

"And you're telling me this because …"

"I don't know. I guess because I want to be like them." I pushed aside a heavy pine bough so we could pass. "Do you think we can ever be like that?"

"Is that what you want?"

"Yes. Yes, I do. What about you?"

We walked along in silence, the question floating in the air between us. "I'd given up on the idea after leaving Harry. I'm honestly not sure I could handle another relationship like that."

"I'm not Harry."

"I know, Steven. I know." After a pause, she added, "And I'm not Ellen."

We reached the edge of the lake and I put my hands on her shoulders.

"I wasn't suggesting you were. What are you afraid of?"

"You look up to Bill and Ellen as the perfect couple. Who knows? Maybe they are. You've been friends a long time, and maybe all you see are the good things about their marriage. I have to admit, I'm a little jealous. But just not ready to commit to a long-term relationship. Not yet anyway. Can you understand?"

I felt my shoulders droop. "Yeah, I guess."

She lowered her eyes. "We're from different worlds."

I took her hands in mine. "Isn't everyone? Ellen comes from an upper-class family. She had everything: money, connections; you name it, it was hers for the asking. When She and Bill started dating, her parents nearly disowned her. Bill's family is blue collar, like mine. Did she tell you how they met?"

She shook her head.

"Bill worked his way through college juggling two or three part-time jobs to pay for tuition. He was working at a gas station when she pulled in to fill up her dad's Lexus one day. When she came inside to pay, Bill wouldn't let her walk out without getting her phone number. That was eighteen years ago. They're as different as a bull frog and a lap cat."

She smiled for the first time since we left the cabin. "So, what's your point? Because we're different, we're just like them?"

"Haven't you heard? Opposites attract."

"And you really think we can make it as a couple."

"We'll never know if we don't try. Seems we've been getting along just fine, or am I missing something?"

"No. You're right." She let go my hands and turned to look off into the twilight descending on the ponderosas. "But just because the sex is good doesn't mean we're meant for each other."

"Of course not. I learned that the hard way from Michelle. But I've watched Bill and Ellen grow closer over time. I think we *can* be like them. I think there's a reason we met again after all these years, and I want us to give it a chance."

"Give what a chance?"

"Love."

The breeze suddenly kicked up, sending a chill through the air. She leaned into me, and I wondered if she could hear my heart pounding above the din.

"I wish I could be as certain as you," she whispered in sync with the wind.

Then, as if some dam broke inside of her, she twisted around, burying her face in the crook of my neck, and started crying.

***

It only lasted a few seconds, not long enough as far as I was concerned. When she pulled back, she wiped the tears with her sleeve before snaking her arms around my waist and kissing me. Wet and warm, I thought it would turn into something more intimate, but she disengaged before I could reach down to caress her. In a slick move, she grabbed my hand and twirled beneath my arm; she started walking, dragging me along like a cocker spaniel.

We followed the path circling the lake. The rising moon laid down a runner of liquid light before us, as if inviting a stroll across the waters. The towering pines on the far side seemed to float at the edge of the lake. Mirrored on the water, their images merged with such perfect symmetry they appeared to be attached at the base of the thick, brown trunks like Siamese twins.

"Is this where you and Ellen walked this afternoon?"

"Uh-huh."

No time like the present, right?

"What'd you guys talk about?

She didn't answer right away, choosing to wait until we reached a little wooden bridge. She stopped and leaned on the railing. "This and that," she said. "You know, girl talk. You wouldn't be interested. Why, did she say something to you?"

I put my arm around her shoulder. "No," I lied, "I just sensed a little tension at dinner between you two."

She turned her head and looked at me, her eyes unreadable. "There was tension, all right, but it was between Ellen and Bill."

"Why did she blame you for Bill's involvement in stopping the merger?"

She refocused on the feeder stream below the bridge. "Let's just say she wasn't happy with how it all happened."

"Well, Bill hasn't been all that forthcoming in explaining things to her."

"I know that now."

She went silent, but I wouldn't let it go. "There's more, isn't there."

She spoke slowly, deliberately. "She thought we were … using him."

"We?"

"Well, me. She thinks I'm trying to seduce him."

"Are you?"

She spun around and pressed her finger into my chest. "No, you geek-a-zoid. How could you even say such a thing?"

I backed up and put my hands up. "I'm not. I mean, you know; he's a man, too. You had him eating out of the palm of your hand last week. I'm not suggesting you did it on purpose, I was just wondering—"

"Jesus, you're all the same. Is that really all you think about? Sex?"

"No. There's football, too."

"*Arghhhh.*"

"Okay, okay. I'm sorry. I'm just sayin' maybe Ellen's picked up some vibes from him."

"If she did, it wasn't because of anything I did. Can we stop this now?"

"Sure. I just wanted to know how it went."

"It went *fine.*"

~19~

Dateline, Washington, DC October 3, 2021

The Washington Post reported today that the FBI, in conjunction with their counterparts in Europe and Japan, have instituted a new, sophisticated algorithm to track illegal financial transactions. In a joint release, a new cooperative effort between the G-8 countries, along with their respective central banks and the IMF, they pledged to 'intercept, interrupt, and interfere with the lifeblood of drug carrels, terrorist organizations, and organized crime syndicates.'

Further details about the program were unavailable at the time of this press release.

***

Sunday morning in Boston dawned windy and brisk. The steady drizzle outside Harry's office window only served to punctuate Delbert Carter's cold stare from across the desk. He fiddled with his pen, a silver-plated Mont Blanc some clueless HR director had given him as a gift before being summarily fired following another successful acquisition. As C&C's front man, Harry was paid a lot of money, and he had no problems flaunting it.

"How'd the meeting go in Phoenix with Salvatore," Carter asked brusquely.

"He's an idiot, like all the rest of them," Harry said, "a pompous jerk. But he's manageable. Just like that asshole in Dallas—what was his name? Stenson? Hampton? Anyway, he's concerned we'll come in slicing and dicing. He's afraid we'll gut his sacred cow, some outreach program he claims stabilizes the neighborhood. A real goody two shoes, that one."

"And what did you tell him?" Delbert demanded.

"Standard line. We're there to help, to make improvements, not disturb the status quo, blah, blah, blah."

"And?"

"He played it to the hilt. Must have read *The Ten Commandments of Tough Negotiators*. He tried to get assurances in writing about not closing down his pet projects, so I rifled through the papers on the table and *accidentally* showed him the new comp plan. I left it there long enough for him to spot his projected raise and bonus. Then I re-shuffled the spreadsheet to the bottom of the pile. That did it. Right on cue, he started focusing on his role in our new management team."

"You're telling me he won't make any noise?"

"Nah, not till after the merger when we fire his ass."

"Good job, Steinham." Carter stood up. "Keep me posted." He walked to the door and opened it but didn't leave. "By the way. A charge showed up in accounting for The Venetian in Vegas, about the time you were heading back from Arizona. You know anything about that?"

A cold shiver ran up Steinham's back, but he answered without hesitation, "Yeah. I met a local investment broker. He was at a conference in Vegas, so I stopped on the way back. I'm thinking about buying a vacation home in the desert. The winters are milder, and it doesn't rain nearly as much as it does here. When do you think the final merger paperwork will be ready?"

Carter studied Harry's face before answering. "Three weeks, four at the most."

Harry squirmed in his seat but met Carter's stare coolly. "Good. I can't wait to start downsizing the place. Especially Salvatore. I want to see the look on his face when I hand him his pink slip."

Carter's eyes were inscrutable as ever and Harry held his breath. They both knew he was expendable, but Carter merely nodded and left without another word.

He didn't take another breath until he heard the *ding* of the elevator.

~20~

Force of habit woke me up at sunrise to the unaccustomed chill in the room. Donna was still asleep, wrapped in the quilt, which left me clutching the bedsheet in a vain attempt to ward off the goosepimples spreading uncontrollably all over my skin. She was breathing softly, and her hair covered most of her face, so I gingerly got out of bed, dressing quickly and quietly to keep from waking her. She stirred slightly when I opened the bedroom door and I froze, but she simply shifted her weight. The steady, easy breathing resumed, so I closed it behind me, heading into the great room. The soft glow of the digital devices along the walls provided all the light I needed to find my way around. I was still shivering, but I paused to survey the room once again, noting the odd conflict between old-world charm and modern-world swagger on display here.

There's more here than meets the eye.

I thought about brewing some coffee in the kitchen, but the smell of java might rouse someone, bringing unwelcome company. I found my coat on the rack near the front door and stepped out into the brisk mountain air. My breath formed little clouds that floated and then vaporized as they rose on a gentle breeze. Dew glistened in the faint starlight as I made my way to the car, turning the heater on full blast as soon as the temperature gauge indicated the engine was warm enough not to spit out cold air through the vents.

The engine hummed almost imperceptibly as I eased down the driveway, trying to keep the crunching of stones beneath tires to a minimum. By the time I hit the main road, I was able to turn the heater down and settled in for the short ride into the town of Snowflake.

I kept the radio off. It was Sunday morning, which meant continuous talk-shows. Some were religious, some were talk-shows about current issues, and still others were infomercials hawking the latest cure for testosterone deficiencies. None of that interested me this morning.

Coming around a sharp curve in the road, the lights in one of the small restaurants on the main street glowed brightly so I pulled in, parking beneath the faded "World Famous Coffee" sign. Jasmine's was empty, except for the waitress at the counter. I ordered a cup of coffee, tipped her more generously than it merited, and found a booth against the front, glass wall so I could watch the sunrise.

The sun wasn't quite over the horizon yet, but the low clouds captured its glow in blooming orange, red, and yellow streaks against the pastel blue sky. It mesmerized me and, for a moment, I was able to separate from the disturbing scenarios playing out in my imagination.

Finally, I turned my attention to my journal which sat open and inviting in front of me.

Yesterday didn't exactly go as I hoped. Ellen went for a walk with Donna, but instead of an endorsement, Ellen came back unimpressed. I'm pretty sure she didn't level with me and that's disturbing. At dinner, the tension between them sucked. I don't know what happened in the woods, but I need to get to the bottom of it. Bill and Ellen started arguing about what was going on with C&C, and I thought for sure the whole damn thing was going to fall apart. I hate conflict, and this threatens everything. I just wanted Ellen and Donna to get along, and for all of us to work together.

Donna and I went for a walk after dinner, and when I suggested we might try to make it as a couple, she ended up in my arms, crying. As far as I was concerned, the world could have stopped turning right then and there. I'm sorry, Ellen, you're a good friend and I know you mean well. I trust you implicitly. But I have to follow my gut. No matter what anyone says or thinks, I need this, more than I need to breathe. I'm tired of being alone and I think Donna is, too. She's strong because she's had to be. She's feisty and independent, but there's a need, deep down inside of her, too, the same as me. How do I convince her we're really the same? Together, we're much more than we could ever be alone.

If we do this, if we can stop C&C from taking over SCM, maybe that will prove it to her. I don't know if we have a chance in hell of pulling it off. Who are we kidding? But it doesn't really matter. Someone has to take a stand against these bastards. I'm willing to risk it all for her. Somehow, we've got to figure out how to send Carter and Steinham packing.

I stopped for a moment, re-read it, then added.

There's something disturbing about Bill's sudden extravagance. He's risking everything with this attempt to stop the takeover yet is acting like a little kid on a trip to Disneyland. What's the story behind this cabin? And the separate mailbox station and virtual phone and fax? Not to mention his access to information no one else seems to have. What am I missing here?

I put the pen down and closed the notebook. The sun rose crisp and bright in the distance, and it promised a warm, invigorating day. I sat for about fifteen minutes more, considering my options. When nothing useful showed up in my mind, I got up, exchanged my ceramic mug for a fresh cup of coffee to go, and headed back to the cabin.

***

Sunday breakfast consisted of omelets—eggs, veggies, cheeses, and spices—and an assortment of muffins and breads from town I'd picked up on the way back. It was downright cold out, and I missed the nearly triple-digit temperatures of Phoenix, if that's even possible. The chill was nevertheless a good excuse for people to sleep later than usual, snuggled under down comforters. The smell of eggs cooking and coffee brewing in the kitchen, however, was sure to lure even the most comfortable from their toasty beds.

Bill and Ellen were the first to drift into the kitchen.

"You two sleep okay last night?" I asked.

"Like babies," Bill answered. "What about you? I don't remember hearing you come back from your walk."

"We ended up walking clear around the lake. I'm not sure what time it was when we got in. Thanks for getting the fire going; Donna fell asleep in front of it. I had to carry her into the bedroom."

Just then, she walked in wrapped in a fuzzy, blue bathrobe. She sniffed the air like she just discovered she had a nose.

"Speak of the devil," I said. "You sure slept like a rock last night."

"The walk and the fireplace did me in," she said. "I hope you weren't too disappointed in our lack of extracurricular activity."

"No, not at all. It was kind of nice, just watching you sleep. I'm glad you were able to let go and relax." She put her arms around me and kissed me, long and deep.

"Okay, you two, we get the point. Can you cool off long enough so we can eat breakfast?" Ellen said.

"I guess so." Donna let go and I reluctantly returned my attention to the stove. "Bacon's almost ready. Donna, can you put out the muffins and butter from the fridge?"

"Yes, dear."

"Bill, if you and Ellen don't mind, you have table-setting duty again. Anyone allergic to vegetables, cheese, or oregano?"

"Nope," they all said in unison.

"Great. I'll make more omelets, and you can compliment me later. Just make sure to leave me at least one cup of coffee in the pot. I need more caffeine."

21

Arnold Stromble searched through the spreadsheets, flipping back and forth from screen to screen. Tacked on the walls of his sparse office were newspaper clippings from around the country depicting nefarious schemes, large and small, to siphon the coffers of the treasury.

He tapped his pencil on the government issue legal pad, occasionally stopping to scratch down a few notes. Otherwise, his desk was bare except for a carafe of ice water and a half-filled glass.

"What's your game?"

He laid the pencil down and took a sip of water before rolling up the limp sleeves of his previously starched white shirt.

817 facilities populated his current list of statistical outliers. As deputy director of the Medicare fraud division, he was responsible for identifying irregularities and assigning field agents to investigate the most compelling anomalies. At present, he had more than 375 open cases.

Near the top of the list was a conglomerate out of Boston. In just under three years, it gobbled up dozens of hospitals and critical care centers, nearly tripling in size. It wasn't unusual for significant changes in hospital billing footprints during the first six-twelve months under new management, but they eventually returned to pre-acquisition levels.

"How are you doing it?"

He brought up a graph of the last two years and overlaid it with the baseline composite.

"Damn. Standard deviation's nearly one-point-eight."

He circled back to gross billing chart, then made another note in the middle of the legal pad and circled it several times.

"This has got to be it."

He pulled the pink phone message from his shirt pocket.

"Call From: Mr. Bill Phillips
RE: C&C proposed merger with SCM in Arizona

Phone:602-275-0073

Message: Mr. Phillips claims to have information concerning upcoming C&C merger. Please call ASAP."

"Who are you, Mr. Phillips? And what do you know?"
He reached for the phone.

22

The remainder of the day passed uneventfully as if the problems we'd faced the day before never existed. The cool air felt invigorating, and the subject of takeovers and mergers didn't get raised once. Instead, the hours were filled with brisk walks, lively gossip about friends and co-workers, and a marathon session of bridge on the porch. We polished off the rest of the beer and wine, along with the remaining deli meat and assorted snacks. Except for Donna, of course, who kept away from the alcohol and ate less food than the sparrows who made off with their fair share of crumbs.

The ride home was equally uneventful. We took the faster and less scenic route 79 home, though the scattered clouds to the west painted a colorful mosaic of the setting sun. We reached the outskirts of Scottsdale when Donna turned her cell phone back on.

"Shit!"

"What?" I asked, thinking maybe she spotted some obstacle on the road I'd missed.

"There's a message from Harry."

"A call or a text?"

"A text. Or should I say a sext. It's a picture of him, naked!"

***

"You survive the weekend, buddy?" Bill asked when I answered my cell.

"Yeah, it was great. Thanks for the invite. I may have to consider getting a place of my own up north. The country air did both of us some good."

"Careful, you're sounding awfully domestic."

"So? What's wrong with that? It seems to have worked out well for you," I chided.

"Yeah, well I was lucky. I met Ellen."

"And I've met Donna. Better late than never, right?"

"Agreed, though Ellen seemed to think you should take it slow."

I took a deep breath and let it out slow. Real slow. "Is that what she told you?"

"It's what she told me she told you."

"Hmph. And you agree with her, I suppose."

"I've learned not to *disagree* with her. The secret of marital bliss is to use those magical words, 'Yes, dear,' early and often, as if you're voting in a Chicago election."

"Okay, okay. I get it. Did you hear from our good friend Harry?" I asked, putting my feet up on my desk.

"Yes," he said, "but I have to tell you first about my new friend, Arnie Stromble."

"Huh? Who the hell is Arnie Stromble?"

"Only the lead investigator for the Medicare fraud unit in DC," he said, sounding quite pleased with himself.

"No shit. Did he have anything worthwhile to say?"

"Plenty. He's been investigating C&C for nearly two years now and was *very* interested in what we were doing."

"Interested? How?"

"Interested in, like, maybe he's willing to work with us. He's friends with the regional FBI director located right here in Phoenix. He said he'd put us in touch. He'd love to catch Harry red-handed as much as we do."

I straightened up and put my feet back on the ground. "Why don't we just turn the whole damn thing over to them?"

"We're already in too deep," Bill said. "Stromble thinks we have a good hook. If we back away, Harry's likely to cut and run."

"Good hook? Cut and run? Since when are you Dick Tracy?"

"Hey, hold it there, Steve. This was your idea, remember? Save the world from Carter and company?"

"Yeah, well, I just don't want to see anything happen to Donna."

"Oh? You getting cold feet?"

"No. But I want to keep her as far away from Harry as possible."

"Well, I have news on that front." I heard him typing on his computer. "I'm sending you a secure e-mail. Steinham faxed me the projections, as promised. I'm guessing these are as phony as a three - dollar bill. It appears our dear doctor has taken the bait."

"Okay, so why can't we turn it over to your new friends?" I asked.

"Because he said he's coming back to Phoenix next week, and he wants to meet some of my investors."

I started tapping my pen on my desk. Investors, my ass. He's coming for one reason, and one reason only, the horny bastard. "Really. And where are we going to get investors to meet with him?"

"That's where the FBI comes in. They can put together a team of undercover agents to pose as investors. Harry's worried the merger will close before he seals the deal with Jim Adams."

"I think that's not the only deal on his mind"

"Wait, what? What do you mean, 'not the only deal?'"

I took another deep breath, then let out a long sigh. "On the way back last night, Donna got a text from Steinham. He sent her a nude photo of himself."

There was a short silence on the line. "Oh my God."

"I almost ran into a tree when she showed me. I had to pull off the road for a while to cool down."

"What did she do? She didn't answer him, did she?" Bill asked.

"No, but she was pretty upset."

"Shit. Does she want to back out?"

"No, but she doesn't want to ever see Harry again, and, quite frankly, neither do I."

"Hmmm. I understand. This could be why he's rushing us. Our little scheme worked too well. He believes she wants him back."

"I'll kill him first," I heard myself say.

"Not a good idea. We want *him* in jail for fraud, not *you* in jail for homicide, no matter how justifiable."

"Got any great ideas how to handle this?"

"Let me think on it. Meanwhile, we need Donna to keep leading him on—"

"No fucking way," I said. "I don't care about Carter or C&C anymore. I don't want to put Donna through this."

"Have you asked Donna her opinion?"

"I don't need to. I don't want her having anything to do with that freakin' bastard."

"She doesn't have to. We'll work this out. Meet me for lunch. Hannah's, at 11:30. And have Donna forward the text to me. We'll deal with Harry ourselves."

"How?"

"Like I said. Let me think this through. Just be there at 11:30."

"All right, I will. But I don't want Harry getting within a thousand miles of her. Ever."

"I have an idea. If it works, she won't need to. See you in four hours."

The line went dead.

***

I slid into the booth across from Bill. Hannah's was busy, as usual, crowded with the locals from the surrounding factories and offices. We stood out like sore thumbs in our starched shirts and ties but over the years, the stares subsided, and we'd become just two more patrons of Hannah's down-home cooking.

"Did you get the text from Donna?"

"Yeah. About an hour ago." He pulled it up on his phone. "I hope he was better looking when they got married. Why on Earth would he think anyone would consider him desirable now?"

"No clue. Probably thinks his money will stand up longer than, well …." I pointed at the Viagra enhanced self-portrait.

Bill almost gagged on his coffee but managed to swallow before laughing.

"So what's this great idea of yours? Does it involve torture? If so, I'm in."

"No, no torture, at least not the physical kind. We'll need him in one piece to turn on Carter."

Our waitress stopped by, bringing a fresh cup of coffee for me, then took our orders. When she was gone, Bill continued, "I want Donna to act like nothing happened. I picked up a disposable cell phone on the way over here, and I want her to text him back on it. I wrote out the script for her." He handed me a typed page,

"Harry, I don't know if you tried to reach me, but I lost my cell phone this weekend. The phone company gave me a new one and suggested I change numbers so no one can use it and run up a huge bill. Here's my new number:555-228-8827. Jim said you were coming to town again this week. If you're free on Tuesday night, I can meet you at the Kierland in North Scottsdale, at the main bar. Say 8 o'clock?"

"What the hell is this? I'm not going to let her get within a hundred miles of that asshole!"

The people at all four tables near us turned their heads to look at me.

"Relax." Bill waved his hand at me. "I have no intention of her going to the meeting. I just want him to believe this is her new phone. After she hangs up, you're gonna give it back to me, and I'm gonna give it to my friend Jeremy."

"Jeremy? Why"

"His girlfriend is an experienced exotic dancer. She'll peak Harry's, uh, interest. Meanwhile, Jeremy said he can use it to upload a tracking cookie onto Harry's phone, so we can monitor his calls."

"He can do that?" I asked, half afraid to believe such software existed.

"The things he can do would scare the shit out of you."

"But he's on our side, right?"

"He's on his own side, but he trusts me, and I trust him, so he'll do this for us."

"Okay. I'll have Donna text Harry tonight. What should she do with her real cell phone?"

"Jeremy will block Harry's phone from calling her old cell number. If he tries, he'll get a recording saying the phone is no longer in service."

I held the throw-a-way phone in my hands and shook my head. I considered myself tech savvy, but this Jeremy character was light-years ahead of me. "Okay. Okay, I'll explain it to her." I put the phone in my pocket. "Now, back to our other problem. How are we gonna get the FBI to conjure up these nonexistent investors Harry's expecting to meet?"

"Ask him yourself."

"Huh"

Bill was staring over my left shoulder. When I turned around, there was a lanky, middle aged man standing behind me.

"Say hello to Ryan Billings."

If there were a cliché for a career law-enforcement officer, he would be its poster child: crew cut, grey suit, laced black Oxfords, and a chiseled, no-nonsense face. He sat down next to Bill with a finality that left no doubt about his intentions. I had no idea why the FBI would humor a couple of amateurs like us, and a new pod of butterflies stormed my stomach. My appetite gone, I let the chicken scampi grow cold as Bill droned on with the details of our plan to our new-found accomplice.

At first, it all seemed like an adventure, the kind you play on the computer; a real cat-and mouse psychodrama thriller video game where you collect clues and flush out the secret agent before he discovers you're on his tail and kills you in an ambush outside your apartment. Now? Now we're meeting with an FBI operative, caught in a serious sting on a large and ruthless organization. Steinham may not be a Soviet spy, and C&C may not be a terrorist organization, but intimidation and outright murder weren't outside the realm of possibility if their billion-dollar empire were threatened—especially by two low-level nobodies like Bill and me.

I wanted to tell Billings to call the whole damned thing off when I tuned in to the conversation.

"It would be better for you to continue the charade. If one of my agents stepped in to replace you now, this Steinham character might balk, and we'd lose him. You've done a damn good job laying the groundwork, and we're months away from anything actionable. The merger's moving too fast to stop it any other way. Can you forward me a copy of Steinham's fax?"

"Sure." Bill pulled out his cell phone and made some notes. "I'll have it couriered over to your office, along with my other notes." He reached to grab the pen from my hand. "For the umpteenth time, will you please stop clicking your stupid pen?"

"Sorry."

Bill looked at his phone again, as if reviewing a file. "My best guestimate is Steinham has between thirty and forty million dollars stashed overseas somewhere, not including the money he has tied up in C&C stock and options. That's enough to leave the country, establish a new identity and disappear."

Billings nodded agreement.

"On the phone, you said you could assemble a team by early next week. Is that still a go?"

Billings pulled his phone out, and I could see him checking his calendar. "Uh, looks like I can have them ready by Wednesday."

I looked back and forth between them, wondering whether they needed me at all. "Isn't that a little too late? We're expecting Harry in by Tuesday—"

"We'll set him up on Tuesday. The real meeting won't be till at least the next weekend, right Ryan?"

"That's the plan. You two need to hold him off till we can set up the sting."

"We'll do our part. Just make sure Harry doesn't see it coming." Bill looked like he was going to jump in, but I waved him off. "I like eating regularly, and Ellen and the kids wouldn't enjoy witness protection. I don't want us spending the rest of our lives looking over our shoulders."

"Nothing in life is guaranteed, Steve. Harry only knows me as Jim Adams. I'll drop out of sight as soon as Ryan's men have Harry cornered." Bill tapped the table in front of Billings. "What about it? Can you at least keep Steve out of the spotlight?"

"It seems you've managed to keep him out sight thus far." Billings replied. "I see no reason to involve him beyond what he's done already."

"See? You can relax. Here's your pen."

I put it in my shirt pocket and pushed the dish of now-cold chicken pasta aside. Billings stood, and I joined him, shaking his hand and walking out before I could tell them I was done with the whole thing.

***

"I've been giving a lot of thought to what you said this weekend," I began, avoiding her eyes, "and I'd like to ask you a question."

"Is it a good thing I'm sitting down?" she asked, "or are you going to wax romantic on me before we get to the eggrolls?"

P.F. Chang's, the Chinese restaurant on Scottsdale Road, was busy, but worth the wait. I didn't feel like cooking and wasn't in the mood for takeout. I intended on filling in Donna on our meeting with Billings. After all, she was the nexus of this plot to overthrow Carter and company. She deserved to know just what direction our venture into corporate espionage had taken. Nevertheless, the question of her feelings for me—or the lack thereof—held me in its debilitating grip.

"I thought you liked when I waxed romantic?"

"I do, but you obviously have something else on your mind." She cut a small portion from the eggroll on her plate and dipped it in the sweet and sour sauce.

I did the same, eating it quickly and washing it down with some sake. "I want to know what happened when you and Ellen went for a walk. Did you two fight about something?"

She put the fork aside, the tidbit of eggroll still speared on the tines. I felt the blood drain from my ears, as if they were unwilling to stick around to hear what came next. "You really believe you're in love with me, don't you?"

I folded my hands on the table and looked directly into those dark, cavernous eyes of hers. "With all my heart."

"You're so certain, so sure I'm the one." She looked away, biting her lower lip. After a minor eternity, she re-engaged. "I wish I could fall in love as easily as you."

"I didn't ask you if you loved me. I asked you what happened with Ellen."

"She's worried about you. She thinks you're taking this all too seriously, and she doesn't want to see you hurt."

"You mean she doesn't want to see you hurt me."

Her head bent downward. "Something like that."

I reached over and took her free hand. Without lifting her chin, she lifted her eyes to meet mine. "I'll tell you the same thing I told her. I'm a big boy, and I can take care of myself. I know what the stakes are, and

I know I still have a long way to go to convince you we belong together. I respect Ellen's opinion, but it's yours that matters most to me, okay? So, whatever happened out there, don't let it influence you."

She sat up straight, picking the fork back up. "Nothing happened out there. It was just girl talk, that's all." She ate the morsel of eggroll, barely chewing it, then took a sip of hot tea.

Evidently this part of the conversation was over, regardless of my unquenched curiosity.

Time to resort to Plan A. "We met Billings today, the FBI agent I told you about."

"What did he have to say for himself?" Donna asked, cutting another piece of eggroll and dipping it as before.

"He confirmed what Bill already uncovered independently. Carter and Steinham have been on the government's radar for quite some time, precisely for the reasons we suspected."

"And? Is he going to help us?"

"I think it's more like we're going to help him, which suits me just fine. I feel much better knowing law enforcement is in control."

"Are you saying we're backing out of it now?" she asked, the hint of a smile on her lips.

"No. No, not so much. Billings liked the idea of trapping Harry in our little investment charade, and since we've already laid the groundwork, he thought it best we see it through, with his advice and consent, of course."

"So, I still have to play nice with Harry?" Donna's smile faded, morphing into a frown.

"Yes, but not directly. According to Bill, Jeremy's friend has been keeping Harry busy on the throw-a-way cell. So long as you don't take any calls from the good doctor, you shouldn't have to interact with him anymore."

She sighed. "I thought my cell number was blocked so he couldn't call?"

"It is, but if he happens to call your old number from a different phone, he might get through, so you probably shouldn't answer any numbers you don't recognize for the next few weeks, at least until this thing is over."

"But he'll get my voicemail. He'll know it's me."

"You recorded the same voicemail message on both phones. He won't realize he called the wrong one. Just make sure you let Bill or me know if you get a message so we can forward it to Jeremy."

The waitress brought the main course, and Donna surprised me by asking for the check and a take-home box, even though we hadn't even begun to eat. It was clear she wasn't very hungry, and we'd take the lion's share of her food home tonight.

I reached for my wallet to pay the tab. "After this is all over, win or lose, I want you to come with me to San Diego."

"What's in San Diego?"

"There's this great big ocean, and it's lined with beaches and boardwalks. I thought we could start walking and make our way north. If, by the time we got to L.A., you weren't convinced I'm the one for you, you can come back to Phoenix and go on without me. I'll let go, and I won't look back."

"And if it turns out we really are meant to be together?"

"I'll find us a shack on the beach, and I'll never leave you. We'll make love in the sand every night. We'll put on a such a show the man in the moon will have to look away. Deal?"

"You'll just have to wait and see," she said, smiling for the first time all night.

~23~

The Kierland resort in Scottsdale, Arizona consists of an upscale hotel surrounded by posh shops, theatres and exclusive eateries. Located just two miles south of the PGA Tour's winter tournament site at the TPC, it didn't surprise anyone that Harry would choose such an extravagant and expensive locale to close the deal, especially since it wouldn't be on his dime. As an added incentive to make sure he showed up on time, and in a festive mood, Donna's stand-in had implied seductively she would be there as well.

Bill "Jim Adams" Phillips had no difficulty tracking him down. After parking the car, he began his search in the hotel bar, and sure enough, the good Dr. Steinham was nestled in a corner booth nursing a half-empty glass of Jack Daniels. He felt a little uneasy wearing the FBI wire, but he reminded himself he'd done no differently when they taped and recorded Harry at Tiani's. Why the FBI used actual wires under his shirt rather than wireless technology befuddled him, but he had little choice if he wanted their involvement.

He buttoned his jacket and slipped into the booth, extending his arm. Instead of a handshake, Harry simply slapped an envelope in his hand.

"These are the receipts for the airfare and rental car. The hotel said you already supplied a credit card, so no need to worry about that. I'd appreciate cash or check, made out to me if you don't mind, Jim-boy."

Bill folded the envelope and slipped it inside his jacket pocket. "I'll write you a check before I leave. I looked over the reports you faxed me, Harry, and I have some questions."

Before the man could answer, the waitress—a buxom brunette with long legs and a short skirt—stopped by and took Bill's drink order.

"Anything to eat tonight?" she asked, flashing a smile at them.

"Just you," Harry said, his mustache twitching uncontrollably.

"You couldn't afford me, honey."

She winked at Bill then sashayed away. Harry's eyes followed her till she disappeared around the corner of the bar. Sighing, he turned his attention back to Bill.

"I thought you might." Harry drained the glass. "Where's Donna?"

Bill pulled several folded papers from his side pocket and smoothed them out on the table. "The numbers in these spreadsheets look good. Too good." He pointed to several red circles with handwritten notes next to them. "These projections are nothing but smoke and mirrors; overly optimistic at best, downright hallucinations at worst."

"Good insights, my friend," Harry said without even looking at the copious notations. "And under ordinary circumstances, you'd be right. But you see, Jimmy, C&C does more than just cut fat and update procedures. We install a whole new control structure. We eliminate marginal programs that do little for the community, or the bottom line, and focus instead on those areas offering the best returns. Coincidentally, those tend to be the most needed by the local communities we serve."

"Give me an example"

"An example? Certainly." Harry launched into a practiced speech on how medical insurers squeeze hospitals, negotiating ever smaller reimbursements for each and every procedure performed. "These negotiated fees are often below reasonable market rates, but ineffective administrators have been cowed into accepting these ridiculous contracts which restrict revenue. This is because they have no leverage, no bargaining powers of their own."

Just then, the waitress came back with Bill's soda water, which looked just like Vodka on the rocks, along with a refill for Harry, who pulled out his wallet and laid a Ben Franklin on her tray. "That's for you, you little fox. And there's more of those, enough to satisfy even you."

She picked up the bill, held it up to the light, then stuffed it into her bra. She placed her free hand on Harry's arm. "I like round numbers. You think of a nice one, and I'll be back to check on y'all in a little while."

Harry tried to grab her arm and pull her towards him, but she blithely twisted out of his grasp and walked away. He watched her intently until Bill banged his hand on the table.

"Hey, remember me?"

Startled, Harry sneered at him, then straightened his back and pasted a smile on his face. "Sorry. Where were we?"

"You were saying something about bargaining power."

"Yes, yes, my boy. Bargaining power. There's clout in numbers. By acquiring multiple facilities, we now have negotiating muscle with these behemoths. With centralized operations, our purchasing power has gone up exponentially. We've successfully renegotiated more than twenty-two contracts with the major insurers, representing millions of households. Each incremental increase in reimbursements translates into hundreds of thousands of dollars in increased revenues per hospital, all of which falls to the bottom line."

Harry took another long drink and Bill wondered why he was still conscious.

"That's all well and good," Bill countered, trying to sound unconvinced, "but it only serves to prove my point. You can only renegotiate so many contracts, and when you're done, where does the growth come from?"

"We're an aging population, Jimbo. With age comes infirmity. That's just a fact of life. We are aggressively reoutfitting our hospitals for the onslaught of retirees from the baby boom generation, many of whom have substantial assets. The older ones have medical insurance plans and Medicare supplements from their previous employers, which are quite lucrative. Younger retirees rely more on Medicare and standard supplement plans, which they purchase on their own. In either case, the increase in sheer volume of new patients over the next two decades is staggering. You want growth? Old age is a growth engine for the medical industry."

"You think you can keep this going for decades?"

"Absolutely. And with the installation of new technologies to keep track, bill and collect promptly for each admission, we see sustainable growth in double digits for the foreseeable future."

"What about my clients. What kind of returns can they *really* expect?"

"They'll get a fair return, between eight and ten percent on initial investment, with a payback period of six years. In addition, they're convertible into shares of C&C, so if they want to participate in future growth, they can simply convert after the three years."

"The notes are convertible?" Bill acted as if he hadn't read the phony documents thoroughly.

"Yes. It's an added feature we included to sweeten the pot. Besides, once your investors see how successful we are, they'll want to own a piece of the action for themselves."

"Do you have a prospectus you can give me to look at?"

Harry hesitated a moment, taking a moment to simply stare at Bill. A prospectus or offering statement is required in every security transaction involving stocks or bonds. Since this was an illegitimate transaction, Harry could produce neither.

"Sure. I'll have one shipped right away from our investment department in Boston. Meanwhile, time is running short. If your investors are serious, I strongly suggest they decide quickly. Once the merger closes, they'll be out of luck. You don't want them to miss out on this once-in-a-lifetime opportunity."

"And when is that?"

"Within the next ten days."

"That's not a lot of time, Harry. My investors need time to digest this. I don't think they'll be able to study this, much less raise the money that quickly. We may have to take a bye. When's the next merger scheduled? Do you have another property in mind?"

The smile disappeared from Harry's face. "You said this was exactly the type of investment you and your investors were looking for. Where else are you gonna get this type of return on your money with a top-rated firm like C&C? You're damn lucky I was able to convince the finance committee to let me offer these to you. Now you're waffling? You pass on these, and not only will you be kicking yourselves for missing out on a first-class opportunity, but you'll never see me again. I've got better things to do than waste my time with redneck tire-kickers like you. Either you're in you're not. I need to know right now!"

"Okay, okay," Bill said, holding his hands up in fake submission, "I'll sell it to my clients. What's the next step?"

"The paperwork I sent you has to be signed and notarized, and they'll need to wire funds to our investment bank before the closing is completed." His eyes narrowed. "Has the list changed? I expected to meet them myself while I was here."

"There just wasn't enough time. Don't worry. I'll get you those contracts."

"If there's anyone else who needs one, email me the name and I'll have the additional papers drawn up and FedEx'd to you."

"No, no one else. The list you have is accurate."

Just then, the brunette appeared out of nowhere with another double for Harry.

Harry eyed the waitress hungrily. "In that case, let's drink a toast to our future success." She smiled back and casually placed a slip of paper in front of him before turning and walking away, swaying even more seductively than before.

"Now tell me, where's Donna? She told me she'd be with you tonight."

"Oh, I'm sorry. Didn't she text you? She came down with a sore throat this afternoon and couldn't make it. She sounded awful when I spoke with her."

Harry pulled out his cell, typed in a few keys, then grunted, "Huh! Sore throat." He picked up the slip of paper in front of him and, after reading it, said, "Tell her I had other plans anyway." With that, he bolted down his drink in a single long guzzle, not even bothering to take a breath, then got up abruptly and walked off in the direction of the elevators without bothering to say goodbye.

Bill watched, wondering how long it would take before Harry realized that FBI agent Fleming wasn't going to show up at the hotel room.

"These are the completed forms for Harry," Ryan Billings said to Bill, handing him a stack of manila envelopes. "Each of the eight agents have established aliases and are fully briefed."

I couldn't believe how hot it was in the conference room. I guess the government couldn't afford to pay the air conditioning bill, so we sat around the table drinking iced tea and sweating.

"They have fake social security numbers and individual bank accounts to use for the wire transfers. Everything will be monitored by our field office in Boston. If Harry does any checking, he'll find they each have LinkedIn identities, as well as established credit reports from the three rating agencies. The addresses are all legitimate, and the phone numbers ring to a special bank of recorded lines monitored 24/7 by staff. We've created one for you, too, Bill."

Bill sat across from me, flanked by Arnie Stromble, who'd flown in from DC, and agent Diane Fleming. Dressed in a conservative pinstripe skirt and jacket instead of a revealing waitressing outfit, she still commanded the attention of the men at the table.

"What if Harry tries an end run and contacts them directly?" Bill swiveled his chair in her direction, checking her out for perhaps the fifth time in as many minutes.

"They'll just tell him they prefer to work through you," she said. "We've done this before, you know."

I cleared my throat. "Well, *I've* never done this before, so I hope you don't mind if I ask a dumb question once in a while. If this blows up, it's our jobs on the line. What if the good Doctor wises up and sends his own investigators to check us out?"

"I doubt he will," Billings said. "First of all, there isn't enough time. Secondly, based on what you've told us, he's sloppy. In my experience, amateurs like him get cocky, and they think no one can pull a fast one on them. Besides, if he was suspicious at all, he would have investigated Jim Adams by now and, unless there's something you haven't told us, he bought your act hook, line, and sinker. In fact, if you need a job when all this is done, look me up. We could use field agents with your financial backgrounds who can lie with a straight face."

Ignoring the implied insult, Bill said, "Thanks but no thanks. I like my current job just fine."

"How are you planning to spring the trap?" I asked. "Are you just going to arrest him when he receives the signed documents back?"

"No." Billings answered. "We won't move in until he wires the funds offshore."

I took a sip of tea. "Isn't that a little risky?"

"Yeah," Bill interjected, "in the previous cons, the funds were quickly rewired to other destinations, and no one was able to trace them."

"Ever since 9/11," Billings answered, "the FBI, in conjunction with law enforcement and intelligence agencies around the world, devised a computer algorithm to track illicit funds movement. We've successfully confiscated drug monies from several major Mexican cartels and snuffed out four terrorist cells by following the money right to their secret hideouts. We plan to do the same thing here. Every day, more and more central banks install our software on their mainframes. Once Harry wires the funds, we'll intercept and recover them. We can then charge him with both wire fraud *and* money laundering. Added to the potential jail time for running a financial con game, he'll be looking at fifty years in prison. That should be enough to get him to turn on his friends."

"What about the banks that don't cooperate? Like the ones in Iran and Syria?" Bill asked.

"Let's just say the algorithms are able to embed themselves in unfriendly depositories," Fleming interjected.

"Since Steinham is a principle at C&C, can't we just implicate the entire management team as accessories?" I asked, absent-mindedly clicking my pen, eliciting angry stares from Bill.

"Not enough proof," Billings said. "If Harry is acting alone, as it appears to be in this case, then they can claim no knowledge and simply throw him to the wolves."

"Besides," Arnie chimed in for the first time, "what we're really after is the Medicare fraud. Let's not forget, that's the *real* crime here. We need Harry's cooperation to close them down."

"Okay, but how are you going to implicate Harry?" I asked, putting my pen down. Bill seemed to relax at that. "He does everything through a P.O. box outside of Boston. For all we know, he uses an accomplice. How will you catch him wiring the funds?"

"We're not going to let him do this through the mail. You're going to convince him that he has to meet your investors in person, in Boston, to consummate the deal."

"*What!*"

"Here's what you're going to do ..."

~25~

Dateline, Phoenix, Arizona October 6, 2021

The upcoming merger of SCM Hospital with C&C Healthcare out of Boston will spell the end of an era in the Phoenix Metropolitan area as the last, privately owned and funded major health facility is swallowed up. Rumors are swirling about the impact on the takeover. This reporter's inquiries to upper management of both companies were met with enthusiastic platitudes about the benefits to the community but were notably skimpy on details. In the ongoing aftermath of the Covid-19 Pandemic, serious questions have arisen about the ability of local hospitals to handle another onslaught of hapless victims.

Requests for an interview with C&C's CEO Delbert Carter weren't answered.

***

Harry put the finishing touches on the staff reductions report and sat back in his custom-made leather chair. Looking around at the intricately detailed mahogany furniture in his office, he breathed in the extravagance of it all. The fully stocked wet bar with its Waterford crystal tumblers and stemware. The intimate conference table with built-in tablets at each of the six positions. The fifty-inch retractable LED screen on the far wall, which was currently tuned to a financial news station flashing the latest stock quotes from around the globe. C&C stock had been rising steadily in anticipation not only of the current merger, but also of continued expansion west and south, adding to the impressive growth projections touted by the analysts.

Satisfied with his handiwork, he got up and locked the office door, then hooked up his personal laptop to the screen via the outlet located in the hidden recess of the front drawer. As some of his favorite porn flicks flashed by, he poured himself a drink and started fantasizing about the fifteen million dollars he'd harvest from Adams and his

Arizona pigeons—*Do they have pigeons in Arizona,* he wondered, *or just lizards?*

After this heist, he'd have enough to give Carter the finger and disappear off into comfortable obscurity. Along with the bonus money and stock options he'd cash in after the SCM takeover, he'd have somewhere north of fifty million bucks, a respectable stash by anyone's standards, especially in the third-world nations that offered unabashed erotica and anonymity.

He'd first considered joining the jet-setter community. Buying land on the cheap in Europe would be easy, with the ongoing recession and the wealthy fleeing countries like France, Spain, and Italy to avoid ultra-socialistic tax increases. Mansions and estates could be had for a song. The more he thought about it, however, the less he liked the idea of trying to be respectable. Once you built a facade of wealth and nobility, no matter how fake, it became increasingly difficult to evade the public eye, and especially the local media. No, he wanted to go where nobody knew his name, where no one would think to come looking for him. Hell, he could probably buy a whole town in some poor country in Central America and import enough women to keep him happy for the rest of his life.

"I wonder if the Jensen twins would be interested?" he thought out loud, as he drained the tumbler in one, long swallow.

~26~

Donna and Carol were exhausted after spending the entire afternoon shopping. They treated themselves to dinner and drinks at Emilio's, an authentic Mexican restaurant where the owner's name was really Emilio. Everything on the menu was cooked to order, not thawed and reheated. Located on a man-made lake in Tempe, it boasted a large patio colorfully decorated with piñatas, ceramic parrots, and a variety of artful geckos and lizards adorning the walls and posts.

"You've been awfully tightlipped lately," Carol suggested, sipping a margarita from a fluted martini glass. "What's with you and Steve?"

Donna picked up a warm tortilla chip and dipped it in the dish of mild salsa between them. "It's going all right, I guess."

"All right, you guess?" Carol asked. "What does that mean? I thought you two were a 'thing.' You know, a couple?"

"We are. I think. I don't know." Donna put down the tortilla chip, picked up her fork and played with her salad.

"Jesus, Donna girl, what happened?"

"What do you mean?" she mumbled, her gaze glued to her plate.

"I mean the first time I saw you two at the restaurant …. Hey, *look at me.*" Donna lifted her head slowly, finally meeting Carol's stare. "The first time I saw you two in the restaurant, you looked so great together; he's so into you. What did he do? Did he do something stupid? Tell me. If he screwed with you, I'll hunt him down and kill him myself."

"No, it's nothing like that. He treats me like a princess."

"Then what's the matter?"

"I don't know." Donna paused and looked away for a moment. "I just don't know if I love him, and he really wants to know where I stand. I can't blame him, but I'm not ready to make a commitment."

"So, don't make a commitment. No big deal. He seems like the kind of guy who would understand. Or is he pressing you?"

Donna sighed. "No, he's not pushing, but he did ask me to go to San Diego with him after this merger business is done, to see if we can make things work."

Carol shrugged her shoulders. "What's wrong with that? You're going, aren't you?"

"I haven't decided. I can't get the image out of my head of how he was all those years ago. He was so awkward. He tried being the class clown, always joking around, but it was obvious he was just trying to hide behind it. I remember feeling sorry for him, but I never pictured myself dating him."

"But that was like, what, a million years ago? He's not like that now, is he? I mean he's successful, he treats you well—you said it yourself—and, now he's putting his career on the line for you. What more do you want?"

"Yeah, he's my knight in shining armor."

"Then what's the problem? Is he not very good in bed?"

"He's okay. He won't win any Emmys, but he's passionate and willing to try things. Honestly, that's the best part, I think."

"Well, something's getting to you. C'mon. You can talk to me. Didn't you and he go away for a weekend up north?"

"Uh-huh. We went to his friend Bill's cabin in Snowflake, he and his wife, Ellen."

"Bill?" Carol tilted her head to one side. "Kind of tall, salt and pepper hair, wears expensive suits?"

"Yes. How'd you know?"

"He and Steve were in here a couple of weeks ago working on some big deal."

"Steve and Bill? Here? Did Steve say anything to you?" Donna asked, narrowing her eyes.

"Not much. He was surprised I recognized him. I asked why it took so long for the two of you to get together, and all he said was he didn't recognize you at first but was really glad he met you again."

"Did he say anything else?" Donna asked.

"No, he asked how long we knew each other, and I told him I knew you since you moved here from Boston. I had the impression he wanted to talk more, but he seemed reluctant in front of his friend. What aren't you telling me?" Carol asked, suddenly very serious.

"He said he was glad he met me?"

"Yes," Carol said, scratching her chin, "and he meant it. When you two were eating breakfast here that day, he never took his eyes off you. I wish my guy would act that way. His eyes are always wandering, you know? What's wrong with you, Donna girl? So what if he wasn't Don Juan back then? If he really loves you—"

"I know, I know. But Harry said he was in love with me, too. He was the perfect gentlemen ... well, you know."

"Ah. So that's it. You're afraid of making the same mistake again."

Donna nodded.

"He isn't Harry."

"And how would you know?"

"Have another drink, friend. We're not done talking."

~27~

The flashing emergency lights disappeared behind the doors as they closed against the night. Taking a deep breath, Bill composed himself for the frustratingly long wait ahead of him. The SCM emergency room would be packed, as usual, and that meant doctors and nurses rushing around, trying to care for the most urgently ill, ignoring anyone with less severe injuries or illnesses. In Ellen's case, the fact she woke up with weakness in her left side wouldn't impress anyone here. The paramedics who treated her at the house brought her inside in a wheelchair instead of on a gurney, another unspoken signal she could wait her turn.

"What seems to be the trouble?" the triage nurse asked as she took the first round of vitals.

"My wife has been here before," Bill replied, ignoring her question. "Why did it take so long for you to come by?"

"We're sorry, Mr. Phillips. There were a rash of car accidents involving serious injuries, and we received the brunt of the victims. Several were in critical condition requiring immediate attention."

"It's okay, Bill," Ellen said, waving him off. She reached out and the nurse took her hand. "I got up and felt weakness in my left leg. When I tried walking to the bathroom, I fell heavily against the wall. Bill woke up and felt I needed to come to the emergency room."

"Tell her the whole story, Ellen," Bill said, taking a deep breath. "I helped you to the bathroom, then to the armchair in the bedroom. You said your leg felt weak, almost numb." Addressing the nurse, he continued, "She was slurring her words a little and said she felt a little fuzzy. When it didn't clear up by itself, I called 911."

"And now?" the nurse asked, looking at Ellen.

"I'm fine. I just want to go home."

"You're not fine, so please let the nurse do her job," Bill said.

"Since when are you my doctor?" Ellen asked.

"We can't keep you here against your wishes, Mrs. Phillips," the nurse said politely, "but the paramedic report indicates a possible TIA. I suggest you let us run some tests just to be on the safe side."

"She's had one of those before," Bill said. "You'll find it in your records, probably two years or so ago, I think."

"Bill," Ellen said, "*stop* it!"

"I'm not going through the same thing we did the last time," he said. "I called Stella. She'll watch the kids. Now, let nurse Johnson here do her job."

"I'm ordering some tests for you," she said after taking Ellen's vital signs and having her sign the consent forms. "Stat. An orderly will be here shortly to take you down for a CT scan after we draw some blood. Do you have a list of medications?"

Bill pulled a folded paper out of his wallet and handed it to her. "These are current. She has a diagnosis of—"

"Of PV. Yes, I saw it on her chart." She added the med list the clipboard before tucking it under her arm. "Is there anything I can do to make you more comfortable Mrs. Phillips?"

"No, I don't think so. Did you say they'd be right to take me for a CT?"

"Yes, right after they draw blood. Dr. Sanchez will be in shortly." She handed Ellen the call button. "Call me if you need me."

"Did something change?" Ellen asked when they were alone again.

"I think so," Bill said, looking out towards the nursing station. "That was quicker than last time, and the nurse ordered the tests without consulting the doctor first."

"I meant has something changed with you?"

"Huh? What do you mean?"

"We've been through this before. Why are you snipping at me?"

"I'm not snipping," Bill said, just as Doctor Sanchez walked in.

"Then what do you call it?"

"I don't know what you're talking about." Bill started pacing at the foot of the bed.

"Is this a bad time?" Sanchez asked.

The older physician, maybe in his sixties, sported thinning gray hair to match the white of his coat. The stethoscope hung around his neck, and he carried a tablet glowing green with statistics and graphs.

"No," Bill said before Ellen could respond. "Please come in."

They shook hands, then he scanned the tablet as Ellen continued to glare at Bill. "Looks like you've been a guest here before. You have quite a history."

"Yes," Bill said, jumping ahead of Ellen again. "Seems we're regulars at your emporium. Did you see she has PV?"

"It's in the chart, yes. It lists her primary care physician as Dr. Fallon. Is that correct?"

Bill nodded, reaching for Ellen's hand as the phlebotomist entered the room and started checking Ellen's arm for a promising vein to draw blood from.

"I'll put a call in to him. Meanwhile, the preliminary diagnosis from the paramedics seems to be a TIA of some sort. Has this happened before?"

"Yes," Ellen said, squeezing Bill's hand harder than usual, her eyes darting between him and Dr. Sanchez as the nurse found what she was looking for and proceeded to insert the needle to draw a few vials of precious liquid. "Do you think it might be related to the PV?"

"Maybe, but I'm not an expert on your disease. That's why I want to talk with Dr. Fallon." He checked her heart, peered into her eyes, and felt for the pulse in her neck as the last vial of blood was filled and the needle removed. Just then, a tall man in blue scrubs and caring eyes entered the room with a wheelchair. "Ah, here's your chariot, Mrs. Phillips. The orderly will take you down to get your Cat scan." The doctor turned to Bill. "You can go with her or wait here if you like. Do either of you have any questions for me?"

"No, Doctor," Ellen said. "Thank you for being so prompt. Last time we were here, it took several hours before anyone even looked at me, much less showed up to take me to radiology."

"First of all, you're welcome. It seems like someone upstairs started paying attention to all those patient surveys and decided to do something about it. Let's get you some help. Then, be sure to tell them about your experience when you're discharged. The feedback will keep them on track."

"I will," she said.

Ellen swung her feet off the bed and, waving Bill off. She let the handsome attendant help her into the chair. The three of them moved silently down the long, sterile hallways, following the *Radiation Lab* signs and arrows. Bill walked beside the chair, hand resting lightly on his wife's shoulder. The wheels squeaked on the linoleum, louder each time they turned a corner. Finally, Bill broke the silence. "I'm sorry, Ellen. I've been distracted. If I snipped at you, I didn't mean it."

She managed a smile. "I'm glad you're here, darling. What would I do without you?"

As they rounded the last corner, Agent Fleming stood there, dressed smartly in her dark suit. "Hello, Bill," she said, "the nurse in the emergency room said you were headed this way. Do you have a few minutes to talk?"

***

Hospitals generally are frigid places with temperatures kept purposefully cool to combat bacteria and other infectious diseases which thrive at warmer temperatures.

The orderly pushed the wheelchair a little faster than usual, choosing to forego the usual banter about the weather. Bill kept pace to the side and slightly behind Ellen, who stared at the floor tiles sliding briskly past.

They'd almost made it back before Bill spoke, half to himself, "That was quicker than I anticipated. They're getting mighty efficient around here. Maybe they don't need C&C to come in and—"

"Who the hell was that?"

"Who? You mean Agent Fleming? She's on the FBI task force. She's—"

She glanced quickly at her husband, then resumed counting tiles. "Since when did the FBI start employing Kardashian wannabes?"

"Now wait a minute, Ellen."

"Just what in blue blazes is going on here?" This time, she raised her head and glared back at him. "It's bad enough that your partner in crime is chasing that … that gold-digger, but now you're working with Wonder Woman? Gee, what's a poor wife to do?"

"What? Fleming? There's nothing going on. She's just one of the agents working the project, that's all."

Ellen held up her hand and the orderly stopped pushing. She stood up and faced Bill.

"Ma'am, you're not supposed to—"

"There better not be. I don't need to compete with her, or Donna, or anyone else for that matter. I'm you wife and you'd damned well better never forget it, buster."

Bill reflexively held up his hands. "Calm down, babe. There's nothing going on, and I know you're my wife. I'm here, right? When have I ever let you down?"

She inched her way over to him and placed a finger on his chest. "I know. I know you're always here for me. Just promise. Promise me you'll never …"

He reached out and pulled her into his arms. She nestled her face into the crook between his shoulder and neck and started sobbing.

"I promise."

***

"I got the results back, and I'm afraid they're inconclusive." Doctor Sanchez settled on a stool to the right of Ellen's bed, which was surrounded by three beige walls, the fourth one consisting of a flimsy curtain, as she slept peacefully. Wires and an IV drip line connected to a Christmas tree series of bedside monitors which clicked and whirred rhythmically.

Bill sat on the other side of her, leafing through the thick folder Fleming had handed him. The overhead florescent was off, but enough ambient light leaked into the room from beyond the curtains for him to see.

"Does that mean she *didn't* have a stroke?" Bill asked quietly, nose still buried in the folder.

The doctor recited the signs of minor strokes and shook his head. "They often don't show up on scans unless there's some tissue damage or internal bleeding."

Bill looked up.

"That doesn't mean she *didn't* experience one, only that it left no visible traces behind. If it weren't for the symptoms you reported when you came in, we might not have suspected one in the first place."

Bill closed the dossier and sighed. "So, what do we do now?"

"We wait and watch," the doctor replied. "I want to keep her at least overnight—perhaps a day or two—for observation and additional tests. I'm still waiting to consult with Dr. Fallon. He may want to make some adjustment to her medications. Meanwhile, I'll order a sonogram and have our physical therapy department come up in the morning to evaluate her arm and leg. The fact she didn't lose feeling completely is a good sign."

Bill thanked Dr. Sanchez as he strode out of the room. He watched Ellen's chest as it rose and fell easily. Satisfied she'd be okay for a while, he tucked the folder under his arm, kissed her forehead, and quietly walked out of the room. It was four thirty in the morning, and Steve would be up by now. He pulled out his cell and pressed the speed dial as he retraced the familiar path back to the hospital cafeteria to rejoin Fleming.

***

I recognized the phone number and, noting the hour, was instantly alert.

"You're up earlier than me. That's not like you. What's going on?"

"Figured I wouldn't wake you. I just wanted to let you know I had to take Ellen to the ER last night. We're here now."

I sipped my coffee in the hollow light of the computer screen in my den. The overseas markets were sinking, which meant a negative open on the U S exchanges in a couple hours. Donna was still asleep.

"Omigod! What happened?" I whispered. "Is she all right?"

"I'm not sure. She got up feeling weak and had trouble focusing. The doctor thinks she may have had a minor stroke, but the tests are inconclusive. They're going to keep her here for a day or two."

"Jesus, Bill, I'm sorry. Do you need me to do anything? Who's staying with the kids?"

"Stella's there. She's been through the drill before. The kids have been through it before, too. I'm not worried about them."

"I'll get dressed and head over there."

"No need. She's resting comfortably, and the doc says there doesn't appear to be any permanent damage. What I need you to do is call Billings. Steinham sent me a text wondering where the FedEx'd contracts are. You and he may have to coordinate the responses till I know more here."

"No problem, buddy. I'll handle it. If I need you, I'll send you a text and you can call me when you can. You just take care of Ellen. She's a special lady."

"I know …." His voice cracked, and silence ensued for a moment. "Thanks, Steve."

I got up to pour myself some more coffee, but Donna blocked my way, standing in the doorway in her bathrobe.

"What was that about? Was that Bill?"

I gave her hug and a kiss, careful not to spill the remnants of the coffee down her back. "Yeah. Ellen had some kind of episode last night, and she's in the emergency room."

"Oh, jeez, I'm sorry. Was it her PV?" There was a genuine look of concern on her face as she grabbed the cup from my hand and headed to the Keurig machine.

"Bill said they thought it was a minor stroke. They're keeping her for a day or two. I'm assuming it's not life-threatening, but I'm no expert."

"You're going down there, I assume."

I came up next to her as she loaded the pod into the machine. "Bill told me not to, but I think I'd better get up there as soon as I can."

"I agree. He's your best friend, and I'm sure he'd appreciate the support.'

"You'll have to fend for yourself this morning."

"I'll go in early and catch something in the cafeteria. You go help Bill and tell him I said hi." She turned to head for the bedroom, but I pulled her in close and we embraced as the coffee cup filled with the caffeine kick I knew I'd need.

When the brewing stopped, she kissed me and said, "Say hi to Ellen for me."

~28~

"I'm sorry I couldn't get here sooner." Donna slid the curtain separating Ellen's room from the adjacent nursing station back into place. "Steven told me you were here. I've got an early shift in the OR, but I wanted to check in on you first." She glanced up at the clock above the bed. "I've got a few minutes if you want to talk."

Ellen sat in the recliner next to the bed, a half-empty bowl of oatmeal and a piece of dry toast with a nibble taken out of it. She squeezed a tennis ball in her left hand, barely able to compress it.

"Don't be concerned. I'm sure you're busy, but thanks."

"Is Bill still here?" Donna asked.

"I sent him downstairs to the cafeteria to get some coffee. I love him, but sometimes his hovering can be a bit much. I just needed some space. How's tricks?"

After a strained silence, Donna answered, "Compared to you, I guess I'm doing just fine. Steven said something about a minor stroke. Have they confirmed that? Is it related to your PV?" Donna took a chair near the foot of the bed.

"They're not sure." Focusing all her attention on the ball, she managed to compress it noticeably, her knuckles turning white from the exertion. Putting it down on the bed, she let out a long breath. "It's so frustrating." Noticing Donna had on her scrubs, she continued, "How do you stand it, being around it all day long?"

"If you mean how do I handle being around patients who have to sit and wait for a diagnosis, the truth is, I don't. I'm typically in surgery where the patients already have a diagnosis. I guess you could say I work on the treatment side of things, trying to heal and repair. I wish there was something I could do for you. Did you want to talk?"

"About what?"

"About what happened. About your stroke. I'm not a doctor but, like you said, I've been around hospitals a long time. I'd be happy to listen. Sometimes it's good just to talk about what's bothering you with a stranger, someone who can be a little more objective."

"You mean detached and clinical, like you are with Steve?"

Donna stiffened in the chair. "That's not fair."

"Really. Look who's talking about what's fair. Have you told him yet? Or are you still playing your little game?"

"I told him. Okay? I told him I wasn't ready for a long-term commitment. Isn't that what you wanted?" Donna said, raising her voice.

"That's what you said? 'I'm not ready for a long-term commitment?' Those were you're exact words?"

"Maybe not those exact words, but he understands."

"You mean he's still in the dark, thinking you're for real. Did you think I was kidding when I said I'd spoil your little charade?"

Donna bit her upper lip, then nodded. "I believed you."

"Did you tell him you didn't love him?"

"Yes."

"*Liar.*"

"*I'm not lying!*"

The floor nurse pushed aside the curtain to see what was going on. "Sorry." Donna raised an apologetic hand. "I didn't mean to raise my voice."

"If I hear another outburst from you, I'm going to ask you to leave. Are you okay, Mrs. Phillips? Need anything?"

"I'm okay." Ellen scowled at her guest. "She was just leaving anyway."

The nurse ducked back out of the room, but not before staring for a moment at the SCM badge Donna wore on her surgical scrubs.

"If you want me to leave, I'll leave. But you're wrong about me. I spent a long time thinking about what you said and, the truth is, I think I might be in love with him. I just don't know."

"Well, you'd better figure it out fast. I am not going to let you use him like some old dust broom to wipe up the cobwebs in your empty life, understand?"

"He asked me to go to San Diego with him," Donna blurted out.

"*What?*"

"When I told him I just wasn't ready for a commitment, he asked me to go to San Diego with him after this merger thing is done. He said we should spend some time together, sort things out."

"And then?"

"And then if it didn't work out, I could leave, no hard feelings. Look, Ellen, I know you care about him as a friend. I'm not blind. I can see he's a good man, and he really believes he's in love with me. But you know as well as I, men fall for anyone who looks at them cross-eyed and winks. You're lucky. You and Bill found each other, and it worked out. I got stuck with Harry, and now I've got to make nice to the bastard to try and keep him from screwing me. How do I know Steven won't dump me like yesterday's newspaper when the excitement is over, when it's just him and me with no fires to extinguish?"

Ellen thought about that for a moment. "You're right. Steve can get a little starry eyed. I've wondered about some of the women he's dated since Michelle. He's always jumping at the chance at forever-and-ever. I know he's searching for the right someone. I just don't think it's you."

"Well, I don't know if it's me, either, but I'm willing to give it a try. I just need you to understand. I'm not using him, and I won't hurt him if I can avoid it, but I've got to lead my life, and I have the right to live it my way. If things work out with us, you and Bill will be the first to know."

"So that's the way it is?" Ellen said.

"You say it like I'm doing something immoral. Steven's been married before, too, and he's been burned, just like me. When he followed me that first day, he was looking for one thing and one thing only. Well, turns out I needed it, too, so we ended up in bed." Looking down, she half mumbled, "Nothing wrong with that. We're two consulting adults." Looking directly into Ellen's eyes, she continued, "This thing with C&C, that came up after. Who knows? Without it, we might have gone our separate ways weeks ago. Or maybe we'd still be together, still feeling each other out. Why are you so hell bent to step in like Mother Mary and protect him? He's not exactly the Pope."

"No, he's not. But he isn't Satan, either, and he deserves better."

"You really think I'm a bitch, don't you?"

"I don't know what you are," Ellen replied in a low growl, "but I'm putting you on notice. I simply won't stand for you mistreating him. If I find you've been lying to me, that you're playing Delilah to his Samson, I'll scratch those beautiful brown eyes of yours right out of your head and shove them down your slender, lying windpipe. Do you understand me?"

"Yeah. I understand," Donna said, turning to walk out. As she reached the curtain, she looked back. "What goes on between me and Steven is between me and Steven. Keep your fucking goody-two-shoes meddling to yourself."

Donna's rubber soled shoes squeaked loudly as she spun quickly and left, heading back to the surgical wing. She didn't see Ellen's eyes roll back in her head, or witness her go stiff in the chair, her arms and legs shaking violently.

The hallways at SCM didn't flow geometrically, the way the streets of the city did. Instead, like so many hospitals, the wings and connecting stairwells met at odd angles reflecting decades of jigsaw construction projects. Each addition was built without consideration to whether hapless visitors could navigate from one end of the huge complex to the other.

I wandered, hopelessly lost, until I broke down and asked an orderly for directions. By fortunate circumstance, he, too, was headed to the cafeteria for breakfast, and we walked together, exchanging small talk until we entered the main dining room.

I wasn't ready to eat yet, though the smells of scrambled eggs and sizzling bacon made my mouth water. I grabbed a cup of coffee from the tall urns, paid the attendant, and looked for my friend.

He and Agent Fleming sat in a booth near the back corner. The remnants of their half-eaten meal sat off to the side, and an open folder lay between them, which they were reviewing. They sat alarmingly close to one another. I wasn't sure I could fit the edge of a credit card between them. I knew from experience that the food in this hospital was pretty good, all things considered but, somehow, I didn't believe Fleming was here for the Huevos a la Mexicana.

They both jumped, startled, when I sat down heavily, the coffee sloshing visibly in the cups in front of them. Bill looked like a man who'd been up all night, clothes wrinkled and damp, but the sheepish grin spreading on his face didn't fit the circumstances. Diane Fleming was dressed smartly in a form-fitting business suit, and I wondered how she'd managed to pour herself into it.

"Morning, Bill, Diane. What's up?"

"Things have changed," Diane said. "Billings wants us to go to Boston to meet with Harry Saturday."

"*What*? Why?"

"The timetable has been stepped up. Harry is using a bank in Boston to wire the funds offshore and it seems he wants to get it done sooner rather than later. Billings thinks he's getting ready to flee the country. We agreed, so he wouldn't have the chance to back out."

"But he wouldn't back out on the deal just because we were a day or two late," I stammered, still unable to take my eyes off her.

"We can't know that," Bill said, chiming in.

"Anyway, Billings figures the pressure of getting the funds wired on a Saturday would give us the chance we need to catch him," Fleming added. "We'll be there, along with backup from the local FBI office, to arrest him as soon as the money leaves the U.S."

I turned my attention to Bill. "What about Ellen?"

He stiffened and sat up straighter. "She'll be okay. We've been through this drill before. If I have to, I'll call her mother to fly out. Stella will help with the kids. They'll all be fine."

"Don't you think you should stay here? You know, just in case?"

"I said she'll be fine. I don't want to blow this. We've worked too hard." He played with his coffee cup for a minute, spinning it around, but not taking a drink. "Besides, with Ellen here now, it really hit me. What if they win? I don't even want to consider the consequences. No. Postponing this isn't an option."

"And when Ellen comes home?"

"Her mom will be here by then."

"You called her already?" Fleming asked.

"Not yet. I'm not ready to deal with the drama."

"But if you need to go to Boston …." I took a long drink of hot coffee, not minding the burning sensation in my throat.

"Yeah, I know. But not yet. I need to know the extent of the problem before I call. No sense getting her mother all riled up and have her fly out here if it turns out Ellen doesn't really need her."

"Ellen might have different ideas."

"I'm sure she will. I'm hoping she'll volunteer to call herself and let me off the hook."

"It's settled then," Fleming said. "I'll let Billings know. He said he had the seed money ready, a cool fifteen million."

"That's a lot of scratch," I said.

"At least it isn't ours," Bill said.

"Still, once it leaves the country …."

Diane grabbed one of the documents from the folder and slid it over to me. "You were there at the last meeting. The new tracking software can follow it even through the banking system's sink holes in the most depraved third-world countries on the planet."

I scanned the pages of flow-charts and encryption protocols, barely making sense of them despite my years in finance. "And Billings is willing to bet fifteen million on this?

"That fifteen million could net a hundred million or more in restitution," she said, "and if we can convict under the organized crime statutes, it could be treble damages. You're a broker; you'd bet that much for a three thousand percent return, wouldn't you?"

"Only if it's someone else's money I'm betting," I said.

That got a chuckle out of Bill.

"I still think you're out of your mind," I said.

"Maybe," Bill answered.

"What?"

"Maybe I am out of my mind."

"Did they figure out what happened?" I asked, trying to change the subject.

"Yeah, they found out Harry has an accomplice at the bank," Diane said, putting her hand gently on Bill's shoulder.

He looked up, and their eyes met.

"I meant to Ellen."

Bill cleared his throat and Fleming folded her hands on the table. "There didn't appear to be any discernable cause. I guess the good news is there wasn't any brain damage. They'll keep her here for observation. Then they'll send her home for outpatient therapy."

I'm more concerned about the hot spots in your *brain, Bill.*

"Ellen needs you here."

"She'll be better off with her mother here, and I'll be better off doing something useful. Work will keep me from going nuts."

"Ah, the bliss of married life," I said, shifting my eyes to Fleming. "Is this what I've been missing all these years?"

"I wouldn't know," she replied. "I deal with outlaws, not in-laws."

"Ever been married?" I asked.

"Just to my job." She smiled, and I felt my pulse quicken.

"So why did you come to the hospital?" I asked, trying to find out exactly what was going on here. "You could have called *me* to break the news."

"I thought it would be better in person, especially under the circumstances."

"How did you know Bill was here?"

"She was going to the house when she saw the ambulance pulling away," Bill answered for her. "She followed us here. What's eating you all of a sudden?"

"Nothing. Just worried about Ellen, like you ought to be."

Bill stood up. "That was uncalled for."

"Hey, guys, cool it. It's okay," Fleming said, standing up as well. "I was just leaving. I didn't mean to cause any problems. Bill, I'm sure Ryan will understand if you don't want to go to Boston. We'll figure something else out."

"No. I'm going. Get me the damn ticket and make sure Harry is there. I intend to nail his ass to the wall."

"Your friend is doing the right thing," Fleming said to me as she turned to walk away.

"That's open for debate," I said, motioning for Bill sit back down.

As soon as she was out of earshot, I asked, "What the hell was that all about?"

"What is your problem, Steve?"

"I'm wondering the same thing about you. Ellen's in the hospital and you're making time with this ... this— "

"Were you listening at all? She's the one who followed me here. She wanted to tell me about the change in plans, that's all. Where do you get off accusing me of anything?"

"I saw the way you looked at her, and the way you managed to sit next to her at Billings' office. Are you really that jealous of me and Donna?"

"You are way off base, you."

"That's why you need to hear all about my exercises in futility, right? Because you think you're better than me. Now that I have Donna, suddenly it's different."

"You really *have* lost your fucking mind, you know? You're the one with the jealousy problem. That girl is in your head, and she's screwing it up. Maybe you and she should cool it for a while."

"*I'm* jealous? Me? Listen to you."

Bill's phone rang, which startled me since he usually keeps it on vibrate.

"This is Bill. What? When? Goddamnit. Okay, I'll be right up."

"What?" I asked.

"Ellen," he blurted out, knocking the coffee cups over as he got up. "Another seizure. Gotta go."

All I could do was follow him at a jog as he raced out the cafeteria door toward the elevators. As if anticipating his arrival, the doors to one of them opened and he jumped inside even before the people inside could shove their way out. I stood aside, letting the handful of startled visitors exit before stepping in. Bill was punching the fourth-floor button over and over. He switched to the "close elevator door" button, stabbing at it repeatedly, swearing at it to hurry up.

The doors finally closed and, as the elevator started moving, I noticed the tears running down his cheeks.

~30~

The sun barely cleared the horizon, but its presence lit up the underbellies of the high, scattered clouds in an eerie glow. If I had any artistic ability at all, I'd grab an easel and some brushes and start painting. I stood for a few minutes admiring the dawn, hoping it might ease my mind, but the best I could manage was to quick click the image with my cell phone from the conference room and head to the gloom of my office.

"Good morning, Cindy," I mumbled as I passed by my assistant's desk.

"Morning, Steven. You have a meeting at eight-thirty with Mrs. Jankowski. Did you want me to pull the files?"

"Huh? What? Uh, sure." She held up a fist full of messages, but I waved her off and stepped into my office closing the door behind me.

The last twenty-four hours still swirled in my mind, and the last thing I wanted to think about was work. By the time I got home last night, I was exhausted. All I wanted to do was unwind with a bottle of wine and some pleasant conversation, but Donna wasn't in the mood to talk. I made dinner while she disappeared into the bedroom to take a shower, but when she finally came to sit down at the table, I told her about Ellen's set-back. She looked sick. She excused herself and went for an extended stay in the bathroom. When she returned to a plate of cold chicken and lukewarm vegetables, she was totally uncommunicative. I asked about her day, about the weather, about everything I thought she cared about, but all I got in return were variations of "nothing much," "not really," and "uh-huh." I gave up and we sat in silence as she rearranged the helpings on her plate into an unrecognizable heap destined for leftover stew.

I sat down at my desk, ignoring the blinking red "message waiting" light. I pulled up the picture I'd just taken and texted it to her with the caption, *"Good Morning Sunrise."* I wasn't sure if she was up, but she'd see it as soon as she turned her phone on. I still didn't understand why she turned the damn thing off at night.

"If it's important, they'll leave me a message."

"But what if it's truly urgent?"

"Anyone who knows me, knows where I live and can send the police. All the other urgent calls about getting my carpets cleaned or my insurance policy reviewed can wait till morning."

I got my journal out and starting writing. Sometimes that's the only thing that keeps me sane.

I stayed as long as I dared with Bill and Ellen, but with the parade of nurses and specialists filtering in and out, I felt uncomfortable. When I left, Bill was sitting next to the bed, holding her hand in both of his, talking softly to her. I couldn't make any of it out, but the look on his face said enough. Whatever was going on between him and Fleming was gone from his mind, and he was trying desperately to bring Ellen back from the abyss she was teetering over.

I don't think it's a good idea for him to leave her now to go to Boston, as much as I want to catch Harry red-handed. Maybe the FBI can pull it off without him. They're the professionals, after all. We did them a big favor setting the whole thing up. I'll call Billings this morning and tell him he has to do it without Jim Adams.

Of course, if it falls apart or Harry smells a rat and skips out, the merger will go through, and Donna will lose her job. What then? Maybe I'll wait till I hear from Bill before making that call. He might need a night in Boston with Fleming before this is all done.

I can't believe I just wrote that.

I nearly jumped out of my skin when my cell phone vibrated. It jumped and crawled across the desk like a confused caterpillar till I put my pen down and grabbed it. Donna's text popped up.

Want to meet me @ IHOP for breakfast, night owl?

***

Carol was on duty, as usual, and gave me a warm smile. "Long time, no see, cowboy. Donna's already here waiting for you in your favorite booth."

"You're trusting my memory to renavigate to the booth?"

"No, I'm counting on your homing instincts to find her wherever she might be."

"Thanks." I looked past her into the main seating area, finally spotting her in "our" booth.

As I passed by, Carol grabbed my arm tightly and whispered in my ear. "She's counting on you. And so am I."

"Counting on what?" I whispered back.

She looked me square in the eye. "Counting on you to do the right thing. She's my friend, and I won't have you playing with her heart. You in love with her?"

"Yes."

"Well, she seems really down this morning. Not her usual self." She buried her finger in my chest. "You treating her right, Romeo?"

"Absolutely," I said. "It's just that my best friend's wife went to the ER yesterday."

"Oh, sorry," Carol said, pulling her finger back. "I didn't know."

"It's okay. It was very sudden."

"That wouldn't be the tall, handsome guy you were in here with a couple weeks ago, would it?"

"Yes, in fact, it is. You've got a good memory."

"Please give him my best. I hope his wife recovers quickly." She reached out and straightened my tie, smoothing it against my shirt. "And take good care of my friend. She really needs you, even if she doesn't say it out loud."

"I will."

"You'd better. Or you'll answer to me." She smiled, then picked up some menus for the customer waiting at the counter while I headed back into the restaurant.

***

She was dressed in her *"Nurses do it better"* T-shirt and as I approached, she rose and embraced me. Her eyes were red, but I don't think it was from lack of sleep. The older couple sitting at the table next to us nodded at us before returning to their senior citizen special of eggs, potatoes, and pancakes. Public displays of affection sometimes bring smiles, sometimes frowns, and sometimes keep-it-private sneers. I stopped paying attention to most of it a long time ago, but for a split second I couldn't help thinking how nice it must be to grow old together.

"You okay?" I asked as we both sat down. There was already a pot of coffee on the table with two cups and creamers.

"Great picture, Mr. Crack-o-dawn," she said, waving her phone at me. She was more animated than last night but didn't meet my eyes when she spoke. I poured the coffee and she immediately picked up the spoon and started stirring.

"Of course. I'm not only a great cook, but an expert photographer."

For a change, she laid the spoon aside and took a sip of coffee. "Did you do your meditation or say your prayers or whatever it is you do at o-dark-thirty?"

"I followed my normal routine, yes. You were sound asleep, or we could've done a few Buddhist chants together to ward off misfortune before I left."

"Any word from Bill?

"Not since I left the hospital. I'm hoping no news is good news."

She bit her bottom lip for a second, then asked, "How bad was it?"

"Not sure. She looked like she was resting peacefully. From what little I could make out from the nurses' comments, it may have something to do with her condition. They were performing all sorts of tests, and I didn't feel comfortable hanging around."

I didn't say anything about Fleming or the conversation in the cafeteria.

"Tell me again why you get up so early every day."

"Years of habit, I suppose. I've found it useful to keep my head together. I just need the alone time. Deep down, I'm an introvert. Besides, the dawn over the lake is amazing."

"And when it gets hotter than hell in the summer, what then?" she asked.

The waitress, Anna, stopped by and we ordered our usual breakfasts: a cholesterol lover's plate for me, and the dieter's delight for Donna. Anna refilled my cup from the pot on the table then walked away.

"You've been to my office. When the weather gets unbearable, I commandeer the conference room. It offers a great view of the lake and the Four Peaks mountain range in the distance. The sunrise is as spectacular there as at the park, and it's temperature controlled to boot."

"Glad to see you're such a trooper. You don't like your porridge too hot or too cold, so why not go to the office every day?"

"I spend enough time indoors perforce. I like being outside whenever it's conducive. Besides, it's all about associations."

"Huh?"

She started stirring her coffee again.

"Haven't you ever noticed? Your mind works through association. When you're at the hospital, your mind enters the 'I'm-a-nurse' mode, and it becomes nearly impossible to focus on anything else but work. At home, it's 'what-do-I-want-to-make-for-dinner,' and so forth. The mind likes routine, associating places with thoughts and emotions. The mechanics of it is so strong that no matter how hard you try, you can't think about housework while you're in the operating room or write a novel while you're paying the bills. Me? I can't really relax and get into a deep meditative mood while I'm sitting down the hall from the office where I work all day long. It isn't logical, but that's how the brain works."

"That's pretty insightful, Steven. Weird, but insightful." She smiled for the first time in two days.

"Thanks. I love you, too."

"Don't get defensive. I just meant most people don't think like that."

"You're right. Most people live in a tick-tock world, going from place to place, emotion to emotion, without ever stopping to figure out why. Years go by without ever stopping to notice the changes going on until, out of nowhere, some unforeseen event jumps up and changes their life forever."

"That's a little deep for breakfast, don't you think?"

"You asked. Feel free to change the subject if I'm boring you."

"No, I'll admit you never bore me. But you do surprise me. It seems I see you for the first time every time we sit down to talk."

I nodded, raising my eyebrows in the hope she'd elaborate.

"You talked about mind associations. We went to high school together. I guess I still see you the way you were back then, but you're not that person anymore, are you?"

"God, I hope not. I sure don't ever want to be that guy again. You're definitely not the same person I knew back then either, or am I missing something?"

"No, you're not missing anything. I have to confess, though, I've had a more difficult time getting over my own … associations."

"Like what?"

"Like, well, still seeing you as a geekazoid. I'm sorry."

"Hmph. I was a geek, wasn't I? But if it will make you feel better, you're forgiven. Now, what brought this all on?"

"I stopped by to see Ellen at the hospital yesterday."

"Oh? When?"

"In the morning. After you left, I figured I'd go in early and get a head start on paperwork, but I couldn't stop thinking about her, so I went down to check. She told me she'd sent Bill downstairs to the cafeteria so he could eat, and she could rest a while."

"Were you there when she had the second stroke?" I asked, confused.

"No," she whispered.

"It happened after you left?"

"I guess."

"I was downstairs with Bill when he got a call from the floor nurse. We hurried right up. They were working on her, but I didn't see you. Are you sure of the time?"

Her mouth dropped open. "Omigod. Is she gonna be okay?"

"Like I said, I left before they knew anything definitive. Why?" I asked, sensing something was very, very wrong.

Donna folded her hands around the cup in front of her and started shaking. I reached out and took hold of her hand.

Her eyes welled up with tears. "We had an argument. We exchanged some, uh, unkind words. But she was all right when I left, I swear."

Then, she started crying in earnest.

31

"Well, it's about time, Jimmy. I've been holding the offering up for your so-called investors. You'd better have good news for me, or this is the last time we talk. Now, where are the contracts and wiring instructions? They should have been here two days ago."

Bill stared at Ellen's picture, the one he always kept in his wallet. The cup of cafeteria coffee had grown lukewarm, then cold, on the table in front of him. She was resting comfortably, the spaghetti matrix of monitor wires and IVs crisscrossed on her chest. The call to her mother had gone as expected. She'd berated him for waiting so long. Somewhere between his meeting with Fleming and this morning, he'd gone into automaton mode, shuffling from task to task like a zombie. Harry was just one more detail to deal with in an otherwise colorless world.

"I've got the paperwork, Harry. All signed and ready for you."

"Then I'll expect them on my desk in the morning. Use the address I gave you and make sure to choose early morning delivery from FedEx."

Bill took a sip of coffee, barely tasting it or noticing its lack of warmth. "There's been a change of plans."

Silence greeted him from the other end of the phone. "What. Kind. Of. Change?"

"Some of my investors want to meet with you in person before they sign the wire transfers."

"*Impossible,*" Harry roared. Bill held the phone away from his ear. "I won't be in Phoenix again till after the closing. I told you that last week. They had the chance to meet me then, and you said it wasn't necessary. What kind of nonsense is this? This isn't the time to play games. Do they want in or not?"

"Calm down, Harry. They're on board," Bill said, resorting instinctively to his natural talent as a practiced deal maker. He'd dealt with enough corporate megalomaniacs not to be threatened by the likes of Steinham. "They're just a conservative bunch, and they don't like to feel bum-rushed. I knew you weren't coming to Phoenix, so I offered to cover the costs to have them fly to Boston to meet with you. When would you be able to spend a couple of hours with us?"

The line went quiet for a second time. Bill half expected Harry to call the whole thing off. Either way, he really didn't care. Nevertheless, he held his tongue. In any high-pressure sales situations, the first person to speak, loses.

"I could do something early Saturday morning," Harry said at last, "but they'll need to bring the forms so I can process them immediately, otherwise there's no deal. Understand?"

Bill picked a crumpled paper from the floor and smoothed it flat as he squeezed the receiver between his ear and shoulder.

All tests indicate a seizure, though they are inconclusive as to the cause. There are no signs of physical brain damage. Patient resting comfortably, though unresponsive. Diagnosis remains TIA; continued observation with intravenous fluids till she emerges from coma-like state.

He read it for the hundredth time before returning his attention to the phone.

"Understood. I'll make the arrangements. Where's your office?"

"No. Not my office. The Langham Hotel. On Franklin Street. Be there at eight a.m. sharp," Harry snapped.

"Langham Hotel," Bill repeated, reaching for a pen. "Franklin Street. Eight a.m. Saturday. We'll be there."

"Goodbye," Harry shouted, slamming the phone down in Bill's ear.

He pressed the flash button on his phone, waited for the new dial tone, then punched in Ryan Billings' number. When Billings answered, he didn't bother saying hello. "It's all set for Saturday in Boston at the Langham Hotel, on Franklin Street. Eight a.m."

"We'll fly out Friday morning," Billings responded. "That'll give us time to make sure everything is set up and to do a couple of run-throughs. Harry won't know what hit him."

"I'm not going with you."

Bill hung up and laid his head on the table, not caring where his tears landed.

Not on My Watch

32

Delbert Carter's office occupied the entire thirtieth floor at C&C's corporate headquarters in Boston. Mammoth oak pedestals supported the presidential-style desk. A finely-honed surface gleamed under quarter inch-thick plate glass, the kind you might find insulating a bank's interior from its customers. The eastern windows framed a breathtaking view of Boston Harbor. From his custom-built captain's chair, he could direct the traffic from Logan airport with the wave of his hand. The well-stocked wet bar dwarfed Harry's, and a conference table with eight leather executive swivel chairs filled the remainder of the office. On the far wall, a fifty-inch LED flat-screen television served as a video conferencing panel from which he kept tabs on his lieutenants nationwide.

A concealed doorway next to the TV opened upon an extravagantly furnished apartment, complete with full bath, dressing room, walk-in closet, and another fully stocked, refrigerated bar for those nights when he worked late or when Madelyn, his mistress, was in town. Paintings by Ralph Goings and Richard Estes, his favorite photorealists, graced the walls. On the other side of the TV, a traditional doorway led to a more formal conference room. Another, larger mahogany desk that sat sixteen comfortably dominated the room. Each location was equipped with built-in video screens and pop-up outlets for computer connections. Speakers were built in to allow anyone sitting at the table to hear Delbert clearly, regardless of their rank or pecking order.

This particular Saturday morning he was working in this anteroom, reviewing the final SCM proposals. As he looked through Steinham's latest staffing modifications, he heard a soft knock at the door. Swiveling in his chair, he spotted a young man in jeans and a C&C golf shirt fidgeting in the doorway.

"Who the hell are you?"

"Um, I'm Aaron Higley, sir. Sorry to interrupt. You asked me to meet you here this morning."

"Higley, you say?"

"Yes, sir. If this is a bad time, I can come back."

"And what, exactly, were we supposed to meet about?"

"I found a data breach. I mean, I think it was … I alerted security and—"

"Yes, yes, I remember. Something about an anomaly in one of our files."

"Yes, sir, Mr. Carter, that's right," he said, nodding like his head was on a seesaw.

Carter pointed to a seat next to him. "Sit down. What exactly did you find?"

Higley walked swiftly to a chair opposite his boss and sat down.

"I'm not entirely sure, sir."

"What do you mean you're not sure? Ortega said you thought our computer files had been compromised. That's the word you used, wasn't it? Compromised?"

"Yes, sir. A number of files appear to have been, um, accessed without authorization."

"By who?"

"I don't know yet. It could just be a glitch. We're still running tests on the data fields."

"Were you able to determine which files were affected?"

"Accounting, mostly. Billing statements, accounts receivable. Nothing's missing and all the files appear to be intact, but the registers indicate a shuffling of the contents, as if someone rifled the files looking for something, but nothing's been erased."

Carter paused at that, studying Higley like he was some alien from outer space. "And what would cause that?"

"Any number of things: data decompression during the backup, a power surge …" his voice trailed off at and his next words were mumbled, unintelligible.

"Speak up, boy, I didn't hear that last bit."

Sitting up, spine straight, Higley seemed to find his courage. "I've seen something like this before, at my previous job. I think someone got past our security, into our mainframe, and scanned the files."

"Someone. You mean someone from the outside."

"Until I can isolate the IP address of the intruder, I can't be sure. I've already contacted all the departments with access to the system and no one remembered, or admitted, accessing the files since the last backup."

"So why can't you just compare the backup to the current file and see what's changed?"

"It's not that simple," Higley said. He went on to explain the complications of a data shadow. "It's not like placing two typewritten pages, one over the other, and looking through them under a bright light to see what words were out of place. Whoever did this was very good; there are no fingerprints, no trail to follow. There are over 10,000 files. Even with the right software, it would take weeks to compare them all, one by one, to find which ones were viewed.

"The hacker didn't insert anything and didn't delete anything." Higley stopped to take a breath. "It would be like trying to find a handful of electronic needles in a huge, computerized haystack, and we don't even know what any of them look like, much less what it means."

Carter considered that for a moment while staring at his own portrait on the wall behind Higley. When he turned his attention back to the nervous geek across the table, he said very calmly, "So, let's erase the whole damn thing and restore the previous backup. You said yourself none of our departments changed anything of significance since the last one."

"That could be dangerous," Higley responded. "Anyone sophisticated enough to do this, would probably have included a virus or worm that could wipe the entire memory clean, or worse. Besides, if we did erase the files without harm, we also would erase the evidence and any hope of tracking the hacker down."

"How the hell did this happen, Squigley?" Carter suddenly bellowed, his face turning red.

"I don't know, sir," Higley stood up, the color draining from his face. He looked nervously at door. "Uh, there's one more thing."

Carter's eyes bulged as he continued to glare at him.

"One of the personnel files was accessed as well."

"Whose?"

"Dr. Steinham, sir."

***

After dismissing Higley with a torrent of four-letter words and a threat to find his replacement if he didn't come up with better answers, Carter punched the intercom button with enough force to visibly shake the massive table.

Stella, his assistant, answered immediately. "Yes, Mr. Carter?"

"Get Steinham in here."

"He's not in, sir. He stepped out around seven-thirty this morning and hasn't been back."

"Then find him. Call him on his cell. I want to see him. *Now*."

Delbert grabbed the red file from the bottom of the stack on the table and opened it. Inside was a report from security about Harry's extracurricular activities. Beside his penchant for women and booze, it appeared he'd taken to running some sort of investment scam wherever C&C acquired new facilities. The latest one was in Texas, and the file contained accounts of the unexpected confrontations with some pissed-off ranchers wondering where their money went.

Harry had played dumb, which wasn't much of a stretch, and the cowboys found no tangible evidence to back up the claims. Nevertheless, it cost time and money for the corporate attorneys to respond to the allegations, and Delbert didn't appreciate the negative publicity. With the SCM deal closing in less than ten days, he didn't need any more bad news. If one of the ranchers from Texas, or some other yahoo from Steinham's other sleazy deals, had hired some cyber-cop to infiltrate C&C's computers, he'd have Steinham's head on a plate.

The intercom buzzed again.

"Well?" Delbert demanded.

"It seems Dr. Steinham has turned his cell phone off, sir."

***

The hotel conference room was more than adequate for the eight attendees. A light continental breakfast was set up against the back wall, including breads, juices, coffee, and assorted teas. The FBI agents-come-investors attacked the spread as if they hadn't eaten in a week. Bill

Phillips surmised they didn't get to eat at a posh Boston hotel on Uncle Sam's dime very often and were making the most of it. He half expected them to ask for doggy bags.

It had taken the better part of Thursday afternoon for Billings to convince Bill to change his mind about attending the meeting, including a promise that Fleming would sit by Ellen's side twenty-four/seven until Ellen's mother arrived. The FBI would cover the cost, both of the vigil and of the flight for Ellen's mom. If it became necessary for Bill to return on a moment's notice to Phoenix, he'd have access to their jet.

"You okay?" Billings asked, putting his arm around Bill's shoulder.

"Yeah, I guess."

"Heard from Diane?"

"She texts me every hour or so. Nothing new in the last four hours. I'm not sure if that's good or bad, but my mother-in-law should be there shortly. If she doesn't cure Diane of any desire to get married, nothing will," Bill quipped.

Ryan chuckled, and was about to reply when Steinham stormed in.

"Good morning, gentlemen," Harry said cheerfully, looking confident and in control, in spite of the generally disheveled appearance of his clothing. Spotting Bill, he went up to him and shook his hand. "Good to see you again, Jimbo. Why don't you introduce me?"

Bill went around the table, introducing the agents by their aliases, which he'd memorized on the flight from Phoenix the day before. Reading each file and absorbing the concocted stories had been a welcome distraction from his ongoing worries about Ellen.

Harry walked over to the beverage cart, poured himself a cup of coffee, then sat down at the head of the table.

"Let's get started, shall we?" he said, suddenly serious. "The merger is scheduled to close in less than ten days, so it is imperative you provide me with the wiring instructions from your banks so we can transfer the funds in time. Bill here tells me there are still some questions, and I want to make sure you are totally satisfied with your investment. This is an outstanding opportunity to participate in another profitable acquisition by C&C. Let me fill you in on some of the exciting new developments."

Bill focused as best he could, reminding himself what was at stake. As Steinham droned on, sounding more like a carnival barker than a surgeon-turned-corporate executive, Bill couldn't believe he'd successfully swindled so many people. A career in mergers and acquisitions had honed his skills at crafting his own words into effective presentations. It was an art form to him. Harry was clearly an amateur, yet he'd somehow managed to steal millions from sophisticated investors in four states. It merely proved P.T. Barnum's old adage: there's a sucker born every minute. Harry didn't need to be good, he just needed to appeal to the lowest common denominator of people's basest emotion: greed.

"So, who's got the first question?" Harry asked at last.

Billings spoke up first, "About these enhanced revenue projections ...."

***

Delbert pulled out his cell phone and called Alex Ortega. The six-foot-three-inch muscleman, who claimed to be fifty but looked no more than thirty, happened to be in his office on the second floor this morning.

When Ortega picked up, Carter didn't bother saying hello. "Steinham's gone AWOL and I need to speak to him. I don't care how you do it but find him. Stella said he left around seven thirty and turned his cell phone off. I want him in my office, and I'm not too particular in what condition. Clear?"

"Absolutely."

Ortega, a CIA operative during the first Iraqi war, entered the shadowy world of corporate security, selling his unique skills to the elite, the rich, and the gullible. Ortega wasn't his real name, of course, but no one at C&C knew that. He was an expert in computers and electronic surveillance and had won Delbert's complete trust and confidence during the last three years in his employ. In their private meetings, Steinham's name had come up occasionally, and it was obvious that Carter considered him a buffoon. "A front man for the dirty work," as he liked to call the man, along with "totally expendable."

Delbert's sudden need to have him hunt down and deliver Harry meant the boss finally realized Harry wasn't everything he pretended to be.

In point of fact, Ortega stumbled across Harry's exploits quite some time ago. Never one to take another man's opinion at face value, he'd compiled an extensive dossier on Steinham and knew all about the cons he'd been running. Evidently Carter discovered them as well.

Time was running out, and if ever there was a time to act, it was now.

Tracking down Harry was not difficult at all. He rarely drove his own car, choosing instead to use a company vehicle, all of which Ortega had personally equipped with hidden transmitters. After signing on remotely to Harry's office computer with the ID and password he'd hacked months ago, he checked the scumbag's personal calendar. A "Saturday" entry titled *"investor meeting"* he'd scheduled at the Langham Hotel, which was only a few blocks away on Franklin Street. Checking the GPS positions of all of the company vehicles, he noted one of the BMWs currently parked in the hotel garage. Ortega grabbed his hat and coat, along with a few items hidden in the false bottom of his top desk drawer before he headed for the elevator.

***

I picked up my phone and was surprised to see it was Bill calling. "Is the meeting over?" It was seven thirty-five in the morning in Phoenix—nine thirty-five Boston time—and fully one and a half hours into the sting.

"No. I excused myself for a restroom visit."

I set my coffee cup back on the kitchen table. "Everything okay?"

"Best I can tell. Steinham won't win any awards for salesmanship, but his swagger's entertaining to watch. He's lying through his teeth, of course, and they're recording every word."

That was a relief. I feared Ellen had taken another turn for the worse. If Bill was talking about Harry, it meant she was okay, at least for the moment.

"Yet, you're calling me. Something's just not right, right?"

Bill paused, and I thought I heard a sigh. "I don't know. I'm sure Billings know what he's doing, but—"

"But what? Talk to me"

"What if he's wrong? What if Harry is smarter than we're giving him credit for? What if he has some contingency plan we're unaware of? He can't be stupid enough to think he'll get away with this forever."

"I see. But what can we do about it? If Harry can somehow outwit the FBI—"

"I think we need to call Jeremy. We need our own plan 'B'."

"I've been trying to tell you that since sometime after Snowflake."

"Yeah, well you might have been right, my friend. Sorry I didn't listen to you then."

"Okay, I'll call him. Anything in particular I should have him look for?"

"Tell him to scan the company's secure email servers. We need incontrovertible proof tying Harry to the Medicare scheme. If Billings can't spring the trap, maybe we implicate Harry, convince him we can hang the entire rap on him. He'll jump at the chance to incriminate the rest of them, including that bastard, Carter. But we can't just bluff him. We'll need some hard evidence." A toilet flushed, and I realized he wasn't kidding about the restroom break. "I better get back to the meeting. I don't want to raise suspicions. Let me know if Jeremy finds anything useful."

"I'll text you."

"No. No texting. Nothing in writing. Just call and let the phone ring twice. I'll see it's you and duck out to call back."

"Ten-four, double-o-seven. I'll tell Moneypenny not to expect you for dinner."

"Cute." Bill said and hung up.

I heard a noise behind me, Donna coming out of the bedroom in her bathrobe, combing her hair.

"Was that Bill?"

"Yeah. He and his FBI groupies are still in the meeting with your ex. Bill wants me to call Jeremy and have him do some more digging."

"Does that mean we don't go out for breakfast?"

"It means we go out for lunch instead. I'll call Jeremy while you get dressed. Besides, it's not my fault you slept late."

"Yes, it is, you sex maniac," she said, settling on my lap. "Imagine … your best friend was sleeping alone in a hotel in Boston, trying to get Harry to indict himself, and all you could think to do was get into bed and ruin a perfectly good set of nylon stockings. You should be ashamed of yourself."

"As I recall, you didn't put up much of a fight. In fact, I believe I heard you moaning once or twice. Anyway, it's your hospital he's trying to save. Aren't you suddenly the pot calling the kettle black?"

"I'll call you anything I want to. Woman's prerogative and all that." She draped her arms around my neck, the bathrobe hanging seductively open in front.

"Does this mean you'll go to San Diego with me when this is all over?"

"You're just going to have to wait and see." Her kiss lingered on my mouth. "You'd better call Jeremy," she whispered, then headed back to the bedroom.

I found Jeremy's card, which Bill had reluctantly provided, and dialed his private number.

"Hey, Steve," Jeremy said, answering immediately.

"Hello, Master Geek. We need your help again."

"Oh?"

"Bill's in Boston. He needs you to go back into C&C's mainframe and do some additional, uh, research. He needs more on Steinham. He wants you to access their email servers, see if there's anything tying Harry to the Medicare scheme."

"Is that all? How 'bout I break into the IRS computers and steal his tax returns, too? Do you have any idea how many firewalls I have to break through to get to the email site?"

"No, but I have faith in you.

"You sound like my father. Okay, I'll let you know when I've got something useful."

"When? Not if?"

"This is a big company, which means there's plenty to hide. Most top execs think they're immune to common thievery, so they put things in emails they believe will never be read by anyone."

"Been there, done that, I take it?"

"How else would I be able to drive a Beemer on a programmer's salary?"

"I wondered. Don't tell me, though. I'm content in my ignorance. Just get back to me toot sweet. I don't know how long it'll be before they're ready to arrest Steinham, and I think we'd all feel better if we had some backup in case the FBI can't make their case."

"Did you say 'toot-sweet?' What century are you from, anyway?"

"Never mind. Just don't get caught."

***

It was a short trip to the hotel, but Ortega took a circuitous route just to be safe. After disabling the security camera at the employee entrance using an encrypted log-on he'd established under Steinham's ID, he slipped out undetected and walked to his personal vehicle, an indistinguishable black sedan. The license plates were registered to an off-shore LLC whose ownership was nearly impossible to trace.

Turning left out of the garage, he drove several blocks north, then east, then north again before doubling back. He parked a half block away and walked casually to the Langham like a tourist in no hurry to check in. At the front desk, he asked where Dr. Steinham's meeting was, claiming to be a participant running late. He was careful to keep his head turned away from the camera behind the check-in desk. Locating the conference room, he listened quietly at the door. Harry was pontificating about some minor issue, and it was apparent he still had another twenty or thirty minutes before Harry closed the deal.

"No reason not to let you finish your con, Harry," he said softly to himself. "Your little overseas bank account will grow by a few million more before we become more formally introduced and I lighten you of your burden." He silently padded back to the lobby and out the front door, pleasantly contemplating what he'd do with Harry's ill-gotten gains.

The BHBC Bank was just across the street and three doors down. According to Ortega's file, Harry used this branch to wire funds out of the country. They kept limited Saturday hours and had international connections through its affiliates. Harry would need to get here in time to have the paperwork signature guaranteed by a bank officer before wiring it. No self-respecting banker would sign what Harry was bringing in. Harry obviously had an inside partner.

Thirty minutes passed before Steinham strode by purposefully, looking through the papers in his hands. Oblivious to the man in the turtleneck sweater and khaki pants standing just outside the bank entrance, Harry swung the door open and walked inside.

Ortega kept his head buried in a newspaper, just another Bostonian catching up on the Celtics. In his hand, concealed by the paper, he held his smart phone. He followed the images it received from the tiny transmitter he'd attached to the bank's front window. Its fisheye lens gave him a clear view of the bank's interior. Harry walked to the far back corner, where one of the pinstriped employees got up from his desk to greet him.

Counting your money, Harry? Ortega thought to himself. *Don't get too attached to it.*

It took another fifteen minutes to complete the transaction, and when Harry rose and started for the door, Ortega slipped the phone into his pocket. He removed the pistol from the holster at the small of his back and folded the newspaper expertly around it. He detached the tiny camera on the window to his right and placed that, too, in his pocket. He glanced up once more at the bank's stationary external camera, which he had discreetly re-adjusted, and waited.

***

"Gone? What do you mean he's gone?" I shouted in the phone. "What the hell happened?"

Half the restaurant turned to give me dirty looks, but I paid no attention to them. Donna's eyes went wide, her mouth opened, and I watched the blood drain from her face.

"He's simply disappeared," Bill said. "After Billings got word the funds had been wired from the FBI seed accounts, he ordered his men to arrest Steinham, but Harry was nowhere to be found. The bank video shows him leaving, but he never made it to his car where three FBI agents waited. He didn't go back to his office. They're checking his apartment now, but how would he get there, if he didn't take his car?"

"Jesus! Why weren't they tailing him? You mean they just let him walk out of the bank and vanish?" Carol walked over and grabbed me by the arm.

"Is everything all right, Steve?"

"Yes. Sorry," I said to her, lowering my voice.

"Sorry for what?" Bill asked.

"Nothing. Nothing at all. What happened?"

"An agent followed him into the bank, watching to make sure he completed the transaction. But they couldn't arrest him till they were sure the funds had moved. If they took him in the bank, it's possible his confederate in the bank might have stopped it and the wire-fraud charges would have been useless."

"They just let him saunter away? What about the bank's external cameras? Surely in this day and age of paranoia they had surveillance cameras outside?" To Donna I said, "They let Harry get away."

"They didn't just let him get away," Bill said.

"I wasn't talking to you; I was talking to Donna. Now, what about those cameras? Surely they showed which way he went?"

"All they got was a shot of Harry walking out the door. Somebody's arm entered the frame and grabbed his wrist. He looked surprised, then scared. Then he walked out of the picture. He never came back into the camera's range after that."

"What about witnesses? This was in the middle of Boston in broad daylight. Didn't anyone see where he went?"

"Harry's *gone*?" Donna asked. "With all that money?"

Carol chimed in "What money?"

"Shush you two," I said. "Go ahead, Bill."

"By the time they realized he was gone, it was too late. There wasn't anyone left who would have noticed him."

"What about his cell? Can't they trace his movements with that?"

"Harry must have been planning something. His cell's been turned off since before he left his office at C&C."

My mind raced to find some logical explanation for this royal screwup. "You think he knew? You think maybe this was his last con before skipping town?"

"I doubt it. He's not that smart. Besides, he's too greedy. The deal with SCM is closing next week. He wouldn't leave before cashing in his stock options. Why would he walk away now?"

As usual, Bill was way ahead of me. "Wait. You said someone grabbed him as he left the bank and he was surprised, and then scared. Does Billings have any idea who it could have been?"

"No. All we could see was an arm. The guy, whoever it was, stayed out of the camera's sight. He must have known Harry would be there."

"The timing is too perfect. Whoever it was knew about Harry's extracurricular activities."

"Yeah, but who? And how do we find them? Without Harry, we have nothing on C&C. We're screwed."

"Not yet. I'll get back to you," I hung up and redialed Jeremy.

~33~

"Slow down, partner," Jeremy said, trying to cut off the emotional freight train I was on, "I got it covered."

"Got *what* covered?" I yelled into the phone. Now both Carol and Donna were staring at me. I mouthed "sorry," and asked Jeremy again, my voice lower, "What exactly have you got covered?"

This was a disaster. Steinham was gone, kidnapped, vanished into the night. A numbing heat racked my body, coming in waves, and I suddenly felt faint.

"I got back into the database, dude." His words sounded distant, though he spoke clearly, confidently. "We're sittin' pretty."

"What?" I asked, trying to focus. "What do you mean? How could this have happened?"

"Look,I know you're not my father, but you're acting like him, so just chill. I got the situation in hand."

"You got the situation in hand?" I mimicked. "How? What did you find? Did you find Steinham?"

"Not yet. But I have a good idea where he is."

I took a deep breath and looked at Donna. "Okay, I'm listening."

"I found an encrypted file on Steinham. Your suspicions were right. He was on the verge of being convicted of felony negligence at that Boston hospital when Carter's people showed up. They had friends in low places who squashed the indictment and expunged his record. Then, they hired him to be their mouthpiece and hatchet man."

"We already knew all that," I interrupted. "It's nice background information, but how does that help us? Where the hell is Harry?"

"Let me finish."

"Sorry. Go on."

"I know you knew all that. So did Ortega."

"Who?" I asked.

"When I found the file, it had already been hacked. Someone else at C&C was looking into Harry's escapades, someone with, uh, skills that rivaled mine. Someone near the top."

"And his name is Ortega?"

"Yeah. Alex. Alex Ortega. He's not listed anywhere in their corporate directory, or in any of their personnel files. My guess is he's either a hired gun from the outside, or they wanted to keep his existence a secret from the rest of the company—an invisible, internal enforcer."

"Could he be the man who kidnapped Steinham?"

"My best guess? Yeah."

"Wait a minute, if he's invisible, how'd you find him?"

"There's invisible, and then there's erasable. He must have been on the system at some point, and somebody erased his files. In cyberspace, however, nothing is ever truly expunged. It took some doing, but I was able to reconstruct some of the deleted files and IP addresses and the name Alex Ortega turned up. Who knows? Maybe he erased his own files to cover his tracks."

"Well, if he's the guy who grabbed Harry at the bank, then he must know about the money, too."

"I was thinking the same thing. He was tracking Harry, same as you, and had his scam figured out. It was probably just coincidence he decided to spring his own trap at the same time you guys were closing in. If that's the case, then my second scenario is more accurate. He erased his own files to cover his escape. More than likely, he's pumping Harry for the access codes to the offshore accounts."

"But that leaves us right where we started," I said, the acid welling up in my throat again. "It's a fine yarn, but we're still left out in the cold."

Jeremy harrumphed. "I thought the FBI had some fabulous new software program to trace the wires Harry sent."

"I thought so too, but, unless there's something Bill isn't telling me, they haven't found it yet."

"Great!"

"What do you mean, 'great?' What are you sniffing on that end of the phone?"

"The smell of money. All that lovely money. It's just waiting for us to claim it."

"Wait. What?"

"Meet me at Sky Harbor airport. Bring your passport and credit card. We're going on a little excursion."

***

"Where did he say to meet?"

We zipped along the 101 heading south to Sky Harbor having abandoned our food at IHOP. Our appetites were gone anyway. I just prayed the highway patrol was busy attending to some fender bender or stalking donuts at the local diner, because I didn't plan to bring the needle down below ninety before the airport exit. More than one infuriated driver flipped the bird at me as I cut them off or weaved between them.

"Terminal four, at the ticket counter. He said there's a flight out in a couple of hours."

"Do you trust him? Does he know what he's doing?" She held on to the door handle for dear life as I maneuvered between lanes.

"What choice do I have? Without Harry, we have a snowball's chance in Phoenix to bring down C&C. Jeremy's sure he's tracked the money."

"But who's this Ortega person? He sounds dangerous. You could get hurt."

"Oh? You're *worried* about me, are you?"

"Of course, I am, you geekazoid. I don't want anything to happen to you."

The car rocked to one side as I nearly sideswiped a utility truck cruising at a mere eighty miles per hour. I didn't bother looking at the driver. I could imagine the scowl on his face. "And if I didn't go, and Harry got away, or got himself killed, you wouldn't care?"

She reached over and touched my arm with her free hand.

"I don't care about Harry. I care about you."

Glancing over, I was pleasantly surprised to see the look of concern in her eyes. Turning back to the road, I nearly missed the I-202 exit ramp. With only one lane heading west toward the airport, I was boxed in, headed in the opposite direction. I clipped the fender of an airfreight semi, and the jolt of the impact shook the car violently. The semi driver blasted the truck's air horn at me as I swerved in front of him.

"Then I assume you'll be waiting for me at the airport when I return triumphant."

"Yes, Hercules, I'll be waiting, as long you don't get us killed before we get there."

Just then, my cell phone buzzed. The car's Bluetooth took over, and we could both see the caller ID.

"It's Bill," she said, turning up the volume.

"Hello?" I heard Bill's voice say.

"Hey. Buddy. I'm here in the car with Donna. We're headed to the airport."

"Why? Where are you going? We have to talk." Bill 's voice belied his panic.

"Jeremy tracked the money down. He said to meet him at the airport. If we find the money, we'll find Harry and Ortega."

"Ortega? Who the hell is Ortega?"

"The mystery man whose arm showed up in your bank video. Apparently, he's some spook working for Carter. He's been tracking Harry, same as us."

"Damn. If C&C is on to us, that's not good news."

"It's bad news all right, but not the kind you think. Jeremy thinks Ortega is acting on his own, trying to steal the money for himself."

"Nice. Carter can't even trust his own people."

"There's no honor among thieves. Serves him right, in a twisted sort of way. What's the situation there?"

"Well, you're about ten light years ahead of the FBI. They're still trying to figure out how Harry gave them the slip. Despite their sophisticated software, they lost track of the money after just two overseas transfers. How did Jeremy manage to track it?"

"I don't know, and I don't care. If he's right, though, we owe him big time."

"Are both of you going?"

"Jeremy and I are going," I said. "Donna's gonna stay here. She can be our liaison in case my cell doesn't work wherever it is we're headed."

"Do you want me to fly out, too?" Bill asked.

"No. No sense putting yourself at risk. Jeremy and I are single." I looked over at Donna, then back to the freeway as I entered the airport grounds. I don't want to be responsible for turning Ellen into a widow.

"Don't do anything stupid, Steve. It's only money. If Harry or this Ortega guy gives you any trouble, walk away. The FBI can clean up the mess."

"Don't worry. I'm no hero. But we've put too much into this to just let them get away. C&C needs to be stopped, and Harry needs to face the music with them." The terminal departure lanes weren't crowded, and I spotted an opening near the curb. "Gotta go."

"Okay. Good luck. Call me when you get there, wherever it is," Bill said.

I screeched the car to a stop right beneath the *Departures* sign.

We looked at each other and she took my hand in both of hers. "You come back to me in one piece, you hear me?"

"Loud and clear." I leaned over and kissed her. It would have lasted a lot longer if the cop hadn't rapped the window with his fist and motioned for us to move along.

She let go and I got out of the car. "Sorry officer. We were just saying goodbye."

"This is a restricted area. You can't stay here."

"No problem, officer," Donna said, as she got walked to the driver's side. "Let me know when to pick you back up," she said to me, with a smile that energized me.

"Love you, too," I said.

***

Once inside, it wasn't difficult to spot Jeremy standing by the escalator, holding a *"Steinham Excursions. Cayman Island Express"* sign on a small wooden stick, the kind limo drivers use to attract their fares.

"So, you're Jeremy," I said, taking in his over six-foot frame, blond hair, blue eyes, and solid build. "You're not what I expected."

"You were expecting a short, skinny, pimple-faced wimp with a shirt pocket full of pencils and a lunch pail?"

I laughed. "Something like that. How old are you, anyway?"

"Twenty-seven. I know, that's old for a hacker, but it takes time to develop the right skills, and I got a late start."

"You can tell me about in it on the plane. We should probably get our tickets."

I eyed the lines at the ticket counter, the only place crowded with an abundance of travelers.

"Already got them. We're heading to Gate C-21 in the international terminal. Did you bring your passport?" He started off in the direction of the C gates.

"Right here," I tapped my coat pocket from the outside to confirm it was still there. Reaching for my wallet, I asked, "What do I owe you for the tickets?"

"I already charged them to your Bank of America Visa card. There wasn't room on your Citibank MasterCard."

"What?"

"Don't worry. I didn't hack *all* your accounts, just those two. I figured it was the fastest way to book the flight. You'll need to swipe your Visa card at the electronic boarding terminal to print our boarding passes."

"I'm not sure I like this. I'm gonna have to have them reissue those cards with a different number now."

"Don't bother," Jeremy said. "The reality is, anyone with average computer skills can get your information and do what I did. The electronic age has made most people's financial transactions less secure, not more. Just change the online user ID and passwords. I won't hack in again unless you need me to take you somewhere else exotic."

"You're not giving me any warm and fuzzy feelings here."

"Hey, you're the one who asked me to invade C&C's computers and get the goods on Steinham, remember?"

"Point taken. I may need to rethink the whole online banking thing." We reached the electronic boarding pass kiosk, and I swiped my card. Sure enough, it recognized me, and after answering some security questions, which now seemed redundant, it printed our boarding passes.

"How 'bout that?" Jeremy said at last. "Society keeps moving toward a cashless society, but once everyone's online, the crooks will steal all their cash, and they'll have their wish."

"Speaking of cash, tell me how you found Steinham's money?" I asked as we strode towards the gate. "The FBI thought they could follow the money with their super-sophisticated software, but it proved inadequate after just two transfers. How'd you manage to do what they couldn't?"

"The simplest approach is always the easiest. I hacked Steinham's checking account. Most people are lazy, and they use the same passwords and IDs on everything. Did you know the most common password is 'password?' Or that the majority of people use some combination of their name and birth date for their online ID? They do it so it will be easy to remember. What they *don't* realize is it makes it easy to decipher. With his ID and password in hand, it was just a matter of creating an algorithm to test every major and minor bank in the world. I have a turbo charged motherboard with quad-processors and two terabytes of RAM. It only took a couple of hours to track down the accounts."

"But why the Caymans? It's almost a cliché to park money there. I would think it would have been the first place the FBI would have looked."

"The money's not in a Cayman Island bank, at least not yet."

"Then why the hell are we going there?""

"Because that's where Steinham's going. Ortega booked a flight just before he grabbed him. My guess? Ortega plans to use one of the island banks to transfer Harry's money from its current location, probably to someplace out of reach, like Switzerland. Afterwards, he'll convert to diamonds or gold and transfer it again to further launder it. That's why we have to get there first."

"Why didn't you just hack into Ortega's files and so we can redirect the money after he steals it from Harry?"

"I would have, except Ortega's intent is unclear. I can see where he's been, but not where he's going."

"But you know which bank they're heading to, right?"

"No. That's why we have to get there first. Based on our respective flights, we should arrive at least thirty minutes before they do. We'll have to follow them to their destination."

"We should alert the local authorities," I said, trying to keep up with my younger counterpart.

"That's your job."

***

Boarding the flight was unremarkable, which is to say the security lines weren't outrageously long despite the TSA strike. Thanks to the new technologies, we were able to bypass the regular boarding queue and use the bio-scan identification process.

"Tell me you hacked the TSA computers, too?" I whispered as we met up on the other side of the baggage x-ray machine.

"Scary, huh?"

"You mean—"

"I mean everyone thinks how safe air travel is, post 9/11, but a second-rate terrorist could hack their systems as easily as I."

"You flying the plane, too?"

He gave me one of those sarcastic millennial smiles. "Nah. Too much work."

We hurried in silence to the gate, which was already in the process of boarding. I couldn't help thinking technology was already out of control. We rely on it as absolutely as we rely on the sun to rise in the east and set in the west, but if an anonymous hacker could manipulate the system the way Jeremy could, I was gonna have to rethink everything I believed about my on-line profile.

"We should arrive thirty-six minutes ahead of our quarry," Jeremy said as we buckled in. His tablet was open, and I could see the flight status of both planes, theirs and ours. I watched his fingers fly across the touch screen as he arranged for a rental car at the airport.

I pointed to the screen. "Hey, that's my Visa card you're using again."

"Consider it a tax write-off. You stock brokerage guys need write-offs, right?"

"Just tell me how to protect myself against people like you when this is all over, okay?"

"Okay, but no guarantees. There's always someone better than me out there waiting to steal your money. Been to the Caymans?" Jeremy asked as he downloaded several maps of the city.

"No," I said, pointing at the street map. "I've never had much need for offshore banks. What's with the driving instructions?"

"In case we lose Steinham and Ortega in traffic. I want to know where the larger banks are located." Next, he pulled up satellite pictures of the island and started pointing out the attractions. "This is the beach you want to find yourself at around four p.m. weekdays."

"Why?"

"Full nudity is permitted," he said. Glancing over at me, he added, "You might want to consider keeping your clothes on."

"Hey," I said, "that wasn't very nice, considering I'm footing the bill for this trip."

"Don't worry. You'll be fully reimbursed, plus some," he said, smirking.

I wasn't sure what he meant by that, but I had to admit I was impressed with his knowledge, not to mention his dexterity. Completing complex instructions using a touch screen keyboard is no easy feat sitting in a cramped airline seat.

"What do we do after we follow them to the bank?" I asked, realizing this had become *his* project, not mine.

"This has a built-in video camera," he said, simultaneously lifting it between us and taking a picture. "I'll film the transaction while you're on your cell phone to the police."

"What if someone spots you? I don't think the banks like people videotaping their clients."

"Neither Steinham nor Ortega knows what I look like, so they won't notice me. You'll stay outside. Harry might have had you followed since you were dating his ex-wife and might recognize you. Besides, you'll need to point them out to the police when they arrive. As for the camera, I'll find a chair in the lobby and pretend I'm reading. I'll have a book or newspaper loaded on the screen. I only need to keep the tablet pointed in their general direction. No one will know the camera is rolling except me."

"How will you recognize them?"

"I downloaded Harry's picture from the C&C personnel file," he said, pulling up the picture on the screen. "This tablet also has feature-recognition software, so even if he's in a disguise or has changed somewhat from his employment photo, the software will fill in the differences for me."

"And when do I send in the gendarmes?"

"Not till after they've wired the money. When they turn to leave, I'll send you a text."

"And the money?"

"Leave that to me. I'll hack into the bank's system and find out where it was transferred to. How are we going to divvy it up?"

"Whoa, there. That's not our money. Harry stole it from unsuspecting investors. That money belongs to them."

"Not the interest earnings."

"The feds may have a different idea about that."

"What they don't know won't hurt us."

"Can you send a text to Bill on that?"

"Sure. What do you want me to tell him?"

"Just set me up. I'll type it out myself."

He executed a few keystrokes and handed me the tablet.

Bill, headed to the Cayman Islands. Tell Billings we're following Harry and this Ortega character. Jeremy thinks Ortega is going to force Harry to transfer the money to him. We'll alert the local police and have them arrested as soon as they complete the transfer. I'll text you the bank name and branch as soon as I can. The Caymans are a British territory, so have him contact his counterpart in England to arrange extradition. Steve.

I pressed "send" and handed the tablet back to Jeremy.

"All done, Dad?"

"Yes. And *stop* calling me Dad."

***

Upon our arrival at the Owen Roberts International Airport in George Town at three thirty in the afternoon, we were now in the same time zone as New York, and therefore on Harry Steinham time. Jeremy checked their flight status again and we were still thirty-four minutes ahead of them.

During the flight, I barely paid attention to all the partygoers onboard, but as they made their way down the ramp en masse, I couldn't help noticing the smiles of excitement on the faces of my fellow passengers. For them, the walk through the sun-filled terminal building would lead to a crystal blue beach at some upscale hotel. I watched as a couple in their twenties held hands and sauntered ahead of us, oblivious to the world, heading to some romantic adventure in each other's arms. I stared jealously after them, wishing I'd thought fast enough to tell Jeremy to buy three tickets instead of two.

I felt a sharp jab in my side.

"We're here to catch Steinham, remember?" Jeremy said.

"Yes, Ke-mo-sah-bee. Where do we go from here?"

He strode off, shaking his head, and I obediently fell in behind. We followed the signs to the rental car pick-up lot.

"I'm a frequent flier."

"I know." Jeremy didn't bother stopping at the rental counter. "The car is in lot six, gassed and ready. They even had your credit card on file, so I didn't have to type it in again. You should probably have your passport ready; they'll need it at the exit." With that, he turned and headed back into the terminal.

"Wait. Where are you going?"

"I'll stake out 'arrivals' to watch for Steinham and Ortega. Get the car and park as close to the taxi pick-up station as possible. We won't have much time once they hail one and take off."

"What makes you think they're taking a taxi? What if they rented a car, same as us?"

"Because it leaves a trail. He'll hire a taxi and pay cash."

"Yeah, but—"

"We're wasting time," Jeremy said as he disappeared into the crowd.

I walked outside into the balmy sunshine. The smell of the palm trees and saltwater was everywhere, despite the overpowering scent of car exhaust. I walked the hundred yards to Row 6, presented my ID to the attendant, and he directed me to the Kia Rio in parking stall A-151.

"Don't you have something with a little more power?"

"Don't be fooled," the neatly tanned agent said in his distinctly British accent. "These have quite the pick-up, and they're small enough to maneuver in the narrow boulevards on the island. It's the perfect automobile for your vacation."

I thanked him and grabbed the keys from his outstretched hand. Just as I opened the door, my cell started vibrating.

"Steinham's plane arriving gate in 4 minutes. Park opposite the exit doors marked '3' on south side of terminal."

"What if Ortega has someone meeting him?" I texted back.

"We'll have to roll with it. My guess is he's working alone. Once they grab a taxi, I'll wave for you to pull forward. Be quick!"

"On my way."

I turned on the car, backed out, and headed to the lot exit.

I sure hope he knows what he's doing.

***

I had no trouble following the signs to the arrival curb, though it was disturbing to drive on the wrong side of the road. Fortunately, I've been to England, so it wasn't my first experience driving on the left. I pulled in behind the line of taxis, noticing the angry eyes in the rear-view mirror of the yellow cab in front of me. I glanced up at my own mirror; another taxi flashed his lights at me as he joined the line. As I watched, he got out and started walking toward my door, gesturing with his finger. Looking back out the front windshield, I saw Harry emerge from the terminal. Beside him was a tall man with closely cropped hair and a dark complexion. He wore a trench coat and, from his position to the left and just behind Harry, I guessed he might have a firearm in his coat pocket.

How did he get a gun on the airplane and through customs?

It occurred to me this guy was extremely dangerous. He had the computer skills of Jeremy, an insider's knowledge of both C&C and the banking industry, the willingness to use lethal force, and the ability to get weaponry on and off commercial airliners. If I had a half a brain, I'd grab Jeremy and head for the beach.

Then Donna's image flashed in my head.

What if this is all just a set-up? What if everything she said was a lie? Is it worth my life?

I kept reeling off "what-ifs" in my head until the passenger door swung open, and Jeremy jumped in.

Harry and Ortega got into the lead taxi just as my window shook violently.

"Hey, you stupid bastard. You can't park here." His voice sounded muffled through the closed window, but the message, based on the size of his knuckles, came through loud and clear.

"There they are," Jeremy said, as if I hadn't seen them. "The taxi in the front. Let's move."

I threw my hands up at the angry cabbie outside my door and mouthed, "I'm sorry."

Jeremy pulled the passenger door shut and I gunned the engine.

"Easy, Dad," Jeremy said, "we don't want to draw attention to ourselves."

"He's got a gun. We need to get out of here and head the hell home," I heard myself say.

"Calm *down*. He's not foolish enough to use it. He wants Harry's money and, until he gets it, he's not going to jeopardize his payday."

"I'm not worried about him shooting Harry. I'm worried about him shooting *me*."

"Don't you have insurance, Dad?" The tone Jeremy used to ask this ridiculous question made me laugh out loud.

"Yes, I have insurance. And stop calling me Dad."

Jeremy pointed to the exit ramp beneath the sign for George Town. "That way, Tonto."

***

The traffic moved rapidly once we got past the exit sign. I had to pay close attention to stay in my lane—the wrong lane, as far as any U.S. driver was concerned—while keeping an eye on the taxi, which looked just like every other taxi on the road. I followed them onto Bobby Thompson Way, which veered west into what I imagined was the main part of town.

"Hey, why would they name a freeway here after an American baseball hero?"

Jeremy didn't bother taking his eyes off his tablet. "Who?"

"Bobby Thompson. You know, the '51 New York Giants. My Dad used to brag about meeting him. Even got his autograph."

"What's that got to do with Steinham or Ortega?"

"Nothing. I just keep seeing my life flash before my eyes, and the sign reminded me of happier times. Did you know that Thompson hit a homerun called 'The Shot Heard 'Round the World' to beat the Yankees for the pennant in 1951?"

"That's what I was afraid of."

"What?"

"You're so last century." Jeremy looked up and saw the taxi exiting toward downtown. "Don't lose them, Daddy-o."

I just shook my head and sighed. We passed an official-looking building, likely a government office, and it struck me. "Wait a minute, Jeremy. It's Saturday. Are the banks even open today?"

"I had the same thought. I've been Googling the banks and most have Saturday hours, though a couple are closed. That narrows it down a bit."

"Based on your maps, do you have an idea which one they're headed toward?"

"Yeah. To the only one on this side of the island that's closed."

"What?"

"Ortega must have something up his sleeve." Jeremy said, as we continued to follow the taxi maneuvering its way through the city streets.

"Maybe he spotted us and is trying to lose us."

"Or he's just being cautious, taking the long way."

We drove in silence the next few minutes, each of us trying to figure out what Ortega was up to. It didn't take long to find out. The taxi pulled up to a Fidelity branch on Dr. Roy's Drive and stopped. I pulled over a few cars back, our quarry's car just visible through the windshield of the cars between us.

"What good is a closed bank?" I asked.

"Maybe that's the plan. Maybe he has an accomplice inside to help with the transfer."

"That would make sense. There'd be fewer witnesses."

"And the cameras will likely be disabled. Ortega's smart."

"It also means your plan to film the whole thing from the lobby just went out the window."

"I can still film them going in and coming out. There's only one reason they're coming here, so the evidence will be the wiring instructions on the bank's computer system."

"Can you hack the bank system here just in case?"

"Working on it," he said, his fingers tapping rapidly on the tablet on his lap. "We'll have to make sure the bank official is arrested, too, as a witness."

Jeremy thought fast on his feet, but how long could he keep ahead of Murphy's Law? Something was bound to go wrong that he couldn't fix on his sophisticated Etch A Sketch.

"Crouch down," Jeremy said as Ortega exited the cab.

Harry got out next and, from the look on his face, he was none too pleased to be there.

"The world's full of crooks," Jeremy said.

"Money's money, my friend. Wave enough of it under someone's nose, and you'd be surprised what they'd be willing to do."

Jeremy aimed his tablet at Ortega and Harry as they walked toward the bank's side entrance. Ortega had Harry by the arm, and he turned and called out something to the taxi driver, probably asking him to stay put till they came back out.

"See if you can get the tags on the taxi, too," I said. "When the police arrive, he'll probably take off, and we'll need to provide the information to the locals."

"Done," Jeremy said. "Speaking of the cavalry, you online with the police yet?"

"Dialing now." I had to dial three times. I was so nervous I kept pressing the wrong keys. "How long do you think before they're done?"

"I'm not sure, but it shouldn't be long, assuming Harry cooperates and gives them the account numbers and access codes."

"What if Ortega decides to shoot Harry?"

"Better him than us."

***

"You won't get away with this, you bastard," Harry said, as Ortega hustled him down the alley to the side door of the bank. A couple walking hand-in-hand took note of the two over-dressed characters walking stiffly away, but quickly turned their attention back to their private conversation.

"I already have. We're in the Caymans, and you're about to give up your treasure trove. But don't worry. I don't want your stock options. You can keep those. I'm sure they'll be worth millions more after the merger. That should be enough for you to live comfortably. After all, you can't go back to the U.S. now, so you may as well find some beach front property somewhere on Bora Bora and live out your life in relative luxury."

"What about Carter? He'll come looking for you."

"He won't find me. You, on the other hand … well, once word of your little scam gets out, I'm sure he'll take more than a little interest in your whereabouts. You might want to cash in those options before he rescinds them, or before the stock price crashes."

"Why would the stock price crash?"

"Oh? Didn't I tell you? Your little friend from Arizona, Jim Adams, has been working with the FBI. His name isn't Adams, by the way. It's Phillips. He hacked into the company's computer and now they have the evidence they need to bring the whole charade down. He was planning on using you to testify against Carter. They nearly had you, there in Boston. It's a good thing I showed up when I did, or you'd be in the lockup by now."

"You're lying. I wired the money from those suckers before you grabbed me."

"Seed money," Ortega snorted.

"What?"

"FBI seed money. They fronted it. For all I know, everyone in that room was an FBI undercover Joe. They intended to trace the money and force you to turn state's evidence. They would have succeeded, too, but I managed to neutralize their tracer software. Serves 'em right, especially after all I did for them."

"What the hell did you do for them?"

"Gave fifteen years of my life to the government in some of the stinkiest hell holes on Earth, gathering information, eliminating threats, and for what? So, they could drink champagne and go to five-hundred-dollar-a-plate fund raising dinners with their trophy wives? I was the best, trained by the best, to keep America safe. And what did I get? A paltry salary and a lousy Certificate of Appreciation, signed by the president, suitable for framing. Well, I quit, and wound up working for Carter. He appreciated my talents, at least till now, and paid me well. I'm not taking anything from him that he didn't agree to. You, on the other hand, are nothing more than a petty thief. I don't mind stealing from you."

They reached the side door of the bank and Ortega gave three short knocks, another two, then one. The door opened, and a distinguished-looking gentleman with graying hair and a mustache opened it. He was dressed casually, this being his day off, but Harry knew he must be someone important, as he exuded authority and purpose.

"Mr. Mason, I presume?" Ortega said.

"At your service, Mr. Ortega. And this is …"

"Dr. Harry Steinham," Ortega said, keeping a tight grip on Harry's arm.

"Ah. Your friend. You mentioned he'd be with you. Since you indicated this transaction required some urgency, I assume you realize it would involve certain … additional costs?"

Ortega nodded. "You can deduct your fee from the transfer. I assume you received my wiring instructions. Were they clear?"

"Yes. All the paperwork's ready. I just need the proper account passwords, and your signatures of course. Please, come back to my office."

"Remember what I told you," Ortega whispered into Harry's ear. "One word, one false move, and whatever money you have left will be used for your funeral."

***

"Here they come," I said, as Ortega and Harry re-emerged from the bank and headed for the waiting taxi. "Where the hell are the cops?"

"Right there." Jeremy pointed to a plain, unmarked sedan parked two cars behind the taxi.

"I didn't see them pull up. And how do you know they're police?"

"I've been monitoring the police band on my tablet. They got here about ten minutes ago."

"And you didn't think to say anything?"

"Sorry, I was concentrating."

"On what?"

"On breaking into their radio frequency to send them descriptions of Ortega and Harry, as well as the taxi ID and license numbers, just to make sure they went after the right people."

"Oh. Is there anything you *can't* do with that thing?"

"It's not the tablet. It's the operator."

"Forgive me, Einstein. I didn't realize I was in the presence of genius."

"You're forgiven. Now let's watch and … Hey. Hey," he shouted.

I looked in the direction of his excited stare just as Harry broke away from Ortega and ran across the street.

"Now what?" I cried out.

Ortega didn't make a move to catch him, nor did he pull out the pistol which surely was still hidden in his coat pocket. Instead, he jumped in the taxi and it took off down the street. The unmarked car followed in hot pursuit.

"The police are following Ortega," I shouted. "They're letting Harry get away."

Jeremy jumped out of the car and ran after Harry. I watched in horror as Harry made it across the street, grabbed a woman climbing into her car, ripped the keys from her hands and slid behind the wheel. He fired up the vehicle and sped off in the opposite direction. He nearly hit Jeremy, who jumped to the sidewalk to avoid being run over.

The tires screeched in protest as I wheeled around and pulled next to Jeremy. He hopped to his feet and ran to the passenger side, slamming the door as he got in.

"Let's go," he shouted, and I floored it. Harry was already two traffic lights ahead of us. "Hold on tight." I've had my share of sports cars over the years and am no stranger to running red lights to escape tickets. For a foreign compact, this car had some guts. Accelerating like a legitimate racecar, I had no problem following Harry. The cars between were sparse and seemed to know to stay out of the way.

It was no contest, however. Harry's stolen BMW easily pulled away, doubling the distance between us in two minutes. I saw him turn right at the fifth light, but when we screeched around the corner, there was no sign of him.

Pulling over in a corporate parking lot, I came to a stop and banged the dashboard hard enough to check my hand for signs I broke something.

"*Shit*," I yelled, "God *damn* it!"

"It's all right," Jeremy said, fingers clicking furiously on his magic glass tablet. "It's a small island. The police have his description. They'll alert the airport and the local harbors. Where's he gonna go? It'll just be a matter of time before they find him." He went quiet for a moment, concentrating on the screen. "Yeah."

"What?"

"They got Ortega. They're taking him to police headquarters." He punched the address into the car's GPS system. "Let's go. I want to meet the man who can hide himself in broad daylight inside a major corporation."

***

The interrogation room they led us to appeared dismal and dark, matching my mood. Of course, the drab arrangement was likely designed deliberately to further depress and confuse those being interrogated, but I'm not sure it would have mattered if it was in neon pink with cheerful quotes on all four walls. I was convinced our efforts had come to an ignominious end. A plain metal table and four uncomfortable metal chairs, circa the first world war, consumed most of the available space. The window on the wall opposite the door was clearly a one-way mirror.

Jeremy's attempts to meet Ortega were flatly refused, and he sat at the table, absorbed in his electronic Ouija board. I didn't bother asking what he was up to now. I didn't care. For all his magic, we lost Harry anyway. The police were conducting a door-to-door search, but to no avail. Even with the apprehension of Ortega, all we had was Harry's money and Ortega's implied guilt in stealing it. Our lynchpin to Carter and his malfeasance was gone. He could claim Harry and Ortega were working in cahoots and blame any and all criminal activity on them, escaping once again from any prosecution. Hell, with Harry's trail of investors stretching from Massachusetts to Arizona, Carter could swear ignorance and claim victim status.

I was about to call Donna and tell her the bad news when my cell rang.

"We got him!" Excitement resonated in Bill's voice.

"You got who?" I asked.

"Harry. *We have him.*" I saw Jeremy perk up, so I hit the speaker button and put the phone on the table between us. "I mean, the FBI has him. He's in custody." He was talking a mile a minute. "They're flying him back to New York as we speak. He'll be here in a couple of hours. And he's talking, too. I think his brush with Ortega gave him religion. He's already asked for protection, and they offered it to him, on condition he rats on Carter."

"What? How?"

"Your text."

"What text?"

"The one you sent me from the plane. The Caymans are a British territory, remember? I told Billings, and he called in a favor from a friend at MI5. They launched a drone in time to spot Harry stealing a car outside a bank in Georgetown. They said they also spotted a little red Kia chasing him. I assume that was you and Jeremy?"

"That was us, all right. But I don't understand—"

"Hey, Bill. It's Jeremy. How'd he disappear? Dad here had him in his sights, then he disappeared into thin air."

"Glad you two are okay. He pulled into a parking garage not five hundred feet from where you two pulled over. You were a stone's throw away and didn't know it. You guys left just before the police arrived and set up a tire-puncture strip in front of the only exit. After they pulled him from the car, he started singing."

"What about Ortega? I tried to talk with him, but they have him buttoned up in solitary."

"He's the army's problem. Seems he faked his death then went AWOL. His real name's Corriega. They're waiting to turn him over to military affairs. He's looking at a long stretch in Leavenworth. Steve, have you spoken with Donna? Does she know what's happening?"

"I was about to call her when you rang in."

"Go. I'll see you when you get back. I assume you two pirates are heading home?"

I pursed my lips at Jeremy. "Assuming there was any room left on my credit card, we'll be on the next flight home."

"Huh?"

"I'll explain when I see you." I clicked off the phone. "So, what do you say. Should we head to the airport?"

"All booked, Daddy-o. First Class. We're riding in style this time."

I wasn't going to argue. "Get us a lift while you're at it. A limo. And stop calling me Dad!"

***

Dateline, Boston, MA, October 14, 2021

"In breaking news, Delbert Carter, the chairman and CEO of C&C and Associates, the healthcare conglomerate, was arrested today and charged with conspiracy and Medicare fraud. In a stunning reversal of fortune, the renowned

turn-around king, known for his aggressive cost-cutting and often referred to as the 'robber baron of wall-street', found himself doing a perp walk. FBI and local law enforcement swarmed C&C headquarters, carrying out boxes of files, and carts filled with computer equipment.

"C&C was the darling of the investment community as Carter built a profitable juggernaut by acquiring medical facilities, revamping their service structures, and producing astounding results. The stock more than quadrupled in price during his tenure. Now, it seems those profits were the result of a deliberate and predetermined scheme to bilk the U.S. Treasury by systematically overbilling the Medicare system by hundreds of millions of dollars for unnecessary procedures.

"Federal Investigator Arnold Stromble, in a statement to the press, said, 'We've had our eyes on C&C for quite some time now. A tip from a confidential source helped confirm our suspicions. They were promoting practices at their hospitals targeting seniors and the indigent in a systematic plan to defraud the government.'

"When asked the magnitude of the fraud, his response was, 'Hundreds of millions of dollars, perhaps more than a billion dollars of taxpayer funds.'

"C&C stock plummeted on the move and, after a halt in trading, reopened at ten dollars and thirty-five cents per share in trading on the New York Stock Exchange today, the largest single-day decline since the Enron era. The board has called an emergency meeting, but no successor to Carter has yet to be appointed. An unnamed source, who spoke on condition of anonymity, told this reporter one of the top executives of C&C, the head of Personnel Evaluations, turned state's evidence in a plea deal. Claiming he was an innocent pawn, he provided detailed information to the FBI, and has been placed in protective custody.

"A proposed merger with an Arizona hospital, SCM, has been scrapped, rejected by the hospital's board, to the relief of local staff and residents alike. Rumor has it the confidential informant was a nurse who worked at SCM, and was somehow related to Dr. Harry Steinham, C&C's executive-turned-snitch. Attempts to find her have been unsuccessful, and the only information the human resources office would provide indicated she quit and moved after the ordeal. Details at eleven."

***

The beach at Mission Bay was nearly empty as the sun burned off the lingering fog. Sitting on the seawall, I watched the waves crashing gently onto the sand, whishing like steel brushes rhythmically massaging a snare-drum. The aroma of a fresh cup of Starbucks mingled with the salt breeze. A curious seagull landed on the wall to my right, thinking perhaps I had some crumbs for him.

"Sorry fella," I said, holding my empty hands. "Breakfast isn't till eight."

A few early-morning joggers padded by, their tanned bodies and toned muscles moving effortlessly in the cool, morning sand. On the boardwalk behind me, an occasional skateboarder sailed by, the click-clack of the wheels rising and fading like a passing train. The shops—with their hats and sunglasses and moo-moos with "San Diego" plastered all over them—were not yet open.

I returned my attention to the open journal in my lap.

Harry had everything anyone could hope for: a successful career as a physician, the respect of the community, and the love an astonishingly beautiful wife who wanted nothing more than to start a family and live happily ever after. Instead, he got lazy, screwed up his career, and wound up a lackey for Carter, a greedy son of a bitch only interested in money. Now he has to start over somewhere in the middle of nowhere, part of the Federal Witness Protection program, with nothing: no money, no respect, no career, no family.

Couldn't have happened to a better person.

By contrast, Bill and Ellen found each other, and despite her battle with PV, they managed to have three kids, live a comfortable life, and helped us put C&C out of commission. What is it that made Harry such a degenerate, while Bill was able to face life's challenges head-on and come out a winner? I'm no psychologist, but it seems you have to have something deep inside, some dedication to a principle, some immovable predilection to follow the path of fairness and compassion. The Buddha would smile at that, I'm sure. Too bad he wasn't Jewish; he could have stayed married and still experienced enlightenment!

"I figured I'd find you here."

I looked over my shoulder at Donna. "I'm nothing if not predictable."

"I think maybe that's what I love most about you." I felt her wrap her arms around me and leaned her head against mine.

"Here," I said, handing her the second cup of coffee I had been guarding from the seagull.

"How thoughtful. Don't tell me I'm becoming boringly predictable too?"

"Predictable? Yes. Boring? Never!"

"I'll have to work on that."

"What, on becoming boring?"

"On my latent predictability. I've got to keep you off guard."

"Well, I suppose you could start a consulting firm to help small businesses fend off unwanted takeovers from greedy corporate conglomerates."

"No, thank you. Once was quite enough. Besides, that's your forte, not mine. By the way, have you heard from Jeremy?"

"Yes, in fact I did." I pulled out my cell phone to show her the latest pictures. "The island is really taking shape. I heard he got it for a steal."

"Ha, ha," she dead-panned. "Didn't he buy it from that C&C executive who went to jail?"

"You mean Delbert Carter? Yup. He needed the money for his defense attorneys. Too bad he'll never know the shell corporation that bought it from him is run by the very man who practically sent him to jail single-handedly!"

"You and Bill had more than a little to do with it."

"Yeah, but without Jeremy, we never would have been able to get the evidence we needed to indict Harry. And, without Harry's testimony, Carter might have wiggled free. What's even more ironic is Jeremy bought the island using the money Harry intended to retire on."

"Have you heard from Bill and Ellen?"

"Matter of fact, they're on a cruise to Hawaii with the kids." I pulled up the pictures he sent me on my phone and showed them to her. "Bill says hi."

"But not Ellen."

"Give it time. She was at the wedding, wasn't she?"

"Yes. Cold shoulder and all."

"She'll come around. I mean, after all, if it wasn't for you getting us involved, the merger might have gone through, and the PV Trial would have likely been trashed."

"A friend of mine at the hospital has been keeping an eye on it. Says it appears to be helping those on the experimental meds."

"See?"

"It's a double-blind study. We can't know if she's getting the new drug or simply a placebo."

"Well, she looked great at the reception, and she hasn't had a relapse since the trial started."

"And what about Bill's little tryst with that FBI femme fatale?"

"Who? Oh, you mean Fleming? Nothing happened."

"Nothing happened. Really."

"Really. Bill's always been an easy mark, and he enjoys the attention, but I told you months ago he's a one-man woman, just like me."

"You better be. If I ever catch you—"

"Yeah, I know. I get the Bobbitt treatment."

"Snip, snip."

"Yes, dear."

We sat watching the waves roll in, sipping coffee and basking in the salty sunrise. She leaned in and rested her head on my shoulder. After a while, she got up and turned to look at our beach condo.

"I know you've told this all to me before, but I still can't get my head around it."

"What do you mean?"

"I mean, all that money; it was dirty money. Isn't Jeremy just as guilty for using the money stolen from legitimate investors?"

"He gave all of that back."

"So how did he manage to keep enough to buy an island in the middle of the South Pacific?"

"The only thing Harry did right was to invest heavily in C&C stock. He nearly tripled the original stake he stole."

"But the stock crashed and burned."

"Yes, but not before Harry sold it off. He was planning on 'retiring' after this last scam, and he figured his leaving might cause the stock to decline so he liquidated it."

"So why didn't the FBI take all of it?"

"Ortega. Remember him? He forced Harry to transfer all the funds to a money market in his name. He intended to turn Harry in when he was done and he figured the Feds would come looking for the money, so he left just enough of the original stolen money, as well as the FBI's seed money, in Harry's accounts. Jeremy hacked Ortega's accounts, leaving the rest for the Feds to find."

"And you're sure that Ortega won't come looking for it?"

"Honestly, I can't be sure. He worked in covert operations, and he gave Jeremy a run for the money. The last I heard from Billings, Ortega was in the custody of the CIA. He'd gone AWOL before turning up in Carter's employ, and in the world of spooks, you don't get to play hooky without consequences. They don't send you to Leavenworth. He's likely at a CIA facility, one that doesn't hold public trials or publish their findings."

"So we really don't know for sure?"

"Nothing's for certain, except death and taxes of course. But Jeremy said he cracked Ortega's server and erased any traces of his own forays into C&C's computers."

"What about us?"

"Ortega never knew we were involved. Why would he come after us?"

"The money. Remember? The ten million dollars Jeremy gave us as a wedding present?"

"He converted it into gold, then into precious gems, and back to cash in a numbered Swiss account, like every self-respecting thief."

"And that means …"

"It's untraceable. Well, just to be safe, I laundered it once more through a Las Vegas bookie who was pleased as punch to take the ten percent commission I offered for laying off my losing bets."

"Huh?"

"Translation: no one's looking for us. Not Ortega, not the feds, not the IRS. I'm retired, we're married, and you look delicious in that bathing suit."

"Up for a morning dip in the ocean with me?"

"You don't have to ask me twice."

"Last one in is a sorry geekazoid!"

About the Author

Howard Gershkowitz's debut novel, *The Operator*, came out in October of 2018. In addition, his poetry and short stories have appeared nationally in a wide variety of print and on-line publications. A financial adviser by trade, his goal is to educate, entertain, and encourage readers to take a closer look at themselves and their universe.

Howard is a graduate of Fairleigh Dickinson University in Teaneck, NJ (BSME), and a volunteer in his local community of Chandler, Arizona.

ALL THINGS THAT MATTER PRESS

FOR MORE INFORMATION ON TITLES AVAILABLE FROM
ALL THINGS THAT MATTER PRESS, GO TO
http://allthingsthatmatterpress.com
or contact us at
allthingsthatmatterpress@gmail.com

If you enjoyed this book, please post a review on Amazon.com and
your favorite social media sites.
Thank you!